THE LADY'S GAMBLE

A Historical Regency Romance Novel

ABBY AYLES

Edited by
ELIZABETH CONNOR

Historical Romance Author

Historical Romance Author

BE A PART OF THE ABBY AYLES FAMILY...

I write for you, the readers, and I love hearing from you! Thank you for your on going support as we journey through the most romantic era together.

If you're not a member of my family yet, it's never too late. Stay up to date on upcoming releases and check out the website for all information on romance.

I hope my stories touch you as deeply as you have impacted me. Enjoy the happily ever after!

Let's connect and download this Free Exclusive Bonus Story!

(Available only to my subscribers)

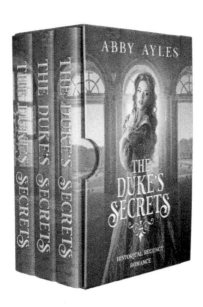

Click on the image or on the button below to get the BONUS

BookHip.com/NVGCDD

ACKNOWLEDGEMENTS
THANK YOUS

Thank you to my parents for their ongoing support. You have turned the world upside down and inside out in order for me to pursue my dreams. I love you.

Thank you to my beta readers Carole Ryall and Danielle Carpenter. Interacting with you is so fun and I am so thankful to have you in my corner rooting for me every step of the way.

Thank you to my editorial team for helping bring my words to life in the exact way I envision them to be said. You push me to be better.

Thank you to the authors who inspire me. There is no world without love, and your books are the reason I'm here now.

Most importantly, thank you to my readers! Whether you are new to my work, or a loyal fan, thank you from the bottom of my heart.

A MESSAGE FROM ABBY

Dear Reader,

Thank you for reading! I hope you enjoyed every page and I would love to hear your thoughts whether it be a review online or you contact me via my website. I am eternally grateful for you and none of this would be possible without our shared love of romance.

I pray that someday I will get to meet each of you and thank you in person, but in the meantime, all I can do is tell you how amazing you are.

As I prepare my next love story for you, keep believing in your dreams and know that mine would not be possible without you.

With Love

♥   Historical Romance Author   ♥

INTRODUCTION

The Lady's Gamble

Miss Regina Hartfield is the youngest of her sisters—
and, if you asked most of society, the least. She's not
good with people and she'd much rather read or sew
than go to a ball. But when her father, a gambling addict,
gambles away their land and titles to a known rake, all
that Regina knows of her world comes crashing down.

Determined to help her family, she enlists the help of
the mysterious and possibly scandalous Lord Harrison,
Duke of Whitefern. Lord Harrison is in love with
Regina's sister Bridget, and in exchange for promising
him Bridget's hand in marriage, Lord Harrison agrees to
teach her to play.

At an upcoming masquerade ball where faces and identities are hidden, Regina can slip into the card game among the men and win back her family's fortune, saving her father's honor and her sisters from destitution... but only if she plays better than anyone else.

For the first time, the sister who was all but ignored is finding herself with the responsibility of her family's future on her shoulders. And that's if nobody finds out about what she's doing, which would only lead to more scandal and Regina's personal ruin.

And then there's the small matter of Lord Harrison herself, the first man Regina's ever found herself drawn to. But Lord Harrison is in love with Bridget, not Regina —isn't he?

CHAPTER 1

Regina Hartfield concentrated on her stitches. Elizabeth was banging away at the pianoforte just one room over. It was threatening to disturb her calm.

She did feel rather bad. It wasn't Elizabeth's fault she couldn't play well. And she wasn't trying to disturb anybody. But every time it gave her such a headache.

"Elizabeth!" Natalie entered the room. Her hair was only half done up. "For the love of all that's holy would you stop! You can hear it through the whole house!"

The pianoforte stopped. Regina breathed out a quiet sigh of relief.

"Honestly," Natalie grumbled. Then she spied Regina. "Oh, darling, you must start getting ready!"

"I don't think I shall be going tonight."

"But you must!" Natalie looked crestfallen. Although part of that might have been her half-done hair. "Regina, everyone will be there."

"Precisely." Regina focused back on her stitching. The idea of being among such a large crowd of people for hours terrified her.

"Have you told Father?" Natalie asked.

Regina didn't answer. She was a horrible liar. And she hadn't told Father. She'd tactfully avoided the subject of tonight's ball all week.

She had been hoping that, being ensconced in the side parlor, she could avoid Father. Then when it was time the flurry of her four elder sisters climbing into the carriage would disguise her lack of presence. By the time Father realized she wasn't there they would hopefully be halfway to the ball. Far too late to turn back for shy mousy Regina.

It was too late for that now. Natalie would be sure to tell Father.

"I think that you should go," Natalie maintained. "It's always such fun."

"For you it is," Regina replied. It was widely maintained that Natalie was the prettiest of the Hartfield sisters.

Regina supposed that depended upon one's taste. Natalie was the only sister with blue eyes. That helped her to stand out, certainly. Paired with a sweet, heart-shaped face and dark red hair, every man in the county wanted to marry her.

Personally, Regina preferred the cat-like green eyes of her other sisters. Not that Regina took after them. She had red hair like all of her sisters. Gotten from Mother, God rest her soul. But Regina had boring brown eyes and far too many freckles. She was tiny as well. Elizabeth liked to joke about Regina being the runt of the litter. What man wanted to dance with a girl when he had to crane his neck down to look at her?

It wasn't her looks that truly made Regina reluctant to go to the ball. She just didn't like people. And all that exercise. She wasn't the adventurous type. A quiet evening stitching and reading suited her just fine.

Not that Father would see it that way.

"It would be fun for you as well if you would make an effort," Natalie replied.

"I'm sure that stitching would be just as fun for you if you made an effort," Regina pointed out.

Natalie sniffed. She'd always hated stitching. "I'm going to finish getting ready. You should as well. Elizabeth!"

Elizabeth appeared, looking peevish. Elizabeth was the second youngest and had taken to it like a martyr. Her red hair was orange and fiery to match her temper and her green eyes were always flashing.

"It's hours yet, Natalie, I don't have to get ready."

"You should start now. You know your hair takes longer to tame."

Elizabeth had also inherited their father's tight curls. It did make her hair rather difficult to get under control.

"Not all of us need half a day to make ourselves fit enough to be seen by society," Elizabeth replied.

Regina focused back on her stitches. She really didn't want to be privy to another spat between Elizabeth and Natalie.

"You could learn from my example. Perhaps then someone would ask you to dance a second time."

Regina shrank a little farther back into the chair. Luckily the spat was ended when Bridget entered the room.

Bridget was the oldest of the five Hartfield sisters. She was also Regina's favorite. Although, it wouldn't do to tell any of her other sisters that. Bridget was everything that Regina wished she could be. Bridget was confident and tall with pale creamy skin and a serene face. She had dark red hair and quick green eyes. Furthermore, she was wickedly funny, well read, intelligent, and could make anyone love her. Natalie was the prettiest Hartfield, everyone said, but Bridget was the wittiest and the most well-liked.

"Elizabeth, please go and get ready." Bridget didn't raise her voice. She didn't need to. "I'll join you in a moment. Natalie, could you remind Father that he needs to speak to the gardener?"

Natalie and Elizabeth looked like they knew exactly what Bridget was doing but they hurried off anyway. Everyone always did what Bridget asked.

Meanwhile Regina was pretty sure that if the house was on fire, nobody would listen to her if she told them to get out.

Bridget smoothed out her skirt and sat down on the settee next to Regina's chair. "That's a lovely set of stitches."

"They're for the Lord and Lady Morrison."

Bridget smiled. "We shan't be seeing them for another two months, at the masked ball."

"Yes, but I want it to be perfect." Regina focused down on her stitches. She'd chosen the flowers for their meanings. They all meant some version of love and devotion, wishes for a happy marriage.

Bridget placed her hand carefully over Regina's. "Darling. You are quite accomplished at that."

"It's merely practice."

"Precisely." Bridget's voice was gentle. "I think that if you practiced just as much at your social skills as at your needlepoint, you needn't find it all so intimidating."

Regina set aside her sewing. She wasn't going to get any more done today. Not if Bridget got her say—and she always did.

"I simply never know what to say," Regina admitted. "I always say the wrong thing. And the men are terrifying. They all think they know better than I do. And they're loud and pompous and I can't bring myself to look them in the eye. Everybody gossips and says nasty things about one another. About Father and about Mother sometimes as well."

Bridget sighed and squeezed Regina's hand. "Father is a good example of how not to deal with grief. And what does it matter what they say about Mother? We know the truth. And they know the truth as well. They just like to pretend otherwise when they're bored and there's nothing else to discuss."

Regina waited. She knew that there was more Bridget wanted to say by that look of discomfort on her face.

Sure enough, after a moment, Bridget spoke again.

"I don't like the idea of you being alone all the time, darling."

"But I'm not alone. And I won't be for quite some time. Unless the four of you have gotten engaged and neglected to tell me so."

Bridget chuckled. "Now darling, you know it won't be long for any of us. Natalie will be off as soon as she finally chooses one suitor."

Regina allowed herself an indelicate snort. Natalie choose just one out of the many men who danced attendance? Not likely.

Bridget leveled her with a stern look. "I have had a talk with Natalie myself about her future."

"Did she listen to a word of it?"

"She shall, if she knows what is good for her. A woman who is known as a flirt quickly goes from many suitors to none at all."

Regina didn't think that Natalie would be inclined to believe this advice until it actually happened to her.

Bridget continued. "And you know that Mr. Fairchild is only waiting for his aunt to pass so that he may marry Louisa."

"His aunt has been stuck with one foot in the grave for two years. Is Louisa willing to wait another two before she passes?"

Louisa, their second-eldest sister, had the carrot-colored hair of Elizabeth but none of her younger sister's fire. Louisa was the gentlest of all of them. It was no wonder she was the first to have been proposed to, even if it must be kept secret for the time being.

"You know as well as I do how quickly one's health can take a turn for the worst," Bridget replied. "Elizabeth will not lack for suitors long, either."

"If she can find one that will put up with her temper."

"She's a spirited girl. She likes riding and long walks. She enjoys trips to town. Many men would pay dearly for such an active and athletic wife. Just you watch, when the shooting season starts and she is in her element, she will have men to admire her."

"And what of you?" Regina asked. She squeezed Bridget's hand in return. "I doubt there is a man on Earth good enough for you."

Bridget laughed fondly. "You give me too much credit."

Regina blushed and looked down at her lap. Their mother had died in quite distressed circumstances. A longtime friend of their mother, had been injured in a riding accident. Mother had raced to his side.

Some said that they were having an affair, but Mother had looked upon the man only as a brother. He had called her 'sister' in his letters to her. Regina had called him Uncle.

Mother's desperation to take care of the man she saw as family had its consequences. She had been caught in a downpour and continued on. She had arrived in time to make the Earl's last few days bearable. But while he lay dying, she was also ravaged. The rain had given her pneumonia.

She had passed away only a week after the Earl. His estate had been far from home and her family. They hadn't had the chance to say goodbye.

Regina had been quite young at the time. Bridget had immediately stepped up as head of the household and as Regina's caretaker. A governess was well and good but did not replace a mother's care. Bridget had provided that.

In her secret, jealous heart of hearts, Regina did not want Bridget to marry. She did not want to lose the woman who was more like mother than sister to her.

"I admit," Bridget said, "My taste is quite discerning. I have turned down quite a few young men."

Each time that Bridget had turned down a man, Regina had breathed a sigh of relief.

"But that state of affairs cannot endure forever," Bridget said. "Already Father berates me for my stubbornness. And I am not entirely impossible to please. There will be a man for me, darling. And when that happens, you cannot endure this great big house alone."

"But Father will need someone to run the house," Regina protested. "I can serve in that. I have assisted you often enough. I like keeping the books."

"And we are both well grateful for it," Bridget teased. She ruffled Regina's hair. "But your place is not here. You must come into your own. You must be a mistress of your own place. And that can never truly be while you are here."

"Did Father put you up to this?" Regina was well aware that Father despaired of finding her a husband when *all you do is sit*—his words, not hers.

"Father might go about it the wrong way but he worries because he cares. And no, he did not put me up to this. You should know better than to think my opinions come from anyone except myself."

Regina could see that her sister was not moving on this matter. "But what if I find no man to suit my tastes?"

"Well then tell me your tastes. I shall help find you a man to suit them."

Regina thought, but she could not think of a single thing. "I do not know."

"Think on it then," Bridget said. "And when you know, tell it to me. We shall find you someone to protect that gentle heart of yours, darling."

She patted Regina's hand and stood. "Now, come. I have a delightful frock for you for tonight. It shall bring out your fine eyes."

Regina didn't think anything could be done to improve

upon her appearance. But neither could she bear to dampen her beloved sister's spirits. So she allowed herself to be led upstairs.

Perhaps, she thought, this ball would be bearable.

CHAPTER 2

Regina had a headache.

The music and lights from the ball only made the throbbing in her temple intensify. Everyone was talking too loudly. It was all a cacophony.

She had allowed Bridget to dress her in a dark blue dress. The fabric was silky to the touch. Bridget had instructed the maid to do her hair up and they'd put a powder on her face to cover much of her freckles.

Looking in the mirror, she had thought she almost looked pretty. Perhaps the ball wouldn't be so bad.

Now she was in the thick of it and it was as awful as she'd remembered.

Natalie and Elizabeth were out on the dance floor. Natalie was laughing, catching hands and tossing them away in turn. Elizabeth was dancing intensely, locking eyes with her partner like a dance was a challenge.

Louisa was sitting off with some close friends and talking. Holding court, more like. Louisa was gentle and quiet and yet it drew people to her. All her friends sat around with bated breath as she talked.

Regina could see Mr. Fairchild hovering nearby. Obviously wanting to ask Louisa to dance—and obviously unable to. Until his wealthy aunt passed he could not let his favor be known. Poor Louisa, Regina thought. To love someone and be unable to have them. At least Mr. Fairchild loved her in return.

Bridget was about somewhere. Regina craned her head, searching for her. Perhaps she could persuade Bridget to call up the carriage to take Regina home. The men about would undoubtedly offer her sisters a ride home when they found them without one.

As Regina made her way through the ball to find her sister, she began to hear whispers. At first, she feared it was about Father again. The gambling habit he'd developed after Mother's death was appalling. Many said it was only a matter of time before he gambled away his estate.

But no, they spoke of something else. Regina listened for a moment.

"Is he really here?" Someone asked.

"Oh to be sure, I saw him over by the foyer. I couldn't bring myself to greet him."

"He's quite intimidating, isn't he?"

Regina wondered who they were talking of. She pushed onward and caught a flash of dark red hair. Bridget!

She hurried forward. Bridget was talking with a man that Regina had never seen before.

Charlotte Tourney was just to the side. Regina came up to her. "Who is that man?"

"Who, speaking with Miss Bridget?"

Regina nodded.

Charlotte was the best person to approach for gossip. She did not disappoint Regina in this matter. "That is the Duke of Whitefern."

"How have I never before seen him?"

"He's quite the mysterious figure. I know hardly a thing about him. Other than his title and that he is heir to a massive fortune. But of course he wasn't born into the latter."

"Oh?" Regina asked. She kept watching her sister and the Duke. She couldn't see the man's face but she was certain he must be enamored of Bridget. What man alive wasn't?

"I heard that his family was quite destitute when he inherited the title. It's said his father was a poor businessman. The Duke had to earn it all back. And he had extraordinary luck about it. If you know what I mean."

"I'm afraid I don't."

Charlotte gave Regina a pitying smile, as though she thought it was sad that Regina didn't know. "Gambling, my dear. He's said to be a master with cards."

Now Regina knew why the smile was pitying. Because of her father. She drew herself up as best she could. Her stomach quaked. "I suppose he has good luck indeed, then."

"Indeed. Not much else is known of him. He is quite good looking but nothing is known of his connections or his family. Of course there is speculation. I heard that his mother was a French duchess."

Regina hummed noncommittally. Not that it deterred Charlotte.

"I also heard that he's won a dozen duels. Nothing to corroborate any of this, but it is rather fanciful, don't you think?"

"Um, yes, rather like a novel," Regina stuttered, and turned to approach Bridget. This headache really was monstrous.

She walked up and cleared her throat politely. "I beg pardon, but I'm afraid I must have a word with my sister."

The Duke of Whitefern turned and Regina's breath caught in her throat. He was tall, though not as tall as some men that she knew. He had dark hair and warm blue eyes. Regina had grown up with Natalie's clear, bright ones. She hadn't known that blue eyes could seem so warm and inviting.

It was more than simply a matter of being handsome— which he was. His entire face was firm, solid, as though he had been carved from stone. The warmth she saw in his eyes seemed quite at odds with the intimidating look of that face.

Regina found herself at a loss for words. He scared her,

somehow. But not in the usual way. She couldn't put a name to it. Still, he scared her.

"Lord Harrison," Bridget said. "Allow me to introduce my youngest sister, Miss Regina Hartfield. Regina, this is Lord Harrison, the Duke of Whitefern."

"It seems that beauty runs in the family," Lord Harrison said. He bowed, taking Regina's hand to kiss it. Warmth spread from the place where his lips had touched.

It made Regina want to snatch her hand away, but she didn't know why. It must have been the headache.

Or perhaps it was the fact that he had inferred that she was beautiful. She did not appreciate flatterers, even less so when the flattery was untrue. She knew what she looked like. Irritation surged up within her, startling her.

"I apologize for the interruption," she said. "May I speak to my sister for one moment?"

"Certainly." Lord Harrison bowed and parted.

"Another suitor, I suppose?" Regina asked. She couldn't help herself. She wasn't quite sure why Lord Harrison was provoking such an emotional response within her. It was unusual.

"He intends to be, I am sure," Bridget said. "I have met

him at other balls and he has made his regard for me clear."

"But you do not like him? He is a Duke."

"He has made his money as a gambler, and we have quite enough of those in our family already," Bridget said firmly.

Regina nodded, secretly quite pleased. She knew it was childish but she really did not want Bridget to marry just yet. "May I take the carriage home? I have the most awful headache."

"You will have to ask Father about that."

That was what Regina had been afraid she'd say. "Where is he?"

"Where else? In the side parlor."

Regina nodded. Gambling again. "If he says yes, do you say yes?"

Bridget nodded. "None of us shall want for offers of a ride home. Mr. Fairchild will take us all if no one else. But Father is not a young, pretty woman."

"Mr. Fairchild will take him as well as Louisa."

"Perhaps. But it's one thing for a young lady to ask a gentleman for a ride home after a ball. It's quite another for an older gentleman to ask another. There is the matter of his pride."

"Very well." Regina sighed. "I shall ask him."

She left Bridget and made her way to the side parlor. It was like stepping into another world. The rest of the house was brightly lit and crowded, filled with noise. The side parlor was done up in dark reds and dimly lit. It was smaller as well, so that the eight men inside seemed to dominate it.

Regina knew all of the men assembled. Lord Harrison was standing off to the side and was the only man she knew by name only. The others she knew both in personality and reputation.

Father was seated at the table with three others. The ones on either side of him were rather young men, a Mr. Charleston and a Mr. Denny. Both looked rather crestfallen.

The one seated directly across from Father—he made her heart sink. Her headache fled completely to be replaced by an awful coldness in her gut.

It was Lord Pettifer.

The man had proposed to Bridget a couple of years ago. He'd only known her for ten days. Bridget had turned him down and he'd called her the most awful names for it.

Natalie had told Regina later on that the man was a terrible rake. He was rumored to have left the daughter of a groundskeeper in the family way up north. He was certainly an unashamed gambler. Unlike most men who pretended they bet only a little—even when they bet a lot—Lord Pettifer boasted of how much he had staked and won.

Lord Pettifer had reason to boast, apparently. He was a veritable card shark. Or so Natalie had told her.

And now he was facing off against Father. Father, who was an awful gambler and had taken up cards as a way to get over his wife's death.

Regina felt a hand at her elbow and looked up into the blue eyes of Lord Harrison. "You shouldn't be in here," he said quietly.

"I know that women aren't allowed," she protested. "I simply have to speak with my father."

"It's not only because women aren't allowed." Lord Harrison's voice was surprisingly soft. There was something else in there too, a protectiveness. "This isn't a good time."

"I only want to ask him a question." What on earth was the matter?

There was a cry from the table. Regina knew that sound —it was her father.

She shoved past Lord Harrison, who was far too surprised to stop her. "Father?"

Father looked very pale, staring at the cards on the table. Lord Pettifer looked far too pleased with himself. Smug, even. Regina thought he looked like a rat.

"It appears as though I've won after all," he said.

Father looked like he might faint. Regina hurried up to him and put her hands on his shoulders. "Father? Are you quite all right?"

"This must be the youngest of your lovely daughters," Lord Pettifer said. "My deepest condolences."

Deepest condolences? Regina looked from Lord Pettifer to her father. "What's going on?"

"Lord Hartfield." It was Lord Harrison. "If I may escort your daughter out?"

Father nodded, still pale and distracted. Lord Harrison turned to Mr. Denny. "Denny, if you'll get Hartfield some water here. Pettifer, do us all a favor and collect your winnings and leave."

"I don't understand." Regina stood firm. "Why must you offer condolences?"

"Regina, please leave," Father said faintly.

"No." She startled herself with how firm her voice sounded. "I want to know what is going on."

"What is going on," Lord Pettifer said, standing, "Is that you are about to find your circumstances wildly changed."

He held up his winnings. There was a wad of notes, a ring, and a piece of paper.

Regina looked closer. No, it wasn't just a piece of paper. It was signed. She squinted until she could read it.

I, Lord Hartfield, do will the holder of this paper the rights and lands owned by me according to the laws of the gentry.

Her father had gambled everything.

And he had lost.

CHAPTER 3

Her knees nearly buckled and only a warm, strong hand at her elbow kept her upright. She looked up to see Lord Harrison looking at her with his brows drawn together. He seemed concerned.

"You should follow me, Miss Regina," he murmured.

Regina yanked her arm away. She had no idea where the impertinence came from. She was never like this. "Father. Have you truly gambled away our lands?"

Lord Pettifer gave an exaggerated sigh. "I did tell him I had a good hand."

"Which you always say when you have a bad one!" Father bellowed.

Regina wrapped an arm around Father's shoulders. He was working himself up into a state. "Father, please, don't yell. Come with me and we'll get you sorted."

"There is no sorting," Mr. Charleston snorted.

"Hold your tongue," Lord Harrison instructed. "Pettifer. Leave. Lord Hartfield, do sit down. Miss Regina if you'll come with me."

"Go," Father said. His voice didn't even sound like his. It was shaking and frail. Regina had never heard him sound so old.

Lord Harrison took her by the elbow again and this time she allowed it.

"Surely this is not legal," she whispered.

Lord Harrison led her out of the room and through to the front door. "It doesn't matter."

He opened the front door and the cool night air hit her face. Only as the wind passed over her face did she realize how hot she had gotten. She was practically shaking.

"Just lean back here." Lord Harrison helped her to lean against the wall of the house. "There now."

Regina looked up at him. "Why does it not matter if it isn't legal?"

Lord Harrison looked away from her. There was light spilling out of the windows of the house on one side. On the other, there were the pearl-white beams of the moon. Both sources coupled with the shadows to play over Lord Harrison's face and place him in contrast: one-half golden and lit up, the other half silvery pale.

Regina wondered which side was true. He looked oddly warm on one half and cold and calculating on the other. It reminded her of the fairy stories Bridget would read to her when she was a child. There were stories about fairy kings in them. They'd enchant you and then whisk you away and entrap you.

She shook her head clear of such thoughts. They were childish and ridiculous. And if there was a time for such thoughts, it wasn't now. She spoke again.

"If I am to be kicked out of my home and my sisters left penniless, I deserve to know why. Surely my father—"

She cut herself off. She had meant to say, *surely my father is not such a fool*. But that wasn't necessarily true, was it? He had been a slave to the cards for years. Regina had eavesdropped on many an argument between Bridget and Father over the matter.

He had lost thousands of pounds over the years at cards. Was it truly so hard to believe that he would lose their home as well?

Lord Harrison sighed and looked back at her. "Miss Regina. You must understand. It is not legally binding. No judge would enforce it. But there is the matter of honor."

"Honor?"

"Your father made a promise in front of others. He swore to honor that promise should he lose. He lost. To back out now would save his land but impugn his honor. He would be looked at with disdain."

"And he shall be looked at with such high regard once he is penniless and without land?"

Lord Harrison inclined his head as if tipping his hat to her. "You see clearly the conundrum you've been left in."

"That I—" Regina's blood froze.

She worried not for herself. She would not miss the balls and the dinners and the like. There was the fear of what it might take to maintain an income. Begging from friends and relying on charity made her stomach churn with humiliation.

But her sisters... her beautiful, stunning sisters. Natalie would wilt when she heard the news. Mr. Fairchild would never be able to marry Louisa now. Elizabeth's sharp wit and fiery temper would become vices rather than amusing virtues.

And what of Bridget? Her sister had rallied them all together when Mother had died. What man would have her now?

Regina had wanted to keep Bridget all to herself but not like this. Not at this price.

Some of her horror must have shown on her face, for Lord Harrison's brow tightened. "I am sorry, Miss Regina."

Her mind raced. "What is to be done? How can this be salvaged?"

"Salvaged?"

"Yes. Surely there is something that we can do to preserve ourselves."

"Well..." Lord Harrison thought for a moment. "Do your sisters have prospects?"

"My three eldest. One is engaged, although it is not common knowledge. The other two have many suitors."

"Then tell them to accept one of them at once. Have their marriages without delay."

"My sister's fiancé cannot marry her. His aunt will not allow it. If they marry she shall rewrite her will to leave him nothing."

"And will he stand by her when the news breaks?"

Regina shook her head. "I do not know."

"If your sisters marry quickly, their husbands can provide for you and your other unmarried sister. Their reputations and income will preserve you until you can be wed."

"How quickly will the news get out?"

"More quickly than you would expect."

Regina passed her hand over her eyes. This felt like a nightmare. It couldn't possibly be real.

But if this was a dream she wouldn't have been able to conjure up a man like Lord Harrison. She couldn't have dreamt such detail. And she could remember every step she had taken throughout the day.

This was all horribly real.

"I shall have to tell them," she said. Her voice was thick and she swallowed quickly. She would not cry in front of a man she didn't even know. "Father will bungle the whole thing."

"Perhaps in the morning. They will be too exhausted to deal with it properly tonight."

Regina nodded. "Bridget will know what to do."

"Bridget?"

Regina looked up at him. Lord Harrison's eyes had lit up in a look that she knew well. She had seen many a man look at Bridget in that way, and Natalie as well. It was how Mr. Fairchild looked at Louisa.

"My eldest sister, with whom you were speaking earlier. She manages our affairs. She'll know what to do."

Lord Harrison inclined his head again. "Well, please give my condolences to your sister and inform her that should she be in need of a suitor, I stand ready and waiting."

"That is rather bold of you, sir," Regina replied. She blinked, surprised at herself. She was not normally so snappish. Perhaps it was the stress. Or perhaps it was that she wanted to protect Bridget.

Lord Harrison chuckled. "There's a feisty one inside of you yet, Miss Regina. And here I had heard that you were the mouse of the five."

Regina swallowed. She knew that she was plain in features. And she knew that she was quiet. But to learn they called her a mouse…

It stung, honestly.

But she would not be a mouse where Bridget was concerned. "My sister is an accomplished woman," she said. "Only the best of men could hope to win her hand."

"And you clearly do not think I am the best of men," Lord Harrison replied. He seemed amused by this, smiling down at her. Regina shivered at that, but not unpleasantly. He looked striking like this, smiling with the moonlight on his face.

"I think that I do not know you well enough to cast judgment. But if you wish to win Bridget, you'd do well to proceed with more delicacy."

"Delicacy?" Lord Harrison chuckled. "Miss Regina, the time for delicacy is at an end. You and your sisters are, as of now, dependent upon the goodwill of others. You must learn to be bold."

"In speaking plainly to you I think that I am being quite bold."

"Miss Regina." Lord Harrison sighed. He briefly

clenched his hand into a fist in frustration. "I apologize if I have offended you. But my offer is genuine. You and your sisters need the protection of a husband since your father can no longer provide any. I am willing and happy to offer your sister my heart and my home. Please convey this to her if it please you.

"You must understand the danger you are now in. I do not wish to see five innocent women thrown out onto the street. My words may be direct but my intentions are good."

He took her hand in his. Regina was surprised both by the size of it and how warm it was. It practically encased her own. It felt oddly as though the warmth and weight of his hand was the only thing anchoring her.

Lord Harrison's eyes bore into hers. She felt a bit like a mouse pinned by a snake, except there was no malice in his gaze. "Believe me, I am only trying to help you."

Regina swallowed. "You have helped, sir, and I thank you for it. The night air has done some good. As has your advice."

She took a deep breath to steady herself. "I must get to my father. My sisters shall stay. It will be remarked upon if we all retire so early. I shall take my father home.

Mr. Fairchild will give my sisters a ride back. Then I will speak to them of this in the morning."

"Good girl," Lord Harrison said. He squeezed her hand. "Have a calm head and act quickly. It is the only way to save yourselves."

Regina nodded. Yes. Stay calm and act quickly. She could do that. Or, rather, Bridget could. She felt certain that Bridget would know what to do.

Then she realized with a start that Lord Harrison was still holding her hand. She slid her hand out of his grasp. Immediately she missed the safe feeling it had given her and the warmth it had provided.

"Thank you again, Lord Harrison. I shall take my leave, if I may."

Lord Harrison made a shooing gesture. "Do what you must. And remember what I said."

Regina hurried back into the house. She could feel Lord Harrison's eyes tracking her the entire way. It felt like they were burning into her back.

CHAPTER 4

Regina returned to the side parlor to find that all the men had cleared it. Save for Mr. Denny, who was sitting with Father.

"Mr. Denny, your kindness will not be forgotten," she said, crossing to Father's side.

Mr. Denny stood at once. "Anything for the Hartfields, Miss Regina. Are you quite well?"

"Yes. Lord Harrison forced me to take some night air. It did me some good."

Regina knelt in front of Father. He had sunk back into his chair and still looked pale. He turned his green eyes to her. They looked watery.

"Father," Regina whispered. "Are you quite all right?"

He shook his head. "I have ruined us," he whispered.

"Don't fret," Regina said immediately. Her voice held a firmness she did not feel. "We shall find a way out of this. Never you fret."

She looked up at Mr. Denny. "If I may take advantage of your good nature once more, sir?"

"As I said, anything."

"Would you please find my sister, Miss Hartfield? Inform her that Father is feeling unwell and I have taken him home in the carriage."

As the eldest, Bridget was known among society as Miss Hartfield. The second eldest, Louisa, was known as Miss Louisa Hartfield. Natalie, Elizabeth, and Regina were all known simply as Miss.

Mr. Denny bowed. "I shall inform her. I hope your father recovers. And..." he hesitated. "If there is anything I can do to assist, please inform me."

"Not unless you are willing to marry one of us," Regina replied before she could stop herself.

Mr. Denny flushed. Regina felt rather like bashing her

head against the card table. When had she become so impudent?

"I was only jesting, of course," she said quickly. "I apologize. Think nothing of it. I fear my mind is not at rights."

"No apology is necessary," Mr. Denny replied, just as hastily. He bowed again and hurried out the door.

Well, there was one man she'd just scared away from her family.

"Up you get, Father," Regina said. It took some tugging but she convinced Father to stand on his own two feet. "I'm taking you home."

She got him out to the carriage without much incident. It was only once they were safely inside that Father broke down.

Regina had never once seen her father cry. She had heard him in his study sometimes. After Mother had died, he would lock himself inside for hours. Regina would creep down at night to see if he was still there. If she pressed her ear to the door, she was able to hear quiet sobs.

She had wondered then what kind of love was so deep it

ruined a man. She had then wondered if any man would ever love her like that.

She doubted it.

But now Father was sitting next to her in the carriage and crying. He was doing it quietly without much fuss. Regina would have expected great heaving and sobbing. But her father merely let the tears run down his face.

It was awkwardly silent. Regina had no idea what to say.

When they arrived home she helped him out of the carriage.

"Here we are," she said, speaking to him as if he were a child. "I'll get the front door."

Father looked down at her. "You know you have your mother's eyes?"

Regina stopped and turned to look at him. "Yes. Bridget has said so."

"The prettiest brown eyes, they were. So soft and dark." Father sighed. "I apologize. You must forgive an old man's ramblings."

"You are not so old, Father." Regina took his hand and led him inside.

"I am old enough to be labeled an old fool."

"I suspect Mr. Charleston called you that and I will have none of it. He is a sour man of little fortune."

Father shook his head. "He was right. Regina, I have just ruined us. And I have been ruining us for years."

"Don't say that." She started to lead him up the stairs. She was grateful the servants were abed so none of them saw Father this way.

"I suppose Bridget hasn't told you." Father let Regina lead him easy as a lamb. "My weakness for cards led us close to bankruptcy even before tonight. It was why I have been urging you girls toward marriage.

"I feel as though I am seized by a devil. I cannot stop myself. Each time I see the cards and think, I shall win. I must win. Surely this time... and then nothing but more loss.

"Your poor sister has been at her wit's end. I have promised her and promised her that I would stop. And I have failed. Now you will all perish."

"Now Father, be reasonable. The whole world knows Lord Pettifer is the most disgraceful of men. It is his title alone that keeps him on invitations. It is not as if Natalie ran off to Gretna Green."

Father shook his head. "No man will have you girls now."

"Lord Harrison asked for Bridget's hand even after your losses," Regina blurted out.

Father stopped on the stairs and stared at her. "Did he now?"

Regina nodded. She felt a little as though she had betrayed Lord Harrison's confidence. But then, he had not asked her to keep it a secret. And he must ask Father's permission before marrying Bridget anyhow.

"I am not sure of him," Father admitted. "I have heard the most wild stories. Nothing about him is known for certain. But he has wealth and seems a good man, if mysterious. Bridget could do worse given our changed circumstances."

"I am certain other men will come forward as well," Regina said. She spoke with a confidence she did not feel. "Now come, we must get you to bed."

She helped him get up the rest of the stairs and into his chambers. It felt so odd, as though their positions had reversed: he the child and she the parent.

Father didn't say anything more as she helped him. Not

until he was in bed and she prepared to walk away. Then he caught her hand in his and said,

"I am glad that one of you took after your mother."

"I have been informed that I am nothing like mother," Regina replied. Elizabeth had hurled that truth at her one day during a fight.

Father shook his head. "No. You and Bridget are like your mother. But you got just a bit more of her, I think."

He raised his hand and gently touched right between her eyes. "Your eyes."

Regina gently set his hand down on the bed and patted it. "Sleep, Father. We shall deal with this in the morning."

She made sure all was taken care of and then went to bed herself. She knew that she should get some rest but for a while she simply couldn't sleep.

She tossed and turned. But everything from the night played back at her. Especially Lord Harrison. She could see his eyes staring straight into hers as he promised that he only wanted to help. She could feel his hand holding hers, making her feel safe.

Regina sat up in frustration. Why should she be

thinking of a man she had just met? It was of Father she should be thinking. Father and her family's future.

She had no inclination to marry. And she did not think her sisters would appreciate being rushed into marriage themselves. To marry a husband for charity? Out of desperation? It seemed so base.

Marriage was to make a good match. It was an economical decision. To marry a man for love alone was folly. But neither was marriage something to be rushed into. It required a careful weighing of pros and cons. It went against Regina's nature to rush herself or her sisters into matrimony.

If only there was a way to get back their fortune and land so that they could rely on Father as before. Then they could marry as other women did, smartly and in proper time. What would society say of them all getting married at once?

Her sisters deserved better than marrying under a cloud of scandal. And Father deserved better than the pity and judgment he would receive.

If only she could think of a way.

Regina distantly heard the sound of the front door. She checked the clock. Her sisters were back earlier than expected.

There was the sound of thumping feet and then the door to her bedroom flew open.

It was Elizabeth, her green eyes all but glowing and her chest heaving.

"Regina!" She snapped. "Care to inform me why Mr. Denny just proposed to me?"

Oh dear.

CHAPTER 5

The sisters all met in Bridget's room.

Louisa sat quietly on the bed, propped up with pillows. Elizabeth paced back and forth. Natalie was curled up on the windowsill. Bridget was on the edge of the bed next to Louisa.

Regina stood in the middle. It felt a little like she was on the stage.

"Spare nothing," Bridget told her.

As simply as she could she told them what had happened. Elizabeth uttered many words that a lady shouldn't know. Natalie clapped a hand over her mouth. And Louisa burst into tears.

Bridget merely stayed silent.

When Regina had finished she looked to her sister for guidance. Before Bridget said anything, however, Louisa cut in.

"Charles can never marry me now," she whispered through her tears.

"There, now," Bridget said, patting Louisa's knee soothingly. "Mr. Fairchild will not hesitate to wed you. I should say this gives him more reason to."

"If only his aunt would hurry up and die," Elizabeth said with an eye roll. When the other four looked at her, she shrugged. "Don't look so scandalized. You're all thinking it."

"You must accept Mr. Denny," Natalie said.

"I am not accepting a man I hardly know," Elizabeth replied.

"He has an income of ten thousand a year and that's all you need know!" Natalie hissed. "I should think you'd put up with half that a year if the man was fool enough to put up with you."

"Squabbling will get us nowhere," Bridget said. "Elizabeth, please consider Mr. Denny's proposal. He is a good man and has been watching you for some time."

"Watching is not half as good as speaking. If he has been watching me as you say then why not ask me to dance?"

"Because you are a harpy that does nothing but insult the man fool enough to ask you."

"Natalie, enough!" Bridget commanded.

Natalie fell silent.

Bridget drew herself up. "You could do well to improve yourself, Natalie. You cannot treat men as playthings. Pick one, and pick now. The time for indecision is over."

Natalie huffed but said nothing.

"And what of me?" Regina asked.

Bridget looked over at her. Her green eyes warmed and she almost smiled. "Don't fret for anything, darling."

"There's no need to play favorites," Elizabeth said. "She's eighteen, that's old enough to marry."

"And how will it look if all of us marry at once?" Bridget replied. "And if the youngest marries before her elders?" She gestured at Louisa.

Elizabeth had nothing to say to that. What Bridget said was true. Two of them getting married at once would raise eyebrows but not too many. Three or four of them?

Everyone would know the real reason they had tied the knot. The gossip would never cease.

As for age, it was commonly accepted—although by no means a rule—that the elder daughters married first. For Regina to marry before Louisa would provoke spinster comments about Louisa. Comments that her sweet sister did not deserve.

"And what of you, Bridget?" Natalie asked. "Surely you have suitors."

"I have. And I shall think on who would best suit me. I shall have to be married first, if Louisa is not. But there is nothing stopping either you or Elizabeth from entering an engagement."

"Let us face the truth, Bridget," Louisa said. Regina was surprised that she had spoken up. She sounded incredibly tired.

"We must face it. Marriage will save us financially. But it will not—nothing can save our reputations. Especially Father's. It will be years before people will stop whispering about it. Any man who marries us will have to take that on."

"The whispers will die down as soon as the next scandal comes," Bridget replied.

"Our lives will never be the same," Louisa countered. "We shall be indebted to our husbands as most women never are. Our wedding days will be covered in clouds. Father might never be welcomed back into society."

"This is how our lives are now," Bridget said. "Perfect marriages they might not be. But they are all we have. Let us be thankful that we have suitors willing to marry us. Not every woman is so lucky."

Again, Regina wished that there was a way to fix this. If only they could win back their land. That would stick it to Lord Pettifer. Then this cloud wouldn't be over her sisters' marriages. Father could hold his head high again.

If only...

"Then prove it to us," Elizabeth said. "Find yourself a husband."

Bridget thought for a moment. "I shall choose my husband the night of Lord and Lady Morrison's annual masquerade ball. It is in a month's time. Is that acceptable?"

The other three women nodded. Regina didn't. She couldn't. A thought had hit her like a lightning bolt. Her skin tingled and her stomach flipped.

Lord and Lady Morrison's masquerade ball.

There was a way to win their land and money back. There was a way to fix all of this.

She had figured it out.

CHAPTER 6

The girls retired for the night to their bedrooms. Louisa stayed in Bridget's room. They all had their own rooms but Regina suspected that Louisa needed a bit of extra comfort that night.

Regina went back to her bedroom and lay in darkness until she was certain the others were asleep.

When she had waited until she could hardly bear it anymore, she rose. She slid on her robe again and opened her bedroom door.

There was no sound throughout the house.

She didn't get a candle. Someone could see it and investigate. Instead she crept down the hall in darkness.

The stairs were tricky. Luckily she had the banister to hold onto.

When she reached the main floor she felt her way using the wall. She had never been in such darkness before. The moonlight slid through the curtains here and there. It created little pockets of silver-white light and tinged the edges of the dark blue. But in between those patches was nothing but deep shadow.

It was a little frightening. Regina found herself holding her breath now and again. Each time she shook herself. She had been reading far too many Gothic novels recently. This was not *The Castle of Otranto* or *The Mysteries of Udolpho*. She was not in a lonely castle on the moors. There was nothing to frighten her here.

Still, she couldn't deny that the house seemed different in the darkness. She moved slowly, carefully. It made everything seem longer. Distance and time were strange and unknowable.

When she finally reached her father's study she let out a sigh of relief. And, thank heaven, it was unlocked.

She slipped inside and latched it. She didn't know what time the servants rose but she didn't want anyone disturbing her. They would tell on her to Father, and that would lead to questions she couldn't answer.

Regina pulled open the curtains to her father's study. The moonlight spilled through, illuminating the room. It wasn't as good as a candle but it would do.

She began to carefully look through the papers on the desk. Surely information about the Duke of Whitefern had to be in there somewhere.

In looking, she found far more than she'd expected.

Father had been right. According to these lists of expenses, their income had been slipping every year. There were tallies of debts far greater than Regina had suspected.

Poor Bridget. She had known about these. Had she not thought to confide in someone? Why had she taken on this burden alone? Regina would have been happy to help.

She understood now why Bridget had spoken to her that morning. She glanced at the clock. Well, yesterday morning. She had known the debts would only get worse.

Regina looked at the papers again. At this rate, it was only a matter of a few years before Father was bankrupt.

How could they have let this go on for so long? Surely

Bridget could have stood up to Father and forced him to stop.

The moment she had that thought, Regina dismissed it. She could not force blame onto others. She too had been ignorant. She had sat sewing and reading, oblivious to the issue. They had all known Father's weakness. She was as much to blame as anyone for her inaction.

She set the papers aside and continued her search. Finally, she found it: in a stack of calling cards that Father kept. She recognized many names, including Lord Pettifer and Mr. Denny. It seemed this was a compilation of the men with whom Father played cards.

Regina took out a piece of paper and wrote down all the names. Then she copied down their addresses. If her plan was to succeed she had to know all the possible men involved.

The Duke of Whitefern was in there as well. It listed him as Lord Harrison, then his title, and an address. Regina was surprised to see the address was in London.

She went to the registry and looked up the Duke of Whitefern. All titled peoples were listed in the registry. There it stated that Whitefern was located on the opposite side of London from her own house.

Regina checked the address again. Perhaps Lord

Harrison had an apartment in London? It was not unheard of.

To be certain, she wrote down two copies of her letter. One would go to the estate of Whitefern and the other would go to the London address.

She thought carefully over what she wanted to say. It wouldn't do to spell out her entire plan. If the letter got into the wrong hands it would spell scandal for her. Well, more scandal than her family was already in.

In the end, she kept it brief:

Dear Lord Harrison,

Pardon my forwardness in writing you. As you may tell from my hand, it is a woman writing and not Lord Hartfield. I hope you allow me to call upon you on your earliest convenience. I think I have means by which my Father may be delivered from scandal. But I shall need your assistance. I hope that you will agree to my request. I promise I shall find a way to repay you for your time.

With best regards,

Miss Regina Hartfield

She addressed and sealed the two copies of the letter just as the sun was staring up over the hills. Every joint ached. Her eyes itched. She wanted to sleep for days.

Instead she made sure the desk was as she'd found it. Then she slipped out of the study and placed the letters in the box to be mailed. She made sure to sign the return address as from Lord Hartfield.

If it was discovered that she, an unmarried woman, had written to an unmarried man—the rumors that would start up didn't bear thinking about. But there were many reasons her father would write to a man such as Lord Harrison.

After that was done, she retired up to bed. She could hear the sound of the scullery maids setting the fires. Regina had been up until dawn before, reading in bed. But that felt different. Curled up in bed with a gripping story was one thing. Dealing with scandal and secrets was another.

She slipped back into bed and pulled the covers up. Her letter would reach Lord Harrison within a day or two. He would help her. He had to help her. Then she could win their fortune back.

That thought was the last she had before sleep claimed her.

CHAPTER 7

Thomas Harrison stared down at the letter in front of him. His breakfast lay untouched on the table. It was probably getting cold but he couldn't tear himself away.

Of all the things—he had not expected this.

When he had gone through his letters and saw that one was from Lord Hartfield, he had not been sure what to expect. Perhaps the man was writing to apologize? Or perhaps to thank him for assisting his daughter?

Instead when he had opened it he had seen that the letter was in fact from the daughter he had helped. Miss Regina.

She had been quite a pretty thing. None of her elder sister's regal bearing or confidence, of course. But nevertheless she had a sweet face. Her eyes were the most striking thing. They were a dark brown and seemed warm and inviting.

The rest of her had been nice as well. She had a fine figure. Her hair was dark red, like her sister Bridget's. She had a tiny face and delicate button nose. Also quite a lot of freckles. He'd thought those endearing.

Her manner had been quite contradictory. All he had heard of Miss Regina suggested a shy temperament. His admiration for her sister Miss Bridget he had ill-concealed. Bridget was witty, capable, confident, and beautiful, all that a man could want in a companion.

But in pursuing Bridget, he had learned about her family as a matter of course. Louisa, the second eldest, he had found to be even-tempered and thoughtful. She was well liked by all.

Natalie, the third, he had danced with once or twice. She was a spirited flirt. He hoped she would learn soon enough that treating men like puppets dancing attendance did not end well.

Elizabeth was the second youngest. He had not talked with her directly but he had heard many stories. While Natalie collected men's hearts, Elizabeth collected their pride. There was hardly a man about who had not been cut by her wit.

Regina he had not seen until the other night.

"A mouse," Miss Charlotte Tourney had said. "Terribly awkward. But I suppose it's natural. She's the youngest of five sisters. Must be quite competitive. And she's not a beauty."

Thomas had to disagree with Miss Tourney on that account. Regina was not a beauty like Bridget or Natalie, true. But she was also far from plain. She reminded him of a little fairy from his childhood stories.

Others had said similar things to Miss Tourney. *Rarely leaves the house. Quite boring. Hardly speaks. No interest in dancing. Blurts out the most frank observations. Clearly the governess gave up on that one. Does nothing but sew. I do believe she is dull-witted.*

All of this had led him to expect a meek child. That was not what he had encountered.

Miss Regina had seemed uncommonly determined to not accept her fate. She had shown fire in the side parlor. He could remember how she had firmly tugged herself away. How she had said that she must know what was going on. How she had declared that there must be a solution.

He thought perhaps that there was more to the youngest Hartfield than people realized.

Despite what he had seen that night, he had not expected this. It was most forward of her. Did she not realize that if he wanted he could circulate this letter? He could use it to spread the most salacious rumors. He could ruin her with it.

It showed quite a lot of trust in him. And she did not know him. They had spoken once. Not to mention that he had taken care that not much of his history be known.

He was not ashamed that he had used cards to regain his family fortune. His father had been a good man. A moral man. But his spine had been as soft as butter. He had no head for figures. Ill friends had swindled him until by the time Thomas inherited there was next to nothing left to inherit.

With the money he had earned from cards he had invested wisely. He had entered into business with good, solid men. He had put many years of hard work into refurnishing his estate. Whitefern had been gutted. All the art and furniture sold to pay debts. He had rebought each piece. Tracking some of it down had taken ages but he had employed determined men who were skilled at such things.

It had taken him the work of a decade but he had done it. He had rebuilt his family home. He had redone the grounds. He had ensured those who lived on his land prospered. He had put the Harrison family and the land of Whitefern back where they belonged: on top.

But not everyone saw it that way. Those who had never had to earn their living saw those who did as less-than. Especially when they had to use cards. It didn't help that people like that blasted Pettifer gave it all a bad name.

Thomas should have intervened. He should have warned Lord Hartfield. Mr. Denny was half in love with Elizabeth Hartfield and had told Thomas all about her father's ill luck with cards.

If only he had spoken to Hartfield and warned him not to play Pettifer. Perhaps this all could have been avoided.

Now Miss Regina was writing to him. She was begging him for help.

He had no idea what she could possibly have in mind that would involve him. Perhaps she had some separate inheritance she hoped to invest? If her deceased mother left her daughters some pounds, those would belong to Regina outright. She could invest them if she wished.

That didn't sound right. There were plenty of men Regina could go to for help with that. Why him?

Thomas couldn't find it within himself to refuse a young lady's plea for assistance. Especially the sister of the woman he loved. He was well aware that Bridget Hartfield hardly thought of him. But then, she hardly knew him. Perhaps with more time...

And how could he refuse a girl who was in the same position he had been as a young man? He had watched his father squander everything. Now Regina's father had done the same. It would make him the worst hypocrite to refuse her.

For Bridget's sake and for the sake of his own sympathy, he ordered for paper and pen to be brought.

Dear Miss Regina,

I have received your letter and am perplexed as to how I may assist. But I wish your family nothing but joy. If you think I may be of assistance then I shall do what I can. As you may know I have a London address. It shall make a fine halfway point between your father's estate and mine. If you can find an excuse to go to London, I can meet you there this Saturday.

With warmest regards,

Lord Harrison

He was tempted to add a postscript remind her to pass his regards onto Bridget, but he thought that might be pushing his luck. He had been rather bold about that the other night.

Still, he could not deny the idea appealed to him. Bridget could hardly avoid to look with favor upon the man who helped save her family. Perhaps, in helping the Hartfields, he could win Bridget.

Thomas finally tucked into his breakfast. He did not even mind that it was cold.

CHAPTER 8

Regina looked down at the address written in her hand. Then she looked back up at the building.

She was in a nice section of London. The streets were broad and lined with trees. The air smelled fairly pleasant for a city. And the houses were fine and sturdy. Yet she couldn't help but feel nervous.

She shook herself. She wasn't in a dangerous area. And Lord Harrison was not a dangerous man. A mysterious one, but not dangerous. There was no reason to be so concerned.

He really was mysterious though. Regina had made careful inquiries over the last few days. She had even spoken with Bridget about him. But nobody knew anything more than what Charlotte Tourney had told her.

"Lord Harrison is a fine man," Bridget had said. "His behavior has been acceptable."

"I had heard that he admired you," Regina had put forth.

"He has made that clear," Bridget had replied. "But I saw nothing in him to interest me. He seemed a gentleman, nothing more."

"But now you must consider him," Regina had suggested. "For as you told Natalie, we can no longer be picky."

"Beggars cannot be choosers," Bridget had admitted. "I shall consider him along with the others. If nothing else his fortune is massive and he is titled."

Now Regina was in front of Lord Harrison's city home. And she was terrified.

She recalled the way he had looked at her and the feel of her hand in his. A shiver ran up her spine. She did not like the way that he affected her. She couldn't even name how he affected her. He just...did.

"Well?" Lady Cora Dunhill asked. "I am happy to go in, my dear, but you look rather like you've seen a ghost. Perhaps it is best if we go for a bracing walk instead."

Lady Cora was what could only be described as a beauty. When she had first seen her Regina's breath had caught a little in her throat, the way it did when she saw a particularly lovely painting. Lady Cora had thick, dark hair that shone in the firelight and dark blue eyes that seemed deep and unfathomable.

She actually looked a little like she could be related to Lord Harrison. They had similar dark hair and blue eyes, although Lady Cora's were dark and mysterious in color while Lord Harrison's were warm and inviting. There was also the sly look to her, and the quirk of her mouth that suggested a private joke.

The thing that most struck Regina about her was the sense of class and style. She seemed the sort of woman to wear the latest fashions before everyone else, as if she had a secret carriage that whisked her to Paris in the night. In fact she was probably the woman who made the fashions that everyone else followed. And the curve of her throat, the slope of her shoulders, the very bones in her face reminded Regina of a statue.

'Classical beauty,' she thought. It was something that Bridget had said once. They had been discussing Helen of Troy. Well, this Lady Cora had that. She was the most beautiful woman Regina had ever seen, barring Bridget.

They had been introduced through Lady Morrison, with whom Regina had quickly struck up a correspondence asking for potential chaperones while in London.

She had failed to inform Lady Morrison that her mother would not do, for it had to be someone who did not previously know Regina.

Regina had called upon Lady Cora first thing after arriving in London. When she had curtsied to her, Lady Cora looked at her for a moment, a strange puzzled light in her eyes.

"You remind me of someone," she had said. Her voice was rich and melodious.

Regina could only think that one of her sisters had crossed Lady Cora's path before. Despite Regina's own opinion that she looked nothing like her sisters, most people only noticed the red hair and assumed they were all related. That must be it.

"I'm told that I look like my mother," she said, "But she has been dead for some time."

"Perhaps I saw her when I was young and that is why,"

Lady Cora replied. "No matter. It is wonderful to make your acquaintance."

It had taken little persuasion for Lady Cora to agree to chaperone Regina. It might have been because Regina had lied and said that Lord Harrison was her cousin, whom she had not seen in years.

"He quite disappeared off the face of the earth," she informed Lady Cora upon their meeting. "My parents wish me to make acquaintance with him once again, in light of his return to proper society."

Lady Cora, as Lady Morrison had hinted in her letters, was a dear friend to Lord Harrison. She had been more than happy to help his 'darling' young cousin and he get reacquainted.

"Honestly, Miss Regina." Lady Cora gently took Regina's shoulder and turned her so that she might look into her eyes. "I know that in its own way, family can be more intimidating than any stranger. If you need another day to brace yourself, then I shall not judge you."

"He expects my coming today," Regina said, unable to confide more without giving the game up.

"I'm sure that he will understand," Lady Cora replied.

As Regina stood there debating, the front door flew open. And there he stood.

Lord Harrison.

He looked more handsome than she had remembered. His eyes shone in the sunlight. They contrasted well with his dark hair. He had a strong stature, one that she could easily picture astride a horse. If they were going by looks alone, Regina was certain Bridget would have chosen him.

Furthermore, he looked every inch a noble. There was something in his bearing that showed it. It reminded Regina of Bridget's confidence. They would make a good couple, she decided. They were both the handsomest people she had ever seen.

"Are you going to hover outside all day?" Lord Harrison asked. "Or are you going to come inside?"

Regina nearly jumped out of her skin. "I, uh, that is—"

Lord Harrison sighed. "Come inside. It won't do for you to be seen hovering outside of my house. Unless you would like two scandals about your family instead of just the one."

"You needn't scare her in such a fashion," Lady Cora

replied, ascending the steps to go into the house. "Banging open doors like a banshee."

"I take it you are her chaperone?" Lord Harrison asked.

"You'd think you were being led to the guillotine," Lady Cora quipped. "Yes. Come inside, Miss Regina. I'm sure Harrison here won't be able to resist giving you the tour."

Regina actually liked the idea of a house tour. She quite liked decorations and furnishings. As if sensing this, Lady Cora groaned. "I was only... oh never mind. Give your tour, Harrison. Make it quick."

The house was very nicely furnished. Regina rather liked the style of it. She was surprised, for she had heard that a house done up by a single man was not often in good taste.

"Whitefern is rather a hodgepodge of generations," Lord Harrison said, as if reading her mind. "My father bought this flat and urged my mother to decorate it how she chose. It is to her taste."

"She had a marvelous sense of style," Regina said. The foyer had a staircase and all was done up in cream and soft gold.

"If you like the foyer, I'm certain that you'll enjoy the

rest of the house," Lord Harrison said. He sounded amused.

Regina looked up at him. "I should hate to think I'm wasting your time."

"It's not a waste. I have so few visitors and I like to show it off."

"Why so few visitors?" She asked. It was only after that she realized it might be a rude question.

"I try not to invite too many people over."

"Because then they might know you as a man and not as a mysterious entity."

Lord Harrison laughed. "I see Miss Elizabeth is not the only Hartfield with wit. Yes, you have hit the nail directly on the head."

He led her into the room to the right. Lady Cora trailed behind them, looking incredibly bored. "This is the dining room." It was done in shades of silver and grey. Regina didn't think she'd seen anything so elegant.

"I have tried to find out about you," Regina admitted.

Lord Harrison directed her through the dining room to a door at the back. It led into a side parlor done in gray with gold trim. "Oh? And what did you discover?" He sounded amused.

Regina moved past him into the next room—and promptly gasped.

It was a library. A wonderful library with a thick lush green carpet. It was all green. And it had a massive lovely fireplace in white marble. The windows had white trim and looked over the back of the house. The view was only of an alley but the position meant the sun would come streaming in from the south.

"I take it you enjoy reading?" Lord Harrison asked.

Regina nodded. She hurried to the shelves before she could stop herself. There were so many titles. All of the books were bound so lovingly. She ran her fingers over the spines.

"We have quite a good library at home," she said. "But it's not so cozy as this."

"It was my father's favorite room," Lord Harrison said. "His favorite color was green."

"It's mine as well," Regina admitted.

"Sometimes I think it would have been all the better if he'd had an older brother. Then he could have whittled away his days in here. He took to books better than he took to business."

Regina turned to look at him. Lord Harrison did look rather sad. "I heard that he lost your family fortune. I am sorry."

Lord Harrison shook his head. "It's no use worrying about it now. It's all said and done with and he has been with the Lord for many years now."

"Do you like to read?" Regina asked. She felt desperate to change the subject. She hated the way the lines on Lord Harrison's face deepened and his eyes darkened as he thought of his father. She was sure she looked the same when she thought about Mother.

"A bit." Lord Harrison's lips twisted upward into a wry smile. "Not as much as I should, and not as much as you, I'm sure."

"If you let me alone in here I should never leave," Regina admitted with a smile.

"Then we should probably continue the tour before I lose you here forever."

She felt her smile broaden and she had to hold in a laugh. Lord Harrison held out his arm for her to take as though they were at a park rather than his house. That made her want to laugh even more.

Regina took his arm and let him lead her through the last room. They had done a circuit now, and through the other door she could see the foyer.

This room was decorated in cream and silver with hints of green. It was a proper sitting room. There was a pianoforte in one corner. In another sat a writing desk. There was another, smaller fireplace on the outside wall.

"My mother used to welcome friends in here," Lord Harrison observed. "Father would be in the library while she was chatting away. The other parlor was used for cards or sweets after dinner."

"I quite like it."

"I should show you the upstairs rooms if I did not think it rude," Lord Harrison said. He winked at her and Regina found herself blushing. "There are four bedrooms. All in different shades of blue."

"They sound lovely."

"Well." Lord Harrison checked his pocket watch. "That took us ten minutes' time. Compare that to Whitefern. My housekeeper enjoys giving tours. It takes at least two hours. More if you let her rattle on. One time a poor family was stuck there for six hours. They were too polite to ask her to move things along."

Regina laughed. "If I ever see it, I shall ask you to give the tour then. You are rather brief."

"Didn't you know? Men are supposed to be brief. I've been told it's one of the failings of our sex."

Regina had to hold in a snort at that. She'd heard Elizabeth say something similar many a time.

"Since the library was your favorite, why don't we retire in there. I can have some tea brought up and we can discuss your reason for visiting."

Regina nodded. She'd like that very much.

They settled themselves in the library. Lord Harrison had a fire made up and sure enough tea was brought. Lady Cora seized upon a book and informed them she would be in the sitting room, where the light was better. "The doorway is open," she warned Lord Harrison, as if he were going to try and rob Regina or something while Lady Cora's back was turned.

Regina was secretly glad that Lady Cora was giving them some distance. She seemed to assume that private family matters would be discussed, such as where Lord

Harrison had been all this time. That suited Regina just fine.

Lord Harrison sat down and turned to face her. The playful light faded from his eyes and his voice grew somber.

"Now," he said. "Your letter was quite mysterious."

"Says the man that nobody knows anything about. Two people told me you had a secret wife. Another said you had engaged in piracy."

"I fear everyone is making me into someone much more exciting than I actually am."

"But I do hope one rumor is true: that you are a devil with cards."

Lord Harrison blinked as if surprised. "Yes. That is."

Regina waited. Lord Harrison seemed poised on the edge of something. It was like he was standing on a cliff and considering jumping off.

After a moment, he spoke.

"I am rather mysterious, as you say. But I can promise you most would prefer half-baked rumors to solid facts. At least where I am concerned.

"My father was terrible with business. He squandered

all of our fortune. When he died this London house was all we had. Whitefern was ours in name only. It was gutted. Empty. Everything had been sold off. Only my mother's love of this place kept it safe. Father wouldn't bargain it for anything.

"When he died I was told to sell this house and use the money to invest what I could. The bankers were quite insistent. In time, they said, I could slowly rebuild Whitefern's glory. But what good is a Duke without income? Destitute nobility are worse than a pauper. A pauper has many ways of earning his wages. A noble has but few.

"If I had pursued normal means it would have taken my entire life to rebuild my family name and fortune. But I saw another way. I was brilliant with cards in school. I even got into fights because the boys thought I was cheating. The professors sent letters home to my parents about it.

"I knew the kind of money that was spent at the tables at balls. I thought that through these means I could obtain the necessary capital. I'd make more money and faster. And, I admit, part of my motivation was preserving this house. It was my mother's pride and joy. She attended to every aspect of its decoration. You should have seen it at Christmas. The magic of it was unparalleled."

Lord Harrison gestured into the front sitting room. "The tree would be placed in there. Wreaths and garlands everywhere. Candles and sweets..."

A look of rapturous wonder stole over Lord Harrison's face. For a moment, Regina could see the boy he had been. But then he shook his head as if shaking away cobwebs.

"In any case. This was my mother's home and all that I had left of her. My father's library was all I had left of him. And I am rather fond of this place myself. I enjoy the hustle and bustle of London. And Whitefern is quite large. Preserving it and its history is of course important. But living in it overwhelms me. It is not mine. This house is.

"I gambled and won enough that in a year I could pay off all of my family's debtors. The next year I made enough to invest in proper ventures. Those ventures tripled my investment. I then began the arduous task of rebuilding Whitefern.

"I admit that this took all of my energy. Despite inheriting eight years ago I have not been seen much in society. All my attention has gone to restoring Whitefern. And I have accomplished it. I can now rest on my laurels.

"Hence," Lord Harrison chuckled. "My return to society these past six months and the wild speculations about my whereabouts for the previous eight years."

"If I may ask, when did your father pass on?"

"When I was eighteen. I am six and twenty now."

Eighteen. That was Regina's age. She thought it ironic that she and Lord Harrison had been the same age when they were forced to rescue their family name from ruin.

"Why are you confiding all of this to me?" She asked. "We have only met once before. I have come to you with quite an odd request in mind. Yet it is a request that I have yet to speak of to you. How do you know you can trust me?"

"Because you're in the same situation that I was," Lord Harrison replied. "And... I am about to be quite blunt here, Miss Regina. You must forgive me for it. I am earnest in my desire to wed your sister. If you know my story and my true history then perhaps you can speak of her kindly to me. At the least you can dispel for her any unsavory rumors."

"That is what I have come to discuss with you," Regina said. "If I may."

"Of course. I have to admit I'm dying of curiosity." Lord

Harrison winked at her. It made Regina feel warm all over. She ruthlessly shoved that feeling aside.

"My sisters know of our plight. Mr. Denny has proposed to my sister Elizabeth."

"Good man." Lord Harrison nodded. "He has cared for her for some time. I see this gave him the push he needed."

"Bridget has urged Elizabeth to accept him. Natalie must also choose one of her suitors. Bridget will select one as well—but I shall get to that presently."

Regina took a deep breath. "But marrying ourselves off will not solve our problems. We shall be marrying in haste. It will be one sister after another. Everyone will know why we're doing it. And it won't stop us from losing our home and lands. Father will still be looked down upon. And our husbands will have a time of dodging snide remarks. It isn't fair to anyone."

"I suppose not," Lord Harrison acknowledged. "But what is to be done?"

Regina drew herself up. "In a month's time, there is the annual masquerade ball hosted by Lord and Lady Morrison. They are dear friends of our family. We are sure to be invited no matter what scandal follows us. Lady Morrison was of great comfort to Bridget when

Mother died. And Lord Morrison comes to our house for shooting every year. We have them over whenever time permits.

"I know that women are not allowed to play at cards. But I also know that the masquerade ball is a time when rules are bent. Or broken outright. Everyone is wearing a mask. This way, identities are hidden. Reputations are preserved. Nobody would stop a woman from playing on that night."

Lord Harrison drew himself up as well. His eyes flashed. "Miss Regina. Are you certain of what you are saying."

"I am." She tilted her chin up and dared him to defy her. "Lord Pettifer will be invited to the ball. He is a horrible rake but he has both money and title. The Morrisons will have to invite him. He will be there and he will play. I shall play him. I will be masked, no one can stop me. I shall play him and win back the Hartfield deed. I can win back a good deal of our income besides."

"And what if you lose?" Lord Harrison pointed out. "The cards can go either way. If you play, Miss Regina, you must be prepared to lose everything."

"What else have I to lose?" She countered. "We are penniless. We are to be driven out of our home. My

Father's reputation will never recover. My sisters shall marry under a cloud."

"And what will you bet? Do you have money?"

"I have a small sum bequeathed from my mother. And I had hoped you might forward me a loan. I should repay you, of course."

"And why should I forward you this loan?"

"So that you may watch me play. You will want to see how your protégé has turned out."

"My protégé?" Lord Harrison looked as though he'd been struck by lightning. "Are you saying that I will teach you?"

"Yes." Regina nodded.

"And why would I do that?"

"Because if you do, I shall convince Bridget to marry you."

Lord Harrison sucked in a breath. His eyes were wide.

Regina nodded confidently. "Yes. Bridget is more like mother to me than sister. I am her darling and I have her ear. I have long conspired that she not marry. Every man she has considered, I have found ways to dissuade her. If I speak to her of your virtues she will be persuaded.

"You just now told me the story of your life. You said that it was because we are alike. I agree. Surely you cannot refuse someone who is in a position so like your own. And you will obtain the key to your future happiness."

Regina took in a steadying breath. She could feel heat pricking her eyes. Her heart was hammering. And her chest trembled.

She forced herself to keep looking into Lord Harrison's eyes. "Bridget is the best of women. She has run our household from a tender age. She has assisted our father in everything. She raised me. She is patient, kind, and well educated. She plays the pianoforte and draws and sings. She reads wonderfully. And she has wit paired with prudence.

"You would never find a better wife anywhere. She would make you so happy it would almost be unbearable. I would not lose her for anything. Except this. I have to save my family. And you can help me. We would owe you everything—my sister's hand is the least I can offer."

Lord Harrison stared at her for a moment. Then he spoke. His voice was deep and slow. It was as if he was coming out of a daze.

"You are not at all what I expected, Miss Regina."

Regina ducked her head. She could feel her face flushing. She knew what he had expected: a mouse. But she couldn't afford to be a mouse anymore. She had to be strong.

Lord Harrison stood up. He crossed over to the fire with his hands behind his back. Regina watched him. She could not read his expression. The light from the fire danced across his face. Once again she was reminded of the stories of the fairy king.

One must always be careful of striking bargains with fairies. That was something all the fairy tales said. They would trick you if you gave them half a chance. Was she striking a deal in a similar way now? Would Lord Harrison trick her in some way?

Regina was wading out into treacherous waters. She knew it. Soon she'd be out in deep ocean with no way to touch the bottom. And she would have to depend wholly on Lord Harrison. He was a stranger to her. Yet her life—and the lives of her family—was being placed in his hands.

She forced herself to keep her breaths deep and even. After what seemed like an age, Lord Harrison turned back to her.

To her surprise, there was a twinkle in his eyes. It was as if he found all of this amusing.

"You really are something, Regina Hartfield," he said. "I think society has quite underestimated you."

"Then you will do it?" She asked. She hardly dared to breathe.

Lord Harrison nodded. "I could not refuse you and remain a gentleman. As you said we have been in similar positions. And I hate to refuse a lady. I shall teach you all that I know of cards. At the masquerade ball, you will win back your family's land from Lord Pettifer. In exchange, you will persuade your sister to accept my proposal and I shall wed her."

Regina nodded.

Lord Harrison approached her and she stood up automatically. He was taller than she was but not so much that she had to crane her neck. It didn't stop him from cutting an intimidating figure.

He held out his hand to her. It took her a moment to realize that he meant for her to shake it. He was offering her a handshake like she was a man. Like she was his equal.

"There are no witnesses," Lord Harrison said. "And we

are not signing any papers. But I shall trust you to uphold your bargain as if we were in a court of law."

"Then I shall trust you to uphold your end," Regina replied.

Lord Harrison inclined his head in acknowledgment.

Regina took his hand then and shook it. Her hand was terribly small in his.

It occurred to her how close they were standing. His hand was as large and warm as she had remembered. His gaze seemed to sink into her skin, worming into the very heart of her. From this distance she could see his soft lashes and the bow of his mouth. She could smell him as well. He smelled like a wood fire: comforting and heady all at once.

As if he realized they had been holding hands for too long, Lord Harrison released hers and stepped back. "We shall arrange a time to meet. We must take care not to be seen together too often. Lady Cora as your escort can only do so much."

"I could not afford to have an escort that knew me," Regina admitted. "My sisters know nothing of my plan. I could not risk anyone informing them of my meeting with you."

"And they shouldn't. No one should know. The more people know of a thing the more likely the truth will out. Lord Pettifer must have no idea what you plan. He is overconfident. If we surprise him we have a greater chance of success."

"In any case my sisters would not approve of the risk."

"I am not sure that I should approve of the risk either," Lord Harrison pointed out. "But I am not quite a gentleman. I am fond of bending the rules. And a little risk excites me."

He paused. A smile flitted across his face as something amusing struck him. "And it appears that you are not quite a lady, either, Miss Regina."

She stood as straight as she could. "If being not quite a lady means I save my family, sir, then so be it. I am willing to pay that price."

Lord Harrison winked at her again. It made that odd heat spike in her blood again. "Then I think we shall have quite a lot of fun together, Miss Regina."

CHAPTER 9

Thomas sank into a chair the moment that Miss Regina and Lady Cora left.

What on earth had he just gotten himself into?

He'd had no idea what Regina wanted when she visited but it definitely wasn't that. Now he had promised to teach her how to play cards. A woman! A *young* woman at that! And playing cards!

He could practically feel Mother's disappointed glare. But what was he supposed to do? How could he refuse her? She had looked so young and forlorn. Those big soft brown eyes and that delicate face with those dear little freckles had warmed his heart. He dared any man to say no to that.

Not to mention—she had been right.

Even if Regina and all her sisters got married tomorrow, there was no true escape from the scandal. Marriage would keep them from being destitute. It wouldn't stop them from being the subjects of gossip.

The only way to truly save her family was to get their home and land back. That meant getting Lord Pettifer to give back the deed Lord Hartfield had given him. But Pettifer would never give that up. He had been looking for years for the opportunity to expand his land holdings.

Besides that, though, Pettifer was a proud man. He wouldn't want to give up what he'd stolen fair and square. But a game of cards—that would be his weakness. Pettifer thought he was untouchable. Probably because he'd never played Thomas. By the time Pettifer had made himself known in society, Thomas had been done with his gambling.

They could play on that. They could play on that very well. Pettifer was overconfident and had an inferiority complex. If he thought a mere woman was showing him up he'd bet everything he had. That would make her bet everything that she had. Then—or so Pettifer thought— he'd strip it all away.

Thomas had to admit it was a clever plan. Pettifer wouldn't be able to do anything to protest. If he did, then Regina could point out his hypocrisy. If he said a bet made was not binding, then the bet made by Lord Hartfield was not binding either.

But first Regina had to win. She had to win and she had to be careful. If anyone guessed her identity at the masquerade she'd be ruined. A woman gambling large sums? A woman alone in a room with a group of men? She'd be ruined.

Well, more ruined that she already was. Thomas wasn't sure if Regina fully grasped the dangerous game she wanted to play. But she was willing to risk being completely outcast by society to save her family. That was a kind of spunk he rarely saw from anyone, man or woman.

For that alone, he probably had to help her. He appreciated boldness of character. And Miss Regina seemed to have that in spades. Besides, she was a lovely girl.

Her face when she had entered the library. Thomas didn't think he'd ever forget that. She had given this little gasp to go with it. And her eyes had been so wide and full of joy. He had never seen someone appreciate his library like that before.

She'd appreciated the entire house, actually. He was glad of that. Most people nodded politely when they entered. The house was done in good taste. He knew that. But it was a simple taste. Elegant, to be sure, but not what people expected from such a prominent family.

Most people preferred Whitefern. The history, the vast lands, the artwork and ostentatious designs... those suited the idea of what people thought a noble's house should look like. But Thomas preferred something simpler. This house suited him just fine.

It was rather nice to find someone who finally appreciated the house the way that he did. Regina had been a delight to show around.

If she was so appreciative, Thomas was sure that Bridget would be as well. Regina had said that Bridget had been more like a mother to her than a sister. He hoped that meant their tastes were similar.

He couldn't deny that he was excited about the prospect of winning Bridget's hand. He knew that it was selfish of him. Theoretically he should have helped Regina no matter what. She was in need of him. It was the gentlemanly thing to do.

But he was also a bit of a selfish man. He wanted Bridget

and now he could have her. Call him a cad for it but it was far less than what some other men had done. And he hadn't even asked. Regina had offered the idea up willingly.

He would help her and he would win the hand of the woman he loved. It sounded like a win-win situation to him.

If only Regina could pull off the card playing.

CHAPTER 10

The first and biggest hurdle for Regina was figuring out a way to see Lord Harrison without causing a scandal. She had to meet with him regularly to practice. The masquerade was only a month away, after all. But she couldn't be seen stopping by his house every day.

Fortunately, their precarious situation worked to her advantage. Louisa was accompanying Elizabeth to visit Mr. Denny's estate up north. Mr. Fairchild would by fortunate coincidence also be there. Louisa and Mr. Fairchild could have some time together to discuss matters. And meantime, Elizabeth could get to know Mr. Denny better.

Bridget had made it clear that Elizabeth was to accept Mr. Denny's proposal. Regina wasn't so sure. Elizabeth was stubborn. Mr. Denny would have to prove himself a man that could stand up to her without belittling her. Regina was a little doubtful of Mr. Denny's ability to manage that.

While Louisa and Elizabeth were gone, Bridget and Natalie would receive suitors for Natalie. Bridget would help Natalie to settle upon one. At the same time, Bridget would be helping Father handle the handover of the estate to Lord Pettifer.

The thought of Bridget dealing with Lord Pettifer made Regina's stomach churn. But what else was there for it? Father was all muddled over the legalities. And even if he wasn't, he was in a state of despair.

That was the hardest part about all of this. Regina had never seen her father like this. He hardly ate. He seemed to have sunk into himself. He was like a husk of a man.

Bridget had determined that Father go to Bath. It was the best place to heal and rest up. The Morrisons were staying there and had happily agreed to take him in. Father would be in good hands with them. And, even better, he wouldn't have to be there to watch his home handed over.

That just left Regina.

She waited until it was late in the evening. Bridget was in Father's study going over the accounts. The candlelight showed the lines of exhaustion on her face.

For a moment Regina simply stood in the doorway, watching. It made her heart ache to see her sister like this. There was so much to do in preparation for the hand over. Not for the first time she felt a spike of hot anger in her chest at Lord Pettifer.

How dare he do this to her family. He knew the situation that she and her sisters were in. It would have been bad enough had one or two of them been married. But all of them single? All of them without home or honor? All of them women unable to enter the navy or the clergy to save themselves?

It was the lowest. Regina would have slapped him if she could. She relished the thought of seeing his rat face go red from the palm of her hand. She wanted to see those beady eyes go wide with shock and fear. She wanted him to cower in front of her.

But there were few circumstances under which she could slap him and escape with her reputation. She would have to settle for beating him at cards. She quite looked forward to the look on his face when she bested him. She knew it would be something to behold.

That is, if she won. And she would have to win. There would be no second chance. The masquerade ball was where the Morrisons got to break all the rules of society. Nobody could say for *certain* that Eliza McAvoy and Edmund Branson sharing passion in the third guest room last year. Nobody could claim for *certain* that it was Lucas DeWitt who'd had too much to drink and splashed about in the fountain.

And so nobody would be able to say for certain that it was Regina Hartfield that played at cards this year.

The masks kept everyone anonymous. That meant that the normal rules of society were gone. Or, rather, as gone as they would ever be. The Morrisons had gotten the idea from Carnival down in Italy. It was especially celebrated in Venice, they said.

If Regina didn't win on the night of the masquerade, she would have to wait an entire year before trying again. And the next time Lord Pettifer would be ready for her. Regina couldn't have that. In a year it would be too late.

She had to act now. This was her one chance.

With that knowledge in hand, she approached her sister.

"Bridget?"

It took Bridget a moment to respond. This was a

sure sign of her sister's exhaustion. She blinked slowly down at the paper in her hand. Then, dragging her head up as if it weighed a ton, she looked at Regina.

"I'm sorry to bother you," Regina said. "But I had an idea."

"You're never bothering me, darling," Bridget assured her. She smiled, but Regina could see the exhaustion in it. "Go on then."

"You said that I need to practice more at being out in society. And I know that you said I don't need to worry about marriage. I am the youngest. But I should make a good reputation for myself. For when, you know, the news hits.

"The Morrisons have a house in London, as you know. I was thinking I could stay there. Mathilda Morrison's mother is there. She can serve as my escort to balls. And I can call on people more easily there. It will give me a chance to become properly known in society."

She added a little shrug. "And who knows? I might even find a suitor."

Some of the tightness in Bridget's face and shoulders seemed to leak out. "Are you sure about this?"

Regina nodded. "It is up to us to preserve our family's reputation. I must do my part as well."

Bridget set down her pen. "As much as it would pain me to be parted from you... how much it pains me that the entire family must split up... it is a wise decision that you make."

She smiled up at Regina. "I'm very proud of you, darling. I know it can't be easy for you."

"It isn't," Regina admitted, and it was true. It wasn't easy to leave Bridget. It wasn't easy to leave the safety of her home. She had never lived in a city before. And she'd never lived alone without Bridget or Father in charge.

But what scared her and what she wanted didn't matter anymore. She didn't matter anymore. What mattered was her family. What mattered was saving them.

Bridget held out a hand. "Come here."

Regina took her sister's hand and allowed Bridget to pull her in. She sat down on Bridget's lap, just like when she was a child. Bridget slowly passed a hand over Regina's hair.

"You know no matter how old you get you shall always remain my baby sister," Bridget said. "It's hard for me to see you grow up. Almost as hard as it is for you to grow up. And perhaps I've babied you too much. But you are a woman. You can make your own decisions. In fact you must. So do what you think is best and don't let me influence you unduly."

Regina nodded. "I won't. But I shall abide by your council. You raised me well."

"I should hope so." Bridget kept stroking her hair. "London is a busy place. It is also full of temptation. Use your head and do what you know to be right. Don't let anyone sway you away from that.

"And," she laid her hand over Regina's, "Protect your virtue. There are rakes everywhere but London seems to have an especially high concentration of them. Keep your wits about you. Don't be swayed by a handsome face or handsome words."

Regina nodded.

Bridget sighed. "I shall hate to see you go. But I think you are wise. London will be good for you. Get out into the world. Establish yourself. You've been cooped up in here for too long."

Regina nodded again. "You know that you have been the best of sisters to me. I told someone just the other day that you are like a mother to me. I couldn't have asked for a better guide than you."

"I am not without fault." Bridget gestured at the papers spread out on the desk in front of her. "Look at this. I should have put my foot down long ago. If I had pressed, I could have cut off Father's gambling."

"He is our father," Regina replied. "And he is the man who owns the land. You couldn't have truly stopped him. Not if he was determined."

"I could have at least tried harder."

"And I think we still would have ended up here." Regina bit her lip. "Bridget?"

"Yes?"

"Have you ever loved like Father has?"

"What do you mean, darling?"

"Well, after Mother died," Regina explained. "That's when the gambling started. Or when it got really bad. I can hardly imagine it. I mean they talk about it in my books. But can you really love someone so much that losing them makes you lose your senses?"

"When it's hard for us to accept a bad truth, we delve into distractions," Bridget said. "And when we lose someone, it is beyond our control. So we try to find things that we can control. Father couldn't control the loss of Mother. So instead he tried to control the cards.

"It's not a bad thing to love someone that much. But I think it's a bad thing to let that love take away your spine. Love shouldn't strip away who you are. It should make you more of who you are. It should embolden you."

Bridget paused, as if running her words back over through her head. "Does any of that make sense?"

"A little."

"And to answer your question, yes. I loved like that once. Or I thought I did."

Regina straightened in her sister's lap. Bridget had never told her of this before. "What happened?"

"We could not marry."

"Why not?"

Regina racked her brain but could not recall a time when Bridget had favored anyone. If her sister had loved, she had done it in utmost secrecy.

Bridget shook her head. "When did you become so curious?"

It was because she wanted to test the waters of Bridget's heart. She wanted to see how easy or difficult it would be to turn her affections toward Lord Harrison. But she couldn't tell Bridget that.

Instead she said, "With all this talk of you all getting married, it made me curious. I know that things have become such that you cannot even marry for affection. Never mind marrying for love. But I do want to know."

Bridget laughed lightly. "I think you have been reading too many of your Gothic stories. But you will deal with marriage soon enough. I suppose it's only fair that you know a bit."

She thought for a moment. Her gaze was far off. Regina waited patiently.

After a moment or two, Bridget spoke.

"There were three things standing in our way. Three very sensible things. The first was that we were young. Quite young. Young enough that marriage at such an age was not prudent. It was considered that we did not know our own minds. And I suppose that may be true.

"The second was that Mother died. And I had a very young, very sweet little sister to raise. Father was beside himself as well. Someone had to look after the household.

"The third was that the family did not approve of me. My suitor was sent away to live with an uncle for a time.

Pains were taken so that our paths should never cross again.

"And that is all there is to say about it, really. We were young, the family did not approve, and fate was against us."

Regina wondered how her sister could speak so plainly about something as deep as love. "I am sorry."

"What for?" Bridget looked at her, startled. "None of it is your fault."

"But if you hadn't had to take care of me—"

"Nothing would have changed the family's disapproval of me. You had no hand in that. And it was a joy to help raise you. You are my darling sister and I would not take back a second by your side."

Regina felt tears welling up and she hugged her sister fiercely. She felt terrible about bargaining for her sister's hand with Lord Harrison. She had used Bridget in that, used her like property. But there was nothing to be done about it now.

"You are the most loving sister that ever lived," Regina promised her. "Not one of us deserves you."

Bridget laughed, holding Regina tightly. "Now, now, what brought this on? No tears, darling. I know it all seems very scary right now. But if we hold our heads up high and persevere, this storm will pass. I promise."

Regina wanted to explain that wasn't why she was crying, but she couldn't. Not without giving the entire game away. Instead she just nodded into the crook of Bridget's neck.

"Have you really never seen that suitor again?" She asked. "After all these years?"

"Never." Regina could feel Bridget's shoulders move as she sighed. "But then I might not even recognize them now. So much time has passed. They are probably married by now anyhow."

"There are other men out there," Regina said. She pulled back so that Bridget could see her face. "Good men. I know you'll find one of them to love."

Something pained flashed across Bridget's face. It was there and gone in the space of a heartbeat—so fast that Regina couldn't be sure she had read it right. "That is very sweet of you. I appreciate your faith in me and in the men of this world."

Regina smiled at the teasing tone in Bridget's voice. She'd do anything to help raise her sister's spirits. "I shall try and find you a man in London," she declared.

Bridget laughed. "If you can, I shall be both surprised and grateful."

Regina slid off of her lap and stood up. "Shall I write to the Morrisons then and ask them?"

"I shall write them," Bridget said. "You may add a note of your own. But as you are still young it is best if I ask formally."

"Thank you!" Regina said. She flung her arms about her sister's neck and kissed her cheek. She felt giddy and lightheaded. It was almost like she was a child again. "Thank you, thank you!"

She then hurried off. She was in little doubt that the Morrisons would say yes. That meant she had packing to see to.

CHAPTER 11

The Morrison house in London was enough to make her jaw drop. Regina always forgot how much money the Morrisons had until it was staring her in the face. She had never been to their London residence before. She had expected—perhaps naïvely—that it would be similar to Lord Harrison's house.

It wasn't. Lord and Lady Morrison had clearly gone all out in their preparations. The house was done up in rich colors. Each room had its own color: soft pink in the front parlor. Powder blue in the sitting room. Red in the dining room. Yellow in the back parlor.

The house was also twice the size of Lord Harrison's. Regina got lost on her first day. The housekeeper had to help her get back to her room. She had to admit that the house was beautiful, tasteful, and showed off Lord Morrison's wealth. There was nothing distasteful about it. And yet, she preferred Lord Harrison's house.

Lord Harrison's house had felt like a proper home. There was love in each decorating choice. The Morrison house felt more like it was designed to be shown off.

Still, she couldn't complain. Lady Morrison's mother was a lovely woman. Regina had expected nothing less. Lady Morrison, née Mathilda Braxton, was a lively woman. She was educated and had a sparkling sense of humor. She also liked to skirt impropriety. She did it in such a way that it entertained people and just barely stopped short of a scandal.

Her mother, unsurprisingly, was the same. She was full of life and energy despite her age. And she insisted right away that Regina dispense with the "Mrs. Braxton."

"I am to be your hostess," she said, "and I want to be one you can properly confide in. Call me Jane, as you would your girlfriends."

"I don't have any girlfriends," Regina admitted. There were just her sisters. And only Bridget could really be called a friend. Louisa was nice enough, but they weren't close. And Natalie and Elizabeth merely tolerated Regina.

"My daughter is," Mrs. Braxton pointed out. "But if you think she doesn't count, then I shall be your first."

Regina wasn't quite comfortable with calling her 'Jane.' Especially with so many years between them. They compromised and had Regina call her 'Aunt Jane.'

"I know the sort of temptations that London is full of," Aunt Jane said. "I only ask that if you grow curious, you tell me. I shall show you how to do things properly."

Regina could only begin to imagine the sort of things Aunt Jane referred to. But she thought she might test the waters slightly.

"What if I wanted to learn something that ladies ought not to learn?"

"Such as?" Aunt Jane asked.

"...such as..." Regina thought. "Well, cooking."

"Then I would say that's an odd thing to want to learn, but I won't stop you," Aunt Jane replied.

"And what if I wanted to keep odd hours?"

"I would ask you not to wake me."

Aunt Jane put her hand over Regina's. "My dear. My daughter had her own time sampling what the world had to offer. As did I. As long as you are smart about it, I see no reason for any of it to cloud your future or your reputation."

Regina was not so sure of that herself. But she was grateful for it if it meant that Aunt Jane wouldn't ask questions.

The Morrison house was, thankfully, only two doors down from Lord Harrison's. It was part of why Regina had asked if she could stay with them. It was easy enough for her to exit through the back door into the alley, then cross over and enter Lord Harrison's from his back entrance.

It meant that the servants sometimes looked at her oddly, but she didn't mind. What could they say? She knew that the downstairs talked and gossiped as much as the upstairs. It wasn't that she underestimated that. She was sure that Lord Harrison's servants and Aunt Jane's servants had compared notes.

But who else could they tell? Why would they bother to tell any other servants? And why would those servants then bother to go tell their employers? It was out of their way and served no purpose.

When she told Lord Harrison this, he handed her some pound notes. "Slip them a few extra coins here and there. Say it's for setting the table so fine. Or for turning up the beds the way you like. Any excuse will do. And take care to learn their names. You can never be too careful. If they like you, they won't betray you. And they'll know the real reason you're lining their pockets."

And so her lessons were to begin.

She waited until late morning when everyone else was out calling. She had a leisurely breakfast with Aunt Jane to start. They discussed society and Aunt Jane started quizzing her on who was who. Then they read the paper together.

Then Aunt Jane set out to call upon her acquaintances. She would be gone for at least three hours. It was perfect timing.

Regina slipped down the alley to Lord Harrison's house. She instructed the housekeeper to tell anyone who visited that she was out making calls as well. That should keep anyone who visited off her trail. Although she doubted anyone would want to call and see her.

When she knocked at the back door, Lady Cora opened it immediately. "In you go."

Regina slipped in past her and let her lead her up the library, where Lord Harrison was waiting.

"I have some letters to write," Lady Cora said, and sat down at the desk in the corner.

Lord Harrison gave her a long-suffering look and then turned back to Regina. "Normally we'll play cards at the table in the side parlor. But first I want to start you on this."

He then handed her a book.

Regina stared at it. Of all things—a book?

Lord Harrison laughed. He looked much more relaxed than when she'd seen him last. His hair was loose and curled around his face. It made him look younger. Boyish, almost.

His posture was a bit more relaxed as well. And while he wore a shirt and waistcoat done up properly, he had no coat to go with it.

Regina thought she liked this look. He seemed so much looser now. Like he'd been holding himself stiff and now he could let go. It suited him much better.

"The look on your face," he said. "It's absolutely precious."

Regina bristled at that. "I am not precious."

"I hate to tell you this, but you really are." Lord Harrington grinned at her. "I think it's your fairy face."

"My what?"

He plopped down onto the sofa. Regina had never seen a man behave in such a relaxed manner. It was quite novel. "You have a fairy face. When I was a child, my mother would read fairy tales to me. I always pictured fairies as looking like you. You have such a delicate pixie face. Plus your freckles."

Regina wanted to bristle more, but he sounded so genuine. It actually sounded like a compliment coming from him. "When I first saw you on the porch I thought you looked like a fairy king."

Over in the corner, Lady Cora made an indelicate sound but didn't look up from her letters.

"I'm going to choose to take that as a compliment," Lord Harrison said. "And I shall take our similar observations about one another as a sign that we shall make a good mentor and protégé."

And a good brother and sister-in-law, Regina thought. She couldn't forget about that. She had tried to put it out of her mind, but it was always present. She had all but sold her sister for this.

Would Bridget ever forgive her? Or would she hate her if she learned the truth?

"Why did you think I was a fairy king?"

Regina was wrenched out of her thoughts and she blinked. "What?"

"Why did you think I was a fairy king?" Lord Harrison had a mischievous smile on. It rather suited him. "I'm quite curious."

"Something about the lighting," Regina confessed. "And the idea of making a deal with the fairy king. You have to be careful or he'll trick you."

"I have no intentions of tricking you," Lord Harrison said. "That I can promise. But you don't look rather like those heroines who went up against the king. You look more like a fairy attendant. Perhaps you can be Puck then."

"I'm Puck and you're Oberon?" She replied, getting into the spirit of it. "We are intending to trick at least one mortal."

"And we'll be masked. One night of the year when we can roam free. Sounds similar to Shakespeare to me."

Regina found herself smiling back at him. It was just so

conspiratorial. Excitement bubbled up in her gut. They were going to do this. They were really going to do this.

And it might even be fun.

"I want you to start with these books, Puck," Lord Harrison said, "Because they're about how to play cards."

He tapped the cover of the books. "You said you enjoyed reading so I thought these might help you grasp the theories."

"There are theories to cards?"

"Just like there are theories to stitching."

Regina thought about that. "So just as how there are patterns in stitching there are patterns in cards."

"Exactly." Lord Harrison nodded, pleased. "I think if you have the theory in mind it'll be easier for you to pick it up. Since you're such a bookworm. Do you think you can get through all those books in an afternoon?"

Regina started. She looked through them for a moment. "I think so."

"Do your best. I'm having some friends over to play a game next evening."

Regina's stomach clenched. She couldn't be seen with Lord Harrison! And playing cards! People would—

Lord Harrison held up a hand. "Now, don't worry. Nobody there will know you. I was very careful in who I chose. I want you to just observe tonight. See how each person plays. There's a lot that you can learn just by watching."

"And who am I supposed to be?"

"I'll pass you off as my cousin from my mother's side. None of them will be the wiser."

"As you say, Lord Oberon." Regina tried winking at him.

Lord Harrison burst into laughter. "Look at you! You're a proper minx!"

"I do my best," Regina replied archly.

"Miss Regina, you are a wonder," Lord Harrison marveled. "I never would have expected this from you. If you can surprise me like this I think we'll make a card player out of you yet."

Regina smiled. This might be easier than she thought.

CHAPTER 12

By the time the afternoon was done Regina was rethinking this entire thing.

Who knew that cards could be so complicated? The only game that Regina had ever played was Bridge. Normally her four sisters would play it while Regina read or sewed. Sometimes, however, Natalie would be off at a ball. Or Elizabeth would be in a mood. Or Louisa would be calling at a mutual friend's to see Mr. Fairchild. In that case, Regina would play.

But this wasn't bridge. This was so many card games that she had never heard of before. Whist, Loo, Speculation... how many card games were out there?

It seemed that Loo was the most popular game. She had

a feeling that would be the game Lord Pettifer would play. In a game of Loo the pot could increase exponentially. That sounded like the perfect setup to rob a man of his fortune and lands.

Supposedly the game was easy to learn, but she could hardly make heads or tails of it. She just hoped that when she watched everyone play it would be easier to understand.

She was left alone for some hours. Lady Cora apparently had many letters to attend to. Her only movement was when she would get up to stretch her legs by speaking to Lord Harrison about something in the other room. Otherwise, it was silent save for the scractching of Lady Cora's pen and the turning of Regina's book pages.

The only proper interruption was when a maid stopped by with some sandwiches and tea. It was quite nice, actually. She had no idea what Lord Harrison was up to but she didn't mind. She felt quite safe.

He presented quite a contradiction. He had been so calm and in charge the first night. And when they had met the second time he'd been extraordinarily serious. But today he had been relaxed. Cheerful, even.

Perhaps it was because he knew he would have Bridget.

Or perhaps it was that he looked forward to having someone to teach. Regina could imagine that he hadn't had much opportunity to pass on his skills. And those must have been hard-won.

But no. It must be Bridget. Now that their bargain was struck and she was starting in earnest, Bridget was all but certain. She would persuade Bridget to marry him either way. Either she won and was in debt to him completely, or she lost and Bridget must marry him to secure them all. She had promised him Bridget's hand in marriage. And so Bridget she would deliver.

Regina threw her book to the ground. She knew it was a childish act. But damn it, she couldn't help herself.

Elizabeth rather liked to swear when nobody but family was around. Bridget had picked up quite a few phrases from her. She'd also picked up quite a few other things. Like Elizabeth's tawdry books. The kind that were paperback that she had to order secretly.

She felt like a heel. Every time she tried to justify it she just made herself sick. Lord Harrison would take good care of Bridget. She would want for nothing. And he seemed a good-tempered man. He certainly understood business.

And if a house spoke for a man, then Lord Harrison's

house spoke well for him. He had a good, comfortable home. Modest but in a way that spoke of discretion rather than lack of funds. Tasteful and maintained in honor of his parents. Regina had no doubt that Bridget would love this home. After all, she did, and she'd only been to it twice.

And besides, what choice would Bridget have if Regina lost? Bridget would have to marry someone and it might as well be Lord Harrison. He was risking much by helping a woman learn to play cards and gamble with the men. His reputation was on the line as well. And he'd worked so hard to keep people from finding out anything too sordid.

But no matter how many sensible reasons presented themselves, she felt awful. At the end of the day she had still sold her sister. And that made her as bad as Father.

"How is it going?"

Lord Harrison's voice was low and warm and right at her ear. Regina jumped. She ignored the tingle of heat shooting down her spine and turned to glare at him.

"You startled me."

"That was rather the goal, Puck." He winked at her. "How's the reading going?"

"Quite well," Regina lied.

Lord Harrison shook her head. "You're going to have to get better at lying than that if you want to play with Pettifer."

Regina's face fell. "I'm sorry. I just—it's harder than I expected."

"You don't have to apologize. You've never done any of this before." Lord Harrison sat down by her legs. The heat of his body was so near hers. She'd never noticed that before. It was like he was a furnace. She wanted to crawl into that heat and stay there.

"I think that once you watch us play tomorrow afternoon you'll realize you learned more than you thought," he told her. "We have a month. There's no need to get discouraged after only one afternoon."

Regina nodded. He sounded so confident. She wanted to have some of that. How did people like Lord Harrison and Bridget have such faith in themselves? And why did they also have such faith in her?

"Off with you then," Lord Harrison said. "I expect you to be well rested tomorrow for the dinner."

And, well, Regina couldn't think of a reason to say no to that.

CHAPTER 13

Regina felt incredibly underdressed given the circumstances. Not that she knew what she ought to wear for card playing. But if she'd known that she would be meeting strangers for the first time while understaking this venture, she'd have packed some nicer things. As it was she was merely in an old gown from last year.

She supposed that she would have to get used to wearing old gowns. Her family wouldn't have much in the way of money to spend on her if she failed in this endeavor.

Call it what it is, she thought to herself. This is a gamble, not an endeavor. It certainly wasn't a proper business move.

But what was business, she thought, if not gambling? A man sent his trading ships out and gambled that they would not be lost to storms or pirates or war.

This was the same thing, she told herself. She was simply going about it a different way.

She checked herself in the mirror that hung on the wall of the larger drawing room, the one done up in cream and green.

The mirror was set just above a beautiful polished wooden table. She ran her hands idly over the smooth surface as she looked in the mirror. She looked small and pale and a bit tired from reading those books all day.

A mouse, she thought to herself. She looked like a freckle-faced mouse.

There was no doubt in her mind that Lord Harrison's friends would be rich and dashing. Lady Cora looked like something out of a painting, and she felt certain that Lord Harrison's other friends would be of the same manner. People tended to draw to them others of a similar nature and appearance. She was sure that she would feel hopelessly drab and stupid compared to the guests.

Unfortunately, there was nothing for it. She didn't have enough time to change and she didn't want to risk being seen going back and forth between her house and Lord Harrison's. And even if she did want to take the risk, she didn't have any time.

She squared her shoulders. If she couldn't handle Lord Harrison's friends in a friendly game in his private room, then how could she possibly handle a game for high stakes with strangers?

Regina heard footsteps approaching from the front door and hurried back into the library. She heard the front door open and there was the sound of people talking in low but cheerful voices. Regina thought she could make out the voices of two women.

Were women playing at this game? She hadn't expected that but she was glad for it. It would help her to feel a little less overwhelmed.

The front door closed and then there was the quiet rhythmic thump of shoes crossing the foyer and through the dining room, into the smaller sitting room for playing cards. She took a deep breath. It was time. No point in hiding in the library.

As if summoned by her thoughts, Lord Harrison stepped in. He was wearing a proper coat now and he looked less disheveled. Yet, there was still something relaxed about him.

His posture was easy and sloped with no tension. His mouth seemed ready to slip into a smile at any moment. If she were but to close her eyes and focus on the feeling she got from him, she would have pictured him in naught but a shirt and trousers.

It must have been because he was in his own home and trusted the people he had invited. She still could not figure Lord Harrison out but they had made promises to one another. She saw no reason for him to betray her. Therefore, if he trusted his guests, then she could trust them.

"Come now, Puck," he told her. "The time for hiding in the library is over."

"Are you certain you should be using such nicknames where guests can hear?" Regina asked.

She crossed the room to him anyway, strangely drawn to him as if she was the moon and he was the earth, his gravity inexorably tugging at her.

"I can assure you, these guests won't mind. They're all reprobates of the worst sort." Lord Harrison winked at her.

"Oi!" Someone shouted from the sitting room. "We can hear you, Harrison!"

"Yet I don't hear you denying it!" Lord Harrison shot back.

He smiled at Regina and held out his arm for her. "Come along. They're all dying to meet you. Partially because they don't believe I have a cousin."

"That's because you don't have a cousin," Regina replied.

"But they don't know that," Lord Harrison said, and then he was leading her into the smaller sitting room— the parlor, he had called it—and she couldn't say anything more about it.

She'd noticed earlier that the sitting room behind the dining room was small, or at least smaller than the other rooms. Now it seemed even smaller but in a cozy, comfortable sort of way.

One of the tables had been moved into the center of the room, and there was a fireplace going. The warm light from the fire highlighted the gold accents in the room and made the gray seem warmer and more inviting.

At the table were seated four people: two women, one of them Lady Cora, and two men. Regina paused as they all looked up at her upon her entrance.

Her hand instinctively tightened on Lord Harrison's

arm. To her surprise he laid his hand over hers, a reassuring gesture.

"Everyone, may I introduce my cousin, Miss Regina."

Regina curtsied politely. The two men stood and bowed to her while the two women inclined their heads.

Lord Harrison gestured to them. "These are the most disreputable companions, I can assure you. Scoundrels, every last one of them."

Regina had never heard anyone call somebody a scoundrel in such a casual, friendly manner. It was obviously an inside joke.

"It takes one to know one," said the first gentleman, the one on the far left. Regina recognized his voice. He was the one who'd yelled just a moment ago.

He was tall, though not as tall as Lord Harrison, with light blond hair and a sharp, thin face. Regina could easily have found herself afraid of him given the severity of his features, but he relaxed it all with an easy smile. His eyes were so pale they looked gray. When she looked at his hands, she could see the pale blue veins beneath the skin.

All in all, he looked almost more like a ghost than a

person. Regina saw a large handkerchief resting by his hand on the table. She wondered if he was quite well.

"The one who won't stop running his mouth is Lord Edmund Mannis, eldest son of the Duke of Whitechester," Lord Harrison explained.

"Not for long," Lord Mannis replied.

Regina was confused. Not for long? Did that mean his father stood to lose his title? Such things had been commonplace back when lords were actively warring for land and for the throne. But nowadays to have a Duke stripped of his title was next to unheard of.

Her confusion, as usual, must have shown on her face, for Lord Mannis laughed. The laugh turned into a hacking cough. One of the ladies, the one Regina didn't know, quickly handed him his handkerchief. The other gentleman gently patted Lord Mannis on the back.

"I'm afraid my younger brother will be the one to inherit the dukedom," Lord Mannis explained. He pulled the handkerchief away from his face and Regina saw a spot of red upon it. The spot glistened.

She felt slightly ill.

"Must you frighten the girl?" Said the unknown lady,

the one who had passed Lord Mannis his handkerchief. "We all know you are dying, you needn't go on about it."

"The lady hiding her undying devotion behind a scolding is Lady Elizabeth Thornby," Lord Harrison said.

Lady Thornby was a tiny woman, the same size as Regina. She had light brown hair and light brown eyes that matched. In contrast to Lord Mannis, Lady Thornby looked the picture of health. Her skin had a robust glow to it and every movement spoke of contained energy.

"Miss Eliza, please," Lady Thornby said. "As if we stand on ceremony around here."

"Miss Eliza is in love with Lord Mannis," Lord Harrison said. "And he with her. Although you wouldn't be able to tell by looking at them."

"Simply because you don't know what love looks like doesn't mean the rest of us have to suffer for it," Miss Eliza replied.

She then smiled warmly at Regina. "I beg you, ignore how we snap at one another. I assure you that Edmund and I are entirely devoted to one another, and our friendship with Harrison is just as strong."

"Why are you not Lady Mannis then?" Regina blurted out. She nearly clapped a hand over her mouth.

"There's the awkwardness everyone was telling me about," Lord Harrison said. He sounded delighted. "I've been waiting for it to show up."

Regina had been hoping that she could get through the evening without saying the wrong thing. Apparently that had been too much to ask of her runaway mouth. Why could she not stay quiet? She managed it ninety percent of the time. If she had to speak why did it always end up being something like this?

Miss Eliza only laughed. Lord Mannis winced but it didn't seem to be because of Regina.

"I'm afraid that I don't have long," he admitted. "Eliza and I have spoken at length and we thought it unfair for me to wed and bequeath all my lands to her and deprive my brother. George will undoubtedly live for quite a long time. And Eliza is sought after by many men. She can marry after I am gone. It is better for both of them."

"He refuses to believe me when I say I shall never love anyone but him," Miss Eliza pointed out.

"I never said you would love again, I said that you would marry again," Lord Mannis replied. "There is a difference."

He looked at her then, his gaze bright and full of love. Regina found that there was a lump in her throat. She swallowed it down. In that moment there was no doubt in her mind that Lord Mannis loved Miss Eliza with a terrible, all-encompassing devotion.

When she looked into Miss Eliza's eyes, she saw that same devotion reflected back at Lord Mannis.

"I am a selfish woman," Miss Eliza admitted. Her voice was softer now. "We are not marrying so that George may become Duke and inherit the lands when his father and Edmund are gone. But I refused to let Edmund leave me without living as his wife, even if it is not so in the eyes of the law."

"And so you will not see us about much in society," Lord Mannis added, turning back to face Regina. "There have been enough to see and object to our closeness even if they do not know the full truth."

"They fraternize with me instead," Lord Harrison said. "Adding to their rakish reputation."

"Oh come now, I am merely a beguiled young woman," Miss Eliza protested. "Seduced by the charms of rakish men. But I myself am not rakish."

"Whatever helps you to sleep at night, my dear," Lord Harrison replied.

"And what are we?" Said the other gentleman. "Scraps for the dogs?"

"Ah, yes, of course, we mustn't forget to stroke your ego," Lord Harrison said. "Miss Regina, this is Lord David Quentin. He's been a friend of mine since childhood."

Lord Quentin was on the shorter side, with a broad chest and dark skin that told with no reservation the truth of him having mixed heritage. His hair was short and curled against his head but he had light green eyes. It startled Regina, for she had expected dark ones.

Regina gathered herself. This man was a lord. She would treat him with the same respect that she would the others.

"I must admit I have not heard of the Quentin family," Regina said, giving a curtsy. "Are you from up north?"

Lord Quentin gave a small laugh, flashing brilliant white teeth. "My father is a baron, but I doubt you will have heard much of us. After he conceived me and then dared to bring me home from the Caribbean and raise me as his own, society has been less inclined to invite him to parties."

"Quentin here and I have known each other for years. He helped me when I was gambling to earn my family's money back." Lord Harrison spoke with a deep fondness and respect.

"They let me keep the title and all for now," Lord Quentin said. "But the moment my father's dead they'll find some way to take it all from me. Best to have an independent fortune I can rely upon."

"I admit, I shall continue to call you Lord," Miss Eliza said. "Even when you have become a lonely 'Mr.'."

"You never call me Lord anyway," Lord Quentin pointed out. "It's all Quentin fetch me this, and Quentin read me that."

"There are some who claim I'm spoiled," Miss Eliza said, giving Regina a conspiratorial smile.

"I am deeply sorry," Regina said, for she was. Lord Quentin would get to have no piece of his family history. And it was because of something he had no control over. He hadn't asked to be born out of wedlock and he hadn't asked to have darker skin.

"Why be sorry?" Lord Quentin asked. "I have good friends and have gambled my way to quite an extensive private fortune. The gentry might not let me own land but I'll never lack."

Regina considered that. It was an unconventional way to

look at things. It was also pragmatic. But it was Lord Quentin's decision and his life. If he was not concerned then why should she be?

"And of course you already know our final guest tonight," Lord Harrison said, "The lovely Lady Cora Dunhill."

"I've had the distinct pleasure of becoming this charming lady's chaperone," Lady Cora said. She looked over at Harrison accusingly. "Harrison has been quite cruel to hide a little sprite from us."

"Perhaps I didn't want my dear young cousin corrupted by such as you," Lord Harrison replied.

Lady Cora laughed. "If she were determined to be corrupted in the way that I am, then I should think she'll have already started without any help from me."

Regina had no idea what they were talking about and decided it was best not to ask and stumble into more awkwardness.

"Now that we're all introduced," Lord Harrison said. "Perhaps we can get on to the reason I called you here?"

He guided Regina to a chair that had been set out for her. It put her with Lord Harrison on her left and Lady Cora on her right. Miss Eliza, as she had insisted Regina call her, was directly across from her. Lord Mannis was diagonally to her left, next to Miss Eliza, and Lord Quentin was diagonally to Regina's right, in between Lady Cora and Miss Eliza.

Immediately, Lord Mannis leaned in and spoke softly into Miss Eliza's ear. Miss Eliza's cheeks grew pink not with embarrassment but with warmth, and she responded with her own whisper.

"They really are in love, poor things," Lady Cora murmured.

"It is rather bold of them, is it not, to risk society's wrath to be together?" Regina asked. "Surely it would be better for their reputations to simply marry."

"Mannis has only a few months to live," Lady Cora replied. "He could marry Miss Eliza and produce an heir, but then his younger brother would be left out. And Miss Eliza would be beset by suitors anxious not for her heart but only for her land and the title. And who wants to leave their love to raise their child all alone?"

Lady Cora shook her head. "This way, Mannis gets to take care of his brother, and Miss Eliza can marry one of her other suitors who will give her lifelong companionship and healthy children. Children who are

not cursed with Mannis's affliction and will live
long lives.

"Furthermore, she will know that the suitor, whoever he
is, married her for her personality and looks rather than
whatever title and land Mannis gave her. It is the wiser
decision all around."

"But until then, they must avoid society," Regina
pointed out. "Otherwise someone might notice their
unusual closeness."

"It is a small price for them to pay," Lady Cora replied.
"A year out of society but with the person they love most
in the world? People have sacrificed far more for love."

Regina wanted to object that it was silly, but then she
would be a hypocrite. Was she not risking herself and
her reputation to save her sisters? Was it not all fueled
by her love for them and her father?

Like her father's love for her mother, however, she still
could not understand such a devastating romantic
attachment. Perhaps one day she would understand. But
today was not that day.

Today, she had to focus on playing well.

As if he was reading her thoughts once again, Lord
Harrison produced a deck of cards. "I believe there was

a reason I gathered you all here. Besides poking fun at Mannis, of course."

"I believe you're confusing me with yourself again, Harrison," Mannis replied.

Lord Harrison began shuffling the cards. "I thought we should start with loo. Miss Regina?"

Regina nodded. Loo was the best game to win against Lord Pettifer. It was considered a rather disreputable game, partially because the stakes could be increased exponentially. Regina would be counting on that when she played him.

As she waited, Lord Harrison began to deal out the cards. Loo was a game that could be played with as few as five people, upwards to as many people as you liked. Although, Regina could imagine that after a certain number it became far too confusing.

Loo was actually the shortened name for the game. Its official name was Lanterloo, which as far as Regina could tell was a nonsense word. It had no actual meaning. Perhaps this was a reflection upon the game itself.

For those who gambled away their fortunes, however, the game could mean quite a lot.

It started with a pool, and then each player was dealt either three or five cards. Regina saw that Lord Harrison was dealing out five cards to everyone.

"Normally the person who cuts the lowest card deals first, but I like to break rules," Lord Harrison said. He finished dealing and set the deck down.

After this, Regina remembered, the play would start to the left. She then saw that Lord Harrison hadn't dealt her any cards.

So that was why he had invited four friends. Including Lord Harrison, that left five. It was the smallest number one could have to play the game.

Regina relaxed slightly, glad that she didn't have to focus on playing at first. Lord Harrison noticed this and flashed her a small smile. It was there and gone in a flash, and Regina liked to think that it was just for her, and only she had seen it.

It didn't occur to her then what a dangerous thought that was, but later on she would look back and think, *oh*.

Lord Harrison turned the top card of the deck face up for the trump. Everyone looked at their hands.

"Go on," Lord Harrison whispered. He nudged her lightly with his elbow. "See what everyone has."

Regina stood up and made her way slowly around the table. The other players must have been informed ahead of time that she would be doing this, for none objected.

The entire time, they kept up a steady stream of conversation. Regina suspected this was partially because that was how it would be when she played Lord Pettifer. It was only polite, and talking meant you could distract other players and win the hand.

She also suspected, however, that it was because all five genuinely enjoyed one another's company.

Having inspected everyone's cards, Regina sat back down. This was the only chance the players had to throw their hand in and walk away without any further losses.

Nobody threw their cards down. Instead they each, in turn, announced, "Play."

So the game was on.

The goal was to have cards that were of a higher value than the card turned over on the deck. To make things trickier, there were bonuses or penalties based on the other cards in one's hand.

For example, if you had four cards that formed a suit with the card placed face up, then you immediately swept the pool and won it all. So if the card turned over was a king of spades, and you had the ten, jack, queen, and ace of spades, then you won.

The card placed face-up was known as the Pam. This, Regina had read, would lead to phrases such as "Pam, be civil." She wasn't entirely sure what all of the phrases meant yet but she hoped to find out tonight.

If nobody had a winning hand immediately, then the player could trade as many of his cards as he pleased. However, once a card was traded, he could not trade it back.

For example, if one traded four cards and got four new cards, those four new cards could not be traded for another four. You were stuck with them.

After this, there was another chance for someone with a winning hand to sweep it all, at which point the others would also have to pay a penalty, adding to the pool.

If not, then the rest of the play would begin.

Lord Harrison looked around the table. "Any trades?"

Lord Quentin slid three cards across the table. "Three, please."

"And I'll take one," Miss Eliza said.

"Cora? Mannis?" Lord Harrison asked.

Both Lady Cora and Lord Mannis shook their heads.

Regina marveled at how they all addressed one another informally. The gentlemen were called only by their last names, with no honorific before it. The exception, of course, was Miss Eliza, who called Lord Mannis by his first name. That was her right, Regina supposed, since they were married in behavior and heart if not in the eyes of the law.

Still, she had never heard a married person call their spouse by their first name where others could hear.

And then the ladies were simply called by their first names. Not even a Miss before it, never mind the honorific 'Lady.' Regina called Miss Eliza as such because the woman had asked for it. Lady Cora had said no such thing, so Regina kept the honorific.

What bound these people together so thoroughly that they spoke as family, without barriers?

It wasn't just the names, either. As the play continued, the group teased and complained and confessed to one another. It reminded Regina of her own sisters.

Except, these people got on better than Natalie and Elizabeth did.

The next part of the game was essentially Whist. After all the cards had been played, the pool was then divided evenly among all those who had made tricks. You had to make at least one trick. Otherwise you forfeited the money and earned none.

Being unable to play a single trick was called being "looed." In the unlimited version that gamblers played, anyone who was looed had to forfeit to the others the amount of the entire pool.

This meant that if the pool was, say, equal to fifty pounds, the person who had been looed had to pay fifty pounds. The sum would then be divided evenly among the others.

It was easy for Regina to see how many men had lost their fortunes to this game. With the stakes increasing, there was no telling just how much money would go into the pool. And it was harder than it looked to play a trick, never mind win one.

Regina watched the others playing. She didn't quite have the hand of the card game. Instead, she decided to focus on how each person played.

Perhaps it didn't matter so much playing the cards well. After all, there was fair element of chance to it. She couldn't control the cards.

But with a little bit of careful work, she could possibly control the players. Or at least know how they worked.

Regina studied the players.

First, there was Lord Mannis. He was a reckless player. He seemed to be reckless in everything. He was constantly making comments and trading barbs. He touched Miss Eliza and whispered in her ear.

He had little time left to live, Regina thought. Why should he be cautious when any day could be his last? The way to beat him, she thought, would be to draw out more of that recklessness. Get him to bet larger and larger sums, teasing him until he thought he had a chance.

The cards would turn against him eventually. All she would have to do to beat him would be to play him and keep herself in the game until the cards turned against him. Then she'd collect everything from him.

Miss Eliza was an erratic player. She would be overly cautious at one round and then play recklessly the next. She seemed to delight in confusing the others.

More than once Regina passed behind her to see what cards she had, only to see Miss Eliza pass up a better card in order to play a card that would not help her along but would confuse and frustrate another player.

She most delighted in bothering Lord Mannis. Her teasing only served to make him smile and kiss her cheek. It was far more affection than Regina had seen between any other couple. Save, perhaps, for Lord and Lady Morrison. But then the Morrisons were a little unconventional, just like these people.

It amazed her that someone could tease their lover in such a manner and get away with it. Miss Eliza was constantly bantering—there was no other word for it—with Lord Mannis. Yet he indulged it. He even delighted in it.

Regina had only ever seen women acting demurely towards their suitors. In the marriages she'd seen, there had been nothing but respect from the wife to the husband. At least, out in public. Whatever discord there might be was kept private.

This wasn't discord. This was harmony, but light and teasing. Miss Eliza and Lord Mannis treated one another like equals.

It did give Regina some hope for Mr. Denny in regards to Elizabeth. If he truly cared about her and would meet her witticisms with the same good humor and love that Lord Mannis did for Miss Eliza, perhaps they would make a good match after all.

However, it also made Regina think upon Bridget's words. Her sister had asked her to think of what she wanted in a suitor. For when the time came.

She wanted this, Regina realized. She wanted someone that she could banter with. She doubted that she would ever gain the confidence to banter with someone in such a fashion. Still, it was something to hope for, wasn't it?

Regina realized she wasn't thinking about the game. She focused back in.

Miss Eliza was an erratic player which meant she couldn't be predicted. However, it also meant she wasn't a threat. She was more interested in throwing people off their game than actually winning.

If Regina were to play her, all she would have to do would be to ignore her. Miss Eliza would fluster other players for Regina, but she wouldn't win much. She wasn't a true threat.

On the other hand, Lord Quentin was a methodical player. He had a way of doing things and he stuck to it. Admirable and logical, Regina thought. It also made him predictable.

He must have won the way he had because his method worked. Or perhaps he'd been more flexible before and was now less so because he was among friends. None of them were playing for real money, after all.

Still, Regina thought having a method put him in a corner. Once she figured out his plan, she'd know what he was going to do every hand. And once she knew that, she could depend upon it. She could play against it and piggyback off him to win.

Lady Cora was a more enigmatic player. Regina thought that fitting since she seemed an enigmatic woman.

The people at the table were all good friends. So much so, they acted more like family. Regina could see why, now: they were all, in their way, outcasts.

Lord Quentin was tolerated for now, but being born out of wedlock and his skin color would cast him out the moment his father died. His father's protection afforded him a pretense of acceptance but it wasn't real.

Miss Eliza and Lord Mannis had to make an unconventional decision because of Lord Mannis's illness. That decision might be the most pragmatic one, but it also put a damper on their love. To have both, they had to exclude themselves from society.

And, Regina thought, could any man as sickly as Lord Mannis truly belong with his peers? So many activities required exertion. Riding, shooting, dancing at balls, these all tired even Regina out. Meanwhile, Lord Mannis was having a coughing fit every twenty minutes, just from talking while playing cards.

He would always be left behind, she thought. Poor man. He couldn't dance, or join the men on their hunting expeditions. In a way, removing himself from society to spend time with Miss Eliza must be the best thing for him.

It amazed her that Miss Eliza should be so willing to abandon society for him. Not that Lord Mannis was not worthy of her affection. He was more cutting in his words than anyone Regina had met besides Elizabeth. But he was also witty, and appeared well-learned, and filled with obvious affection for Miss Eliza.

No, it wasn't his worthiness that surprised her. It was simply that Miss Eliza was giving up a year or so of her life for him. It might seem not overlong, in the grand scheme of one's life, but Miss Eliza wouldn't be at a marriageable age for long.

Regina didn't know how old Miss Eliza was. She appeared to be about one and twenty. But seven and twenty was already considered an old maid. Taking a year off could harm her chances of finding another suiter after Lord Mannis died.

Not to mention that she could not attend balls or hunting parties. She probably couldn't see many of her friends. Regina wouldn't mind such a thing for she had no friends. And gatherings of people, of course, were not her cup of tea. But Miss Eliza was full of energy. She seemed the type to love social gatherings.

The fact that she was willing to give up being social, and risking her chances of marriage, said quite a lot. Regina was oddly proud of her. Lord Mannis was going to die either way. He wasn't missing out on much.

In fact this way he won. He got the woman he loved, and then after his death he knew his brother would be taken care of. He would leave behind no sickly heirs. And he would die safe in the knowledge that Miss Eliza, with her breeding and character, would find another husband.

But Miss Eliza was risking much. What if no man wanted her after she was gone for such a time? What if people asked too many questions about where she had been?

Miss Eliza said something at one point about putting forth the rumor that she was traveling about the continent. This was met with much teasing as the others asked her where she supposedly was now. Miss Eliza said, why Italy of course. Where else this time of year?

Regina thought it still a risk. Not everyone would buy into the fabrication. She applauded Miss Eliza in her head for taking such a risk for love.

In a way it made them similar. Although romantic love and familial love were different, Regina liked to think that her love was no less strong, and her risk no less great.

But then, she knew she'd always have her family. Her sisters would be there whether she got along with them or not. Risking all for someone who had no obligation to you... who might reject and leave you... who might change their mind...

The idea scared her. Perhaps Miss Eliza was taking the greater risk after all.

So it made sense why Lord Quentin, Miss Eliza, and Lord Mannis were all banding together. But what about Lady Cora?

She came from wealth, going by her dress and her jewelry. She carried herself with breeding. She was as pale as Regina. And she seemed to be in quite good health. What set her apart? Why would she choose to spend time with the others? If they were all set to be judged by society, what was her supposed crime?

Finally, there was Lord Harrison.

Regina could understand why he spent time with the others. Lord Harrison had nearly lost everything. He'd had to avoid society, and he had probably been judged by them as a child for his father's losses. He had also professed to know Lord Quentin since childhood.

It was perfectly understandable that he would end up finding friends among people such as these. Choosing to stay associated with them spoke of their closeness.

As for his playing, Regina was at a loss.

Lady Cora was a good player. Regina could not quite make out her style yet. But she knew she would in time. Lord Harrison? She had no idea if she'd ever land upon it.

He played subtly. He was not erratic like Miss Eliza but rather seemed to adjust based upon the mood of the hand. He would tip towards recklessness, baiting Lord Mannis. Then he would withdraw and become cautious, countering Miss Eliza's wild moves. When Miss Eliza became cautious, Lord Harrison grew bold.

Oh, Regina thought. Lord Harrison didn't have his own style of playing. That was it! He based his style of playing off of the others, rather than relying upon himself alone.

All of the others played how they wanted to. Or,

rather, in the way that they thought was best. But Lord Harrison was watching the players around him. He was acting based upon their actions. He let them make their move, and then went cautious or playful or aggressive to play off or counter or benefit from what they did.

Lord Harrison lay down a card, and then gently nudged Regina with his elbow. She turned to look directly into his face. The corner of his mouth turned upward just the littlest bit. He didn't wink, but his eyes gleamed.

"Very good," he murmured, softly. Regina doubted anyone else could hear. The warm, intimate tone of his voice sent a shiver up her spine.

He had noticed that she had caught onto how he played. Regina raised an eyebrow at him. Challenging him. Was this how he wanted her to play?

Lord Harrison flicked his gaze over to Lady Cora. Then he looked back at Regina. His message was obvious: watch her.

Regina went back to paying attention to Lady Cora.

"I don't see why you have to be so hung up on it," Lord Quentin was saying.

He was speaking to Lady Cora. Regina had completely

lost track of the conversation. She had no idea what they were discussing.

"I do not see why you are so hung up on staying here," Lady Cora replied. Her voice was smooth, like velvet. But Regina thought she heard a hard core underneath it.

Something about what they were discussing upset Lady Cora.

"You could go to the continent and be quite content there," Lady Cora went on. "Yet you insist on staying here where they will not accept you."

"You know such a thing would break my father's heart," Lord Quentin replied. "I must stay here as long as he is alive."

"He would not be nearly so fond of you if his wife had managed to give him heirs," Lady Cora replied. The hardness in her voice was more evident now. "A dark-skinned bastard son is better than no son at all, I suppose."

"That was out of line," Lord Harrison said. His tone was quiet but Regina felt a chill nevertheless. This was the dark side she'd glimpsed the night they had met. Lord Harrison using that tone was not to be disobeyed for the world.

Lady Cora felt it as well. She seemed to shrink a little. "I apologize," she said. "I did not mean to offend. I only wish to point out that Quentin cannot chastise me for my sins when his are similar."

"How on earth is fulfilling my father's wishes the same thing as loving a woman you haven't seen for ten years?" Lord Quentin replied.

"Love makes fools of us all," Miss Eliza pointed out. "Some would say I'm throwing away my chances."

"I do believe I've said that," Lord Mannis commented.

"Darling, if you try and be self-sacrificing again and tell me to leave you, I shall have to throw a very dramatic fit," Miss Eliza said primly. She smiled sweetly at Lord Mannis.

Regina could hardly keep up with the conversation. "I'm sorry?" She said. "Did you say a woman?"

Everyone at the table turned and looked at her. Regina swallowed. She'd been rude again.

"Yes," Lady Cora said slowly. She turned back to look at her cards. "What's the term they use for people like me?"

"Deviant was a fun one," Lord Mannis said.

Lady Cora acknowledged it with a hum. "Where you admire a man, Miss Regina," she told her, "I admire a woman. Society doesn't like that."

Regina didn't know what to think. Lady Cora seemed to embody everything a woman should be. She was elegant and poised. She was beautiful. She seemed quite educated.

Lady Cora sighed. "If you're going to start babbling about my going to Hell, child, I hope you will start sooner rather than later. I'm close to winning this hand."

"That's what you think," Lord Mannis grumbled, looking at his cards.

"I don't plan on lecturing you," Regina replied. She didn't think she was in a position to lecture anybody, about anything. She was hardly an expert on theology.

"Lovely. Mannis, prepare to lose," Lady Cora said. She laid down a card that made Mannis call her quite a few awful names.

"I don't understand," Regina said. "You've been in love with one woman for ten years?"

Lady Cora groaned. Miss Eliza giggled. "See, Cora, even she thinks you should move on."

"There is a lovely Frenchwoman," Lord Quentin said,

"Who's acquaintance I have been fortunate enough to make. I've heard rumor she shares your inclinations. Lovely woman, hair like gold..."

"You know full well I prefer redheads," Lady Cora snapped. "And I shall not be set up."

"I'd offer up Miss Regina here but she's too young for you," Lord Harrison said.

"And not interested," Regina added. "I mean no offense, Lady Cora."

"Just Cora will do," Cora said. "And none taken."

"You speak as though you haven't already claimed her for yourself," Lord Mannis said to Lord Harrison. He indicated Regina.

Regina felt her face flushing. She looked at Lord Harrison. He looked as though someone had dumped cold water on his head.

"Miss Regina is my cousin," he reminded Lord Mannis.

"And I'm going to live to be a hundred," Lord Mannis countered. "Good lord, you think we can't tell when you're lying?"

"You can tell us who you really are," Miss Eliza said

gently. "We won't tell anyone. We're hardly in a position to judge."

"She's not here because of me," Lord Harrison said. For the first time since Regina had met him, he sounded wrong-footed.

"Lying is unbecoming," Cora said. She was still looking at her cards. "You two make a perfectly lovely couple, Harrison. I don't see why you flounder so."

Regina wanted to say that they were certainly not a couple. But the words were stuck in her throat. She was so shocked she couldn't speak. They thought she and Lord Harrison were—like Lord Mannis and Miss Eliza?

"Now that we've all got that out in the open," Lord Quentin said, "Where are you from, Miss Regina?"

Regina looked at Lord Harrison. She still couldn't manage to form words so she hoped he would notice her soundless plea for guidance.

Lord Harrison looked at her. His gaze was dark and surprisingly protective. "Rather bad luck here, Puck." The nickname made her feel warm inside. Like it was his way of telling her she was safe.

"Her father is Lord Hartfield," he said. His eyes didn't

leave Regina's as he spoke. "She's the youngest of his five daughters."

Cora finally looked up from her cards. "I do know you," she said. There was an odd note in her voice. "Oh, but you were just a child. You were seven when I last saw you. Or perhaps eight."

"You knew my family?" Regina had never heard of the Dunhills.

"This was before your mother passed away," Cora said. "I should have known. You have her eyes."

Cora gave a little sigh. "She was a most remarkable woman, you know. I was the little spitfire as a child, let me tell you. I admired your mother to distraction. My own mother was a rather stern woman."

"Still is," Lord Mannis quipped. "I'm certain that last time we met she tried to set me on fire with her gaze alone."

"Your mother was so close to her daughters. They all worshipped her." Cora sounded unbearably happy and sad all at once. "I was envious. I wanted a mother like her."

Then she laughed. "Oh you should have heard me when the rumors started. Saying your mother was having an affair. I defended her. Quite loudly and rudely, in fact. I offended a great many people."

"How is it that I have never heard of you?" Regina asked. Bridget had never mentioned them knowing a Lord or Lady Dunhill or their child.

"My parents had already thought your family a bit below our standing," Cora explained. "Once I started making a nuisance of myself over your mother, they found it the perfect excuse to end our acquaintance.

"And I'm not at all surprised you've never heard of us. I fear your sisters quite forgot about the skinny little girl they used to know. Your mother's death threw your household into quite the tizzy. I know Bridget had a time of it. She'd become the lady of the household. And at such a young age."

"What was she like?" Regina asked. "Bridget, I mean."

Cora cleared her throat. "She was—well. I'm sure I don't need to tell you of her virtues. From what I hear she's quite the belle of the ball. She was rather the same as a child.

"I was always getting her into trouble. Poor thing was a saint to put up with me. My greatest joy in life was disobeying my parents. I often dragged Bridget along with me in my schemes. She was too sweet a girl to say no."

"You ought to come and visit her," Regina said. "We are in sore need of friends right now. I am certain she would welcome your presence."

To her surprise, Cora went a little pale. "Oh, no. I'm sure I am not wanted. Your sister has forgotten me, I am certain."

Regina was surprised. Bridget would never forget so dear a friend as it seemed Cora had been. And she knew of no one who wouldn't want to spent time with Bridget.

Before she could say anything, Lord Harrison spoke up. "I thought we'd come to play cards, hmm? I plan to clean you all out by the end."

"You always clean us all out," Miss Eliza replied. "Would it do you injury to let someone else win for once?"

"Come now, you know that would injure his pride," Lord Mannis said. "And in front of his lady, as well."

"She's not my lady," Lord Harrison said. His jaw, Regina noticed, was firmly clenched.

"I'm sure that's why he organized this game," Cora said. "To show off for her."

Regina wanted to protest that this was not why Lord Harrison had organized this game. But then, they would inquire as to why she was there. If she wasn't his cousin or his betrothed, why was she with them?

She couldn't tell them the truth. If more people knew, then the more likely the secret of her plan would get out. She couldn't risk Lord Pettifer knowing about it.

If Lord Harrison hadn't told them the true reason for their visit, then he obviously thought the same thing. They couldn't risk it. Not even such close friends as these could know.

But then what was she to do? They all seemed convinced that she and Lord Harrison were together.

She looked to Lord Harrison. Sensing her gaze, he looked over at her. Their gazes locked.

He really did have such warm eyes, she thought. She felt quite safe when he was gazing at her like that. It made her feel like she could trust whatever he said or did. He'd be taking care of her.

Lord Harrison gave a heavy sigh. Regina thought it a bit too heavy. It was put upon, she realized. He was exaggerating it.

Then he reached up and skimmed his fingertips along her cheek.

Regina froze. In fact she quite forgot to breathe.

He trailed his fingers up her cheek until he reached a lock of hair that had sprung free. Gently, slowly, he tucked the hair behind her ear.

His eyes were on hers the entire time. Regina's heart was racing. She felt oddly warm all over.

"All right, you've found us out," Lord Harrison said. He was speaking to the others but still looking at Regina.

What was he seeing in her, in that moment? Was he imagining someone else? Bridget, perhaps?

"Takes a brave man to admit when he's been found out," Lord Quentin said. His tone was light and he was obviously teasing. "I suppose her family doesn't approve? Hence the secrecy?"

"Among other things," Lord Harrison replied. "It's complicated."

He dropped his hand from Regina's face. She sucked in a great lungful of air. It had felt like she couldn't breathe while he was touching her. She'd been too warm.

"Forbidden love." Miss Eliza nodded sagely. Then she broke out into a grin. "Always the most fun."

"Well come on, then," Lord Mannis said. He waved his hand at them. "Let's see a proper kiss."

Regina gaped at him. She couldn't—they couldn't—Lord Harrison was in love with Bridget!

Lord Harrison fixed them all with a fierce glare. Regina would certainly never want him to glare at her in such a fashion. "I am not going to subject Miss Regina to your schemes and teasing. Have some respect."

"Oh come now," Miss Eliza gestured at them. "You're among friends. Don't pretend that this card game wasn't a clandestine way to introduce her to us."

Regina felt completely trapped. Looking at Lord Harrison, she could see that he felt the same way. She wasn't sure that his friends recognized it. But his jaw was still clenched and there was a tense light in his eyes.

Well, they certainly weren't going to get out of this. The group seemed a determined sort. They liked to tease one another and unless Regina could find a distraction or some way to shut them up, they'd keep poking at this. At least until they got what they wanted.

Considering all she was doing, a kiss was a small indiscretion. Even if it would be her first.

Really, it shouldn't be a big deal. As much as society liked to make a big deal of men and women touching. But she had no idea how to do it. Her inexperience was what scared her.

What if they kissed and everyone could tell that she had no clue what to do? What if she came across as a silly little girl? She hated to be seen that way. It was all that anyone ever saw of her.

There was nothing for it, however. Lord Harrison's jaw unclenched the slightest bit. His lips quirked wryly and she could practically read his thoughts. He'd come to the same conclusion that she had.

Might as well do it to shut them up, she could practically hear him thinking.

She wasn't surprised when his hand came up again. This time it cupped her cheek. Regina tilted her face into it instinctively. His hands were large, she'd always realized that. But now they felt larger. Magnified.

Regina found herself leaning into the warm palm of his hand. Like she was a plant, soaking up the warmth of him. Harrison's thumb gently brushed against her skin, once, twice.

Then he leaned in. Her eyes swept closed, and not just because that was how she'd seen others do it. She herself had never experienced it. Nobody'd ever wanted to kiss her. Why would they when she had four better looking sisters to try for?

But no, she was closing her eyes because she couldn't bear to keep them open. She couldn't handle the look on Harrison's face. Whatever that look might be.

Would he be faking a lovelorn expression? Would he seem amused? Or would she see nothing but hidden frustration?

She was scared to know the answer. So she closed her eyes.

She could feel the heat of Lord Harrison's breath upon her face for just one moment, and then—then it was gone.

Regina opened her eyes to see Lord Harrison pulling away. He looked at the others. "No, I do not think so. I will not risk her reputation just to mollify all of you and your curiosity."

"I think that we have pushed him too far," Lady Cora noted.

"Whatever you may think—and perhaps our

relationship is the way you think it is—I will not provide proof that can be used against Miss Regina later." Lord Harrison pulled his hand away and Regina had to resist the urge to gasp at the loss of the contact.

The other three at the table looked properly chastened.

Regina knew that she should be releaved. She should be celebrating the continuation of her virtue and that Lord Harrison was not willing to risk compromising her. This was a good thing.

Yet in a sudden, humiliating rush, she found herself missing the opportunity to kiss him.

CHAPTER 14

Regina struggled to catch her breath. Everyone else had gone back to their card game as if nothing had happened. And perhaps, for them, it was nothing—just a little friendly teasing taken too far.

And yet, Regina felt a little like the world had tilted underneath her. Everything was now off kilter. It had been nothing, really. Just a hand to her cheek and the almost-kiss. Nothing for her to get so excited over, and certainly nothing to be mourning. Yet the heat in her stomach wouldn't go away.

"Are we going to finish this game now?" Cora asked. She sounded incredibly bored.

"Ah, of course, the game," Lord Mannis said. "Not that it's nearly as fascinating as Harrison's young love here."

For the first time, Regina felt aware of the age difference between her and Harrison. She blushed, heat rising in her cheeks. She was nothing but a girl to him.

Why did that thought upset her?

"I think you've embarrassed the both of us enough," Harrison said. He reached an arm around Regina's shoulders, tucking her into his side.

The warmth of him was comforting, as was the weight of his arm and the solidity of his chest. She knew it was all a lie for his friends. Yet she found herself relaxing into it anyway.

"I'll thank you for leaving alone any comments about Miss Regina and our relationship," Harrison added.

"If you insist," Lord Mannis said. He raised his hands in a gesture of surrender.

They all returned to playing the game. But for the life of her, Regina couldn't remember a single thing about it.

CHAPTER 15

After the card game Regina expected everyone to leave. To her surprise, they all stayed.

Harrison had dinner served and everyone adjourned into the dining room. Regina was once again seated next to him. This time he was on her right. On her left was Lord Quentin.

Directly across from her was Lord Mannis. On the left, Miss Emily. On the right, Cora.

"I hope you will forgive the simplicity of the menu," Harrison said. Regina had taken to calling him that in her head. At this point it seemed silly to keep adding the 'Lord' at the beginning.

"You know I don't care so long as there's wine," Lord Mannis said.

"And he wonders why his health declines so rapidly," Miss Emily said with a heavy, exaggerated sigh.

Regina kept quiet. She'd been quiet throughout the card game. Hopefully none of the others would notice that her quiet had changed after the almost-kiss.

Before, she had been quiet because she had been observing. Harrison had been right, she had learned a lot about how to read other players. But now... now she was quiet because her thoughts were in turmoil.

She was quite embarrassed, for one thing. Kissing was something to be done in private. She also felt oddly ashamed, although she knew logically that she had no reason to be. Kisses were private but not shameful.

It was just—Harrison was in love with someone else. Her sister, Bridget. And now she was reminded that she'd practically sold her sister to Harrison to get his help.

The feelings of heat and anticipation she'd felt when she'd been nearly kissed certainly weren't helping. Regina put that down to it being her first *real* kiss, anyway. And Harrison was a handsome man. There was no denying that.

But to focus on it as anything more than that? Folly. And now she was spending all of this time dwelling on it.

She felt the warmth from Harrison's body before she saw him lean into her. "I hope they didn't embarrass you too much."

He sounded amused but also wary. She looked up into his face and saw his brows drawn together—he was truly concerned about her.

"I apologize if I've been quiet. I just have this... fear, I suppose you might call it. I fear saying the wrong thing."

"You're in good company here," Harrison replied. "I don't think any of us has learned proper manners."

"You certainly are all rather..." Regina searched for words.

"Unconventional?" Harrison suggested. His lips twitched in amusement.

Regina nodded. "Yes. Let us go with that."

He gave a low laugh that she felt all the way at the base of her spine.

"I suppose that is what happens when society and fortune are less than kind. You're getting a taste for it yourself, my little gambler."

Regina felt herself instinctively puff up with pride at the possessive tone in his voice and his choice of words. The 'my' in there made her feel...

She didn't know. It just made her feel happy.

Regina shook herself out of such feelings. Harrison was merely being teasing again. It seemed to be his natural state.

"It seems nice," she said. "That you have all found one another."

"We can be ourselves when we are together," Harrison replied. "We will keep our secret for now, to be on the safe side. But other than our little scheme, you can trust them. You are in good company here."

"Oi, you two, stop whispering sweet nothings," Lord Mannis said.

"I think Harrison is rather scheming with her," Cora said. "He has that look in his eye."

"Planning to run away to Gretna Green, no doubt," Lord Quentin said.

Regina was seized with a desire to one-up them. She wanted to banter with these people. She wanted to prove that she was able to hold her own against them in wit.

"How do you know that we have not already done so?"
She asked, turning to look Lord Quentin in the eye.

Lord Quentin choked on his wine. Harrison barked out
a laugh.

"Quite the little minx when she wants to be, isn't she?"
He said. He reached an arm around Regina's shoulders
again, drawing her to him.

She looked up into his face. Harrison was smiling down
at her. He had a proud and mischievous smile on
his face.

Oberon, Regina thought. She smiled back at him.

"Oh goodness, stop looking sickeningly in love for two
seconds," Cora snapped. "Some of us are pining in vain
over here, you know."

"Don't be bitter, darling, it gives you wrinkles," Miss
Eliza said, passing Cora a plate of potatoes.

"If you did go to Gretna Green and got yourselves
married," Lord Mannis said, "And didn't tell me, your
best friend..."

"Lord Quentin is my best friend," Harrison said.

"And didn't tell me, your best friend," Lord Mannis
repeated with emphasis.

Lord Quentin casually sent Lord Mannis a rude gesture.

"Gentlemen, if we could not go to pistols at dark over something that actually hasn't even happened yet..." Miss Eliza said.

"Dark?" Cora asked. "Doesn't really have a ring to it, does it? Not like 'pistols at dawn.'"

"I hate getting up early in the morning," Miss Eliza explained.

"What I would like," Lord Quentin said, "Is to know a bit more about Miss Regina. All that we know is her family name and that she has at least one sister. Personally, if she's run away with Harrison's heart, I should like to know more about her."

"Hear, hear," said Miss Eliza.

Regina realized that four pairs of eyes were now on her. She wanted to shrink back against Harrison. Perhaps even to bury her face into his chest simply so that she didn't have to look at anyone. But that was not only childish, it was wildly inappropriate.

"There's not much about me to know," Regina admitted.

"Surely there must be something," Miss Eliza said.

"No girl raised by Miss Bridget Hartfield could be boring," Cora stated.

"Oh, but I am," Regina said. "Bridget's the star of the family. My sister Elizabeth, you might have heard of her, she's made a name for herself for her temper."

"And her middle sister Miss Natalie has made a name for herself as a flirt," Harrison added.

"Is Elizabeth Hartfield the one that Denny likes?" Lord Mannis asked.

"Does everyone besides Elizabeth know that he feels for her?" Regina blurted out.

She wasn't surprised that she didn't know about such things. But for Mr. Denny to be pining and Elizabeth to know nothing of it was surprising.

"Poor man has taken great pains to hide it," Harrison said. "Your sister is not known for being gentle with suitors."

This was true. Regina could hardly refute that.

"You mean to say you have three sisters?" Miss Eliza asked.

"Four. I have another sister, Louisa."

"It goes Bridget, Louisa, Natalie, Elizabeth, and then little Puck here," Harrison explained.

"You gave her a nickname," Miss Eliza said. "I am going to be sick in the soup tureen."

"By all means," Harrison replied, not at all perturbed by this announcement. "I hate that tureen, it was a gift from a ghastly great-aunt."

"Surely you have interests," Cora said. "You don't sit around and do nothing all day."

"I like to read," Regina said. "Lord Harrison was kind enough to show me his library. I could spend days in it. I've read every book in our library at home."

"Oh goodness, she still gives him an honorific," Miss Eliza snorted. "Dear, you might as well drop that. A simple Harrison will do if you're not comfortable with his first name."

"Not all of us are ingrates who flaunt Christian names about," Lord Quentin teased.

"Edmund," Miss Eliza replied. "Edmund, Edmund, Edmund. There."

"You are all children," Cora muttered. To Regina she said, "Indeed? Reading? You shall have to tell me some of the books you've read."

Now that, Regina could do. She started with a passionate explanation of the latest book she had read, a most diverting novel written anonymously. The author's name had been given only as "A Lady." She was wildly curious to know who the author was.

"If only so that I might thank her," Regina explained. "Her wit is insightful and cutting. There was this one passage where she spoke of a gentleman whose Christian name was Richard. She said..."

"That he 'had never done anything to entitle himself to more than the abbreviation of his name,'" Cora quoted.

Miss Eliza laughed with delight and Regina smiled. Cora gave her a small, almost private smile. Regina got the feeling that Cora didn't smile very often. She felt special for having earned one.

They continued to discuss books for a while. Finally, a subject that Regina felt comfortable with. She knew a great many books. She had even read some books of law that her father kept.

Technically she wasn't supposed to be reading those. But when she had found herself bored and with no new books or knitting, what else was she supposed to do?

Sometime around dessert she admitted that her other

passion was needlepoint. "I'm afraid I am not one for riding or shooting or any of that," she confessed.

"But you go to balls, do you not?" Miss Eliza asked.

"Very reluctantly."

"Why ever so?" Miss Eliza didn't seem upset or teasing. She sounded genuinely confused. "I'm sure you must find your company sought after."

Regina shook her head. "I am not comfortable with crowds or strangers. I'm not overly fond of dancing. And..."

Her voice trailed off as she thought of the things that had been said of her over the years. How people said she was too drab and quiet. Or they said that she was rude on the few occasions she did speak out.

She thought of how the men were never interested in her. Or if they did speak to her they generally made her uncomfortable. And, more often than not, they were only speaking to her to get close to one of her sisters.

Far from being sought out, she was quite certain that if she had disappeared off the face of the earth, most of society wouldn't have noticed.

Something of her distress must have shown on her face. A moment after, she felt the firm press of lips at the top of her head. She had forgotten that Harrison still had his arm around her, and that she was all but tucked against his side.

"Puck here underestimates herself," Harrison said. "She hasn't been given the chance to shine, that's all."

"And Oberon here has far too much faith in me," she added, and she meant it.

She tilted her head up to be able to look into Harrison's face. He gave her a flat, unimpressed look. His eyes twinkled, though—probably because of the nickname.

"I see nothing wrong with your interests," Cora said. "From what I hear, most people seem to think all that a woman should do is needlepoint and reading. I should think that most would applaud you."

"Men only want a woman to be quiet like that once the wooing is done," Lord Quentin pointed out. "Up until then they want a flirtatious girl who will dance with them. Someone they can easily impress."

"You mean someone who will say yes," Lord Mannis pointed out. "And not just to marriage. If you catch my meaning."

"Darling there's no need to be crass," Miss Eliza said.

"It's the truth," Lord Mannis replied. "I know it pains

you my dear but not everyone is as pure of mind as you. Many men are impatient. They don't want to wait until wedlock."

"Surely that's why brothels were invented," Lord Quentin joked.

"Times like these I am glad that I take pleasure in women," Cora said. "No man will take me for sport."

"I hadn't realized this was so..." Regina searched for the right word. "Prevalent."

"It happens more often than people want to believe," Harrison said. Perhaps she was imagining it but it felt as though his grip on her tightened slightly in a protective gesture.

"Everyone wants sex," Cora said dismissively. "And if one is smart about it there's nothing wrong with that. But men will convince a girl that they shall marry her. They sleep with her, and then leave her. The poor thing is then left heartbroken."

"And God forbid anyone finds out," Lord Mannis added. "Then the girl is ruined."

"Always the girl and never the man," Miss Eliza said.

"I think it can be valuable, as long as both parties are respectful," Lord Quentin said. "Goodness knows I didn't know what I was doing the first few times. Can you imagine if it was with my wife? I'd have disappointed her terribly."

"So you disappointed a prostitute instead," Miss Eliza said.

"They are used to disappointment," Cora added dryly.

Regina was back to feeling uncomfortable. To hear intimacy spoken of so openly? It was unheard of. Especially to have it spoken of as something that could be done between people who were unmarried—to be said that it wasn't necessarily a sin.

"Nothing is either good or bad, but thinking makes it so," Lord Mannis said. "Shakespeare's a little overdone if you ask me but he could be an insightful bloke."

Regina thought about that. "You're saying that sex doesn't necessarily have to be just between a man and wife?"

"It doesn't make sense, does it?" Lord Mannis said. "We're told that it's a sin and then when we're married we're told we must do it. I think sex is commonly an expression of pleasure, and at its best an expression of love."

Regina thought about that. She had snuck some

interesting passages and pictures in her time. She knew generally how sex worked. But she hadn't really thought much about it until now.

She'd had no reason to, after all. She'd had idle little crushes, thinking this person looked handsome and so on. But she'd never truly lusted after anyone. And so why think of sex when she couldn't think of someone to do it with?

"I think we've made her uncomfortable," Cora noted. She was looking at Regina, her eyes piercing. Regina suspected that Cora saw far more than Regina or anyone else wanted her to see.

"Do you play cards?" Miss Eliza asked. "You were just watching us earlier. But I'd like to play again. I want to try and finally beat Harrison."

"I've never played before," Regina said honestly.

"You and I can play as a team," Cora said. "No, Harrison, she can't play with you. That's completely unfair. And you can't monopolize her all night."

"You've caught me out," Harrison said lightly. He tucked some of Regina's hair behind her ear again. "What can I say? I like to keep her close."

It was so that he could mentor her, of course. To Cora

and the others, however, it was a gesture of romantic affection. It was hard for Regina not to see it that way as well.

This was a problem. Regina wasn't the sort that could just pretend the way that Harrison obviously could. She would have to learn so that she could pretend at the masquerade. Pretend to be someone else. Someone with confidence.

But right now, she was still just Regina. And right now, Harrison's behavior was doing things to her. Making her skin feel just a little too tight and hot.

"Cards it is, then," Lord Quentin said.

The servants started to clear dinner while everyone retired back to the parlor. Regina was seated between Cora and Harrison once more.

"All right," Cora said. "The most valuable lesson I can teach you is how to gamble."

"Isn't that the same as learning how to play cards?" Regina asked.

"Oh, no. Playing cards is one thing. How you handle your money is another. You can use your money to intimidate others, or lull them into a false sense of security. You can win everything at once. Or you can build up slowly."

Lord Quentin shuffled this time.

Harrison winked at Regina. "Careful, Cora, I'll think you're trying to steal her away."

"You did say you prefer redheads," Lord Mannis quipped.

"She's far too young for me, as I believe I've already said once," Cora replied calmly. "And if my simple presence is enough to worry you, Harrison, perhaps you have to woo her better."

Harrison laughed. "I assure you I can woo whomever I please."

"Really? You failed spectacularly with me," Miss Eliza pointed out.

"Who said I was really trying with you?" Harrison shot back.

"Children, children," Cora said. She sounded bored. "Quentin, do deal us out, will you please?"

Once the cards were dealt, Cora showed Regina her cards.

Harrison suddenly leaned over, his mouth right at

Regina's ear. She knew it was only so that Cora didn't hear him but she couldn't help herself. His lips were brushing her skin and his voice was low and warm. She shivered.

"Don't look at yourself," Harrison whispered. "Look at the others. Play based on them. That's how you win."

Cora began going over the rules with Regina. Regina tried to listen, but she also kept an eye on the other players.

Look at the others.

As they began to play, Regina paid attention to the others. Lord Mannis was reckless. Miss Eliza worked to throw others off. Lord Quentin was stuck to his methodology.

She could play off of this. They reminded her of her sisters, in fact. Lord Mannis was like Natalie, reckless and in it for fun. Miss Eliza was like Elizabeth—ironic given they shared a name. Both worked to fluster others and knock them off their game.

Lord Quentin was like Louisa, patient and methodical. Sometimes playing it too safe. Stuck in his ways.

That left Cora. Regina was surprised to find that comparing Cora to Bridget made a perfect match. Both were enigmatic. You couldn't tell what they were thinking. They balanced out those around them. And they knew this game inside and out.

Regina let Cora handle the rules. She knew she'd pick them up just by playing enough times. Repetition was all that she needed.

Right she would look at the people. Play against them.

As the game started, Regina would whisper to Cora what she thought they should do. Sometimes Cora would do something else. This would be because her knowledge of the game beat Regina's reading of an opponent. But for the most part, she listened.

It was a kind of rush to have someone listen to her. She still didn't talk much but she didn't feel left out of the conversation. It felt like she was included even if she didn't say a word.

It was very much unlike her previous dealings with groups. If balls were like this she would have liked them a lot more. She no longer felt like a mouse, or the least of her sisters, or judged. She felt valued just as she was.

As she watched the others and made suggestions based on their behavior, their pile of money grew. The pile of money in the middle grew as well.

Before long, the only person who was still holding their own against them was Harrison. He wasn't beating them outright. It was more neck and neck. But when it came to money he was matching them piece for piece.

Regina felt a little thrill. She actively wanted to win. She wanted to beat the others. Was this the gambler's rush that people talked about? Was this why people became addicted?

It felt a little like she was on a hunt. Only in this hunt, she didn't have to spill blood. Money and honor were at stake. And finally, her habit of observing people was paying off.

All those years of just sitting without saying anything. All those times she'd watched and listened. Now it meant she could know exactly what each person was thinking and what they would do. It was almost like she could predict the future in that way.

It was terribly exhilarating.

"I thought you said you hadn't played before," Lord Mannis said suspiciously.

"I suspect that her beau has been tutoring her on the side," Miss Eliza said. She gave Harrison a shrewd look.

"Believe me, I haven't taught her a thing. She's just a natural."

As he said it, Harrison sent her another one of his small smiles. Although the others could probably see it if they chose to look, Regina had a feeling it was meant only for her. It made heat rise to her cheeks again.

Damn it, she thought, mentally indulging herself in a swear. What was wrong with her?

"This game will go on forever if we don't put an end to it," Lord Quentin said. He threw down his cards.

"That's the trouble with loo," Lord Mannis replied. "It only ends when everyone is too poor to play."

"I am happy to declare either Harrison or our two-woman team the winners," Miss Eliza said. "They've quite nearly cleaned me out."

Regina looked over at Harrison. She didn't want to stop playing. She hadn't beaten him yet. She'd never thought of herself as competitive but now she was seized with it. She wanted to win.

She also didn't quite have her brain wrapped around the rules. But those were a matter of practice. She wasn't worried.

"Look at Miss Regina." Lord Mannis laughed. "She wants to keep playing."

"You really must work on hiding your emotions," Miss Eliza said. "You are an excellent first-time player but I can see everything you're thinking."

Harrison chuckled. "Yes, I've noticed the same thing. We'll work on that."

"Don't tell me you intend to throw this girl to the wolves," Cora objected.

"Maybe I would like to be thrown to the wolves," Regina replied.

Cora arched an eyebrow. "You might be more like your sister than I had thought."

Regina didn't know what that meant. She was dying with curiosity about it. She wanted to know what Bridget had been like as a child. She wanted to know what her mother had been like. What her entire family had been like. She didn't remember it very well.

But discussing it in front of the others wasn't a good idea. Not because it was scandalous but it was private. Personal.

Harrison spoke up, anyway, so even if she'd wanted to say something the moment was gone.

"Nobody is throwing anyone to the wolves," he said. "Including throwing themselves. I'm merely helping her to get good at something I am also good at. Can a man not have a protégé? I do call her Puck rather than Titania, after all."

"And that doesn't have any homoerotic undertones," Lord Quentin muttered.

"If you're all going to get into another literary debate," Miss Eliza stated, "I need more alcohol."

"I think that we should all retire," Cora said firmly. It once again reminded Regina of Bridget. Cora was acting as the mother of the group, the same way that Bridget would.

"Probably fair," Lord Mannis said. He pulled out a watch. "Good Lord, is that the time?"

Regina started. She looked up at the clock on the mantelpiece. She had been at Harrison's all afternoon and evening. What would Aunt Jane think? Would she be worried?

"There's no reason for you all to drive home," Harrison said. "You are all welcome to use the bedrooms."

"There are only four of them," Miss Eliza pointed out.

Obviously she and Lord Mannis would share, Regina thought. "Will Miss Regina be sharing with you?"

"Miss Regina's residence is only a short walk away," Harrison answered. "I can escort her."

Lord Quentin stood up. "I, for one, could do with some quiet. It was lovely to meet you, Miss Regina." He bowed to her. "I hope that we shall see more of you in the near future."

"I believe that you shall," Regina replied, curtsying.

Lord Quentin started walking towards the door. "I claim the Ocean Room," he said.

Miss Eliza jumped up at that. "Oh no you don't! You got that room last time and we had to make do with the nursery!"

Lord Quentin started running at that. Miss Eliza took off after him. Judging by the thumping on the stairs, they were racing for the room.

Lord Mannis stood up and sighed. "I suppose I had better stop her from scratching him."

"You say that as if you are any less of a spitfire than she is," Harrison pointed out.

Lord Mannis laughed. "Touché." He bowed to Regina

and Cora. "Ladies. A pleasure to make your acquaintance, Miss Regina. I echo Quentin's sentiment."

He then exited.

Regina looked at Harrison, curious. "The nursery?"

"One of the bedrooms was my nursery when I was a child," Harrison explained. "It has since been converted into a normal bedroom. It is done up in a lovely soft powder blue color. Miss Eliza prefers the darker blues and green accents of the bedroom known as the Ocean Room. As does Quentin. It's an ongoing battle."

"I prefer the Lilac Room myself," Cora said. "It's done up in pastel blues and purples."

For a moment there was a pause. A heavy one. Then Cora spoke once more.

"I hope that you both know what you are doing."

Harrison tried to speak, but Cora cut him off. "Now, far be it from me to tell people who to love. But I have seen the dangers of it. Once I nearly brought ruin upon the woman I loved."

"The one you're still pining after?" Regina asked.

Cora nodded. Her eyes looked heavy. Everything about

her looked heavy. It was as though she wanted to sink into the floor. "We were foolish. We were all but discovered. Fortunately our families had only suspicions. No concrete evidence. It could have gone much worse."

"I can assure you," Harrison said. His tone was a low growl. It sent shivers up Regina's spine and made her skin feel hot all over. She loved that growl but it also scared her. She was glad that she was not on the receiving end of it. "No one will discover anything untoward between Miss Regina and me."

"See to it that they don't," Cora said. Her tone grew icy and hard.

Regina felt caught in the middle. Both seemed deadly to her. Harrison was fire and Cora was ice. But neither were to be trifled with.

"If it is discovered that you and she have shared an understanding, the kind of understanding only a husband and wife are permitted to have, it will ruin her." Cora's eyes flashed. "Not just her. Her sisters as well."

Cora turned to Regina, her expression softening. "You are young. It is easy to see only the goodness of love. I know how when one is with your lover, you can forget the dangers. But you mustn't. It is not worth being thrown away by society."

"Society will not throw her away. Society will know nothing." Harrison made it sound like a command. Like he could order the very universe, make the future bend to his will.

"I understand why you are afraid," Harrison added. "You are sensible. But I will be cautious. We both will be. No rumors shall start of a liaison between Miss Regina and me. I can promise you that, if nothing else."

For a moment they stood there, poised like tigers. Neither one wanting to give an inch. It was like Elizabeth and Natalie bickering, only worse.

Regina couldn't stand it anymore. "Has it occurred to either of you," she said, "That I am in the room and do not appreciate being spoken of as if I am not?"

Both turned to look at her. Shock was writ large on both of their faces.

It felt a little like Regina's stomach had turned inside out. But she'd spoken now. She had to continue.

"I appreciate your thoughtful words, Cora." She took a deep breath. "And I understand why you are concerned. But Harrison and I have taken pains to be undiscovered.

"Nor," she added when she saw Cora about to speak, "Will either of us let our guard down. We'll be vigilant. I promise you."

She then looked at Harrison. "Your protectiveness is appreciated. But I can fight my own battles as well. Or at least my half of our battles."

Harrison laughed. "I told you she was a minx."

"You are right, Miss Regina." Cora inclined her head. "My apologies."

She curtsied to both of them. "I wish you both a goodnight." Then she left the room.

Regina wished she could stay. But it was already quite late. Aunt Jane would be worried.

"Shall I escort you home?" Harrison teased. "It is only a couple of buildings but trouble could still befall you."

Regina laughed. The sound was startled out of her. "Certainly. Why not?"

CHAPTER 16

Harrison offered her his arm. She took it, and he led her down the back servants' steps and through to the back door once again.

It felt like a lifetime since she had entered. Since this afternoon she had started to see an entirely different world. She had met people she never would have thought to meet.

If someone had come up to her yesterday and told her that in the course of the next twenty-four hours she would be dining with such people as this group, she couldn't have believed them.

Yet she had enjoyed the evening. Much more so than she had enjoyed previous gatherings.

The night air was chilly, and she had neglected to bring a shawl or coat. Harrison felt her shivering and drew her closer to him. She sank into his side, appreciating the warmth.

"I must apologize," Harrison said. His voice was somber. "I did not realize they would make such assumptions about us."

"It seems you aren't the best liar either," Regina said. "They didn't buy the cousin bit for a second."

"I wish that they had. It was unfair to you to put you in such a position."

"I think it was unfair to both of us. You can't blame yourself. You did what you had to. I'm just glad they didn't discover the real reason."

"Yes, I agree." Harrison grimaced. "I dislike lying to such close friends. I had no siblings growing up. They are truly like family to me. But if they knew, then they might accidentally let something slip. Whether it was in their behavior or in their words. It would be an accident of course. But it could happen."

"And we cannot risk that," Regina said, completing his thought for him.

Harrison stopped. They were outside Regina's door. "No we cannot."

He looked down at her. Regina smiled. "You look like him now," she told him. Her voice had gone oddly soft. "Oberon."

"You ought to see yourself," Harrison replied. "The moonlight. It makes you a proper Puck."

Regina laughed without quite knowing why. She felt oddly nervous.

"The others should be gone tomorrow," Harrison said. "Although Cora might stay longer."

"I was hoping for it. I want to talk to her about my sister. I have many questions."

"Then you are welcome to them. But we must play as well." Harrison sighed and looked off into the distance. "I'll have to have the others over as often as possible. You must practice every day. The game has to be ingrained into you, or you will never beat Lord Pettifer."

"I held my own well tonight." Regina felt frustration and pride prick at her.

"Yes, in a friendly game where three of the players have never been in a proper gambling hall," Harrison replied.

"Quentin was holding back. As, I suspect, was Cora, although she's never been in a gambling hall.

"When you are in a proper game for real stakes it all changes. It is more intense. People play more passionately. And more ruthlessly. And you didn't come close to beating me."

"You and I were neck and neck."

"I was playing lazily," Harrison admitted. "Please, don't feel discouraged. You did very well for your first time. I was surprised at how well you read everybody. But do not mistake this victory for more than it is. We have won the first battle. Not the war."

Regina rubbed her temples. "Why must this be so difficult?" She asked. She knew she sounded like a child in asking that. "I feel as though needlepoint is the only thing that has ever come easily to me. Everything else I bumble my way through."

"You didn't bumble your way through anything," Harrison replied. His tone was sharp but not out of anger. He actually sounded surprised.

He took her hands in his. It seemed to be a habit with him. "Miss Regina, please believe me. You value yourself at far less than your true worth. You are a beginner at cards. That is true. But you are a brilliant beginner. Everyone must start somewhere.

"And you delighted everyone at dinner. I think they were a little surprised by you. In the best kind of way, I mean. I understand that you are not inclined towards balls and the like. But that doesn't mean you are bad at social situations or that you have nothing of value to say."

It sounded as though he really meant it. Regina found her eyes growing hot. It was a telltale sign of impending tears.

Only Bridget had ever talked to her in such a way. And even Bridget, darling Bridget, had left Regina to her own devices. She'd never pushed her.

Harrison was pushing her. He was demanding more and better from her. But he was doing it because he believed in her. He truly thought that she was worth something.

It made her think that maybe he was right. Maybe she could be something if she kept at it.

"Thank you," she said, and she meant it.

Harrison seemed surprised. "For what?"

"For helping me," Regina said. All right, so he was getting something out of it as well. But he didn't have to encourage her. He didn't have to welcome her into his circle of friends.

He was being kind to her when he didn't have to. That meant a lot.

A fond look stole over Harrison's face and he sighed. He gently squeezed Regina's hands before letting them go. She thought that would be the end, but then he brought his hand up to cup her cheek. It was the same gesture he had done right before he had almost kissed her earlier.

As if in anticipation of that, her breath picked up. Which was ridiculous. He wasn't going to kiss her. Harrison was in love with Bridget. Why would he bother kissing Regina?

She really had to stop with these childish fantasies.

"You have been quite a surprise from start to finish, Miss Regina." Harrison's voice was soft. Intimate. "It makes me wonder all that will occur before we are through with this little venture of ours."

"I hope that the surprises will all be pleasant ones," Regina replied. She wasn't sure what she'd do if they ended up being unpleasant ones. Like if she lost everything.

"I'm certain that they will be."

Regina went stiff in shock as he leaned in to her, but he didn't kiss her. At least, not on the mouth. Instead he brushed his lips against her forehead. It was almost chaste.

Almost. If the rapid beating of her heart didn't try to make it into something else.

"Good night, Miss Regina," he murmured.

Then he turned and walked into the night, back to his house. Regina stared after him longer than she should have. Her heart was still beating wildly in her chest. That heat was back on her skin.

Oh, dear, she thought. She was in terrible trouble.

CHAPTER 17

What was he thinking, Thomas thought furiously to himself.

He walked back through the darkness to his house. He couldn't even begin to explain the strange emotions warring inside of him.

All right, he could explain them. He just wasn't sure that he wanted to.

Thomas had been longing for Bridget Hartfield ever since he had first met her. So had a third of the men in England, it seemed. The third that wasn't lusting after Natalie or Elizabeth. And then, when he had thought all was lost, she had been dropped right into his lap.

By her younger sister, of all people.

But now...

He had been drawn to Regina from the start. This, he could admit. Something about her had intrigued him.

When he had learned of her family's plight he had thought it was because she was a kindred spirit. They were both missing at least one parent. They both had fathers ill-suited to business. And they both had to rely upon their wits and gambling to restore their family's fortune and honor.

Then he had spent the evening with her, and he knew it was more than that.

But was it? How much of what he was feeling was real, he thought. And how much of it was a result of playing the part to his friends?

God, but his friends could be so rude. When they felt like it. They were also the most giving and understanding people he'd ever met. Nothing like a little adversity to make you compassionate towards others.

When they wanted to be pains, however...

Of course they had seized upon the idea that he and Regina were a couple. How could he have been such a fool as to not realize that's where their minds would go?

And did they have the decency to make subtle jibes

about it? No. Instead they had forced him and Regina to kiss.

The poor girl. She must have been terribly frightened and embarrassed. She'd brushed it off as if it was nothing, just now. When he had tried to apologize. But he'd seen the hesitation in her eyes right before he'd almost kissed her.

Would that have been her first kiss? A strange kind of possessive heat swept through him. Part of him wanted it to be her first kiss. He wanted to possess her in that way.

And what kind of man did that make him?

If her first kiss had been a charade, partially coerced, it would have been awful for her. First kisses were for passion. They were for the innocent bloom of first love. They weren't something to do because you had to in order to maintain a cover.

It made him feel a little sick.

But that possessive part of him wouldn't go away. It crowed in triumph at the notion of being Regina's first. The first to kiss her. The first to brush his lips over her forehead. The first to plant a kiss into her hair. The first to brush his fingertips against her cheekbone, as if she were made of glass.

The first to take that first step of intimacy.

Thomas shook himself. No. He was in love with Bridget. He wouldn't let himself lust after her younger sister. A woman who was, by the way, eight years younger than he was. He was a better man than that.

Yet he couldn't help but remember how her skin had felt beneath his fingers. Or how she'd fit so nicely against his side, in the crook of his arm. How he'd loved to push her hair back from her face. She so easily went pliant against him. It showed how well she trusted him. Even if he didn't quite feel that he was worthy of that trust.

A part of him could not help but see how easily Regina would fit into his life. She loved his home and his library. He was sure that she would love Whitefern, too, and that he could get her to love London and society just with some coaxing and some encouragement.

The poor girl merely needed people to believe in her. He would be happy to provide that. He could show her how to be happy and content with who she was.

It would be so easy to picture her in his life—yet he had only just met the girl. How could he possibly be having such feelings for her?

And wanting to take her under his wing like that when he was already tutoring her and helping her to skirt propriety? Nonsense. And what of his fickleness when it came to his own affections? Could he really have forgotten Bridget so quickly? What kind of man was he to think he loved one woman only to then turn his affection rapidly onto her sister?

No. No, he was going to stop having such awful thoughts.

He opened the door and stepped inside, making his way up the servants' stairs to his room.

Bridget. He must think of Bridget. He loved Bridget. With her green eyes, and smooth, cream colored skin. Her full laugh. Her dark red hair.

Try as he might, though, when he tried to conjure her up... all he could think of was Regina.

Regina's warm brown eyes. The way you could get lost in them. The quirk of her mouth. The way she pursed it when she wanted to say something but was scared to speak up. How her hands would twist in her lap or her fingers drum against her leg. Like she ached for something for them to do. Needlepoint, probably.

Thomas stepped into his room. The fourth bedroom was the master bedroom. Done up in various shades of blue, it was called the Sky Room.

He had never felt fully at home in it. Part of him still felt like he belonged in the nursery room. Or the Robin's Room, as it was also called, for the color of the walls was said to match the blue of a robin's egg.

It was just that his parents had used this room. He felt odd for using it now even though it was his by right. He was master of the house now. Not his parents. They were gone.

Sometimes he truly missed them something fierce.

Thomas quickly got ready for bed. As he did so, he continued to war with himself.

He merely conjured up Regina because he had now spent more time around her. She was the girl right in front of him. The moment he saw Bridget again, all thoughts of Regina would flee. He would remember how he longed for Bridget.

Soon, he would know all of Bridget's quirks the way that he knew Regina's. It was all a matter of proximity. He was letting his imagination run away with him, that was all. He had to remember his heart.

For some reason, the arguments felt hollow to his ears. As though he was trying to convince himself to fight a battle that had already been lost.

He crawled into bed and tried very hard to picture Bridget in it. Instead the face he pictured had a myriad of darling freckles, an adorably pursed mouth, and big dark brown eyes.

Thomas sighed and stared up at the ceiling. He was in deep trouble if he did not find some way to get a hold on this.

CHAPTER 18

Regina was not surprised to find that Aunt Jane was asleep when she got home the night before. Indeed, the entire household had been abed.

Having said that, she was equally as unsurprised when Aunt Jane brought the affair up at breakfast.

"I was rather worried, dear," she said. Aunt Jane was ostensibly buttering toast but Regina could tell she was completely focused on her. "I had no idea where you'd gone."

"It was thoughtless of me," Regina said immediately. And it was. She didn't deny that. "I was only a couple of doors down."

"I hope you were with good friends," Aunt Jane said.

"I was with Lady Cora Dunhill."

Regina wasn't sure why she had chosen Cora out of all of them. It had just seemed right. Aunt Jane set down her toast.

"Oh?" Aunt Jane's eyebrows had climbed high up onto her forehead. "I didn't realize you had certain preferences."

"What?" It took Regina a moment to realize what Aunt Jane was getting at. Then she laughed—albeit a little hysterically. "Oh, no, not at all, Aunt Jane. Miss Cora is an old friend of the family."

"That does sound familiar." Aunt Jane tilted her head. She seemed to be in thought for a moment. Then she said, "Ah, yes. She was dear friends with your sister, Miss Bridget."

"Yes, she told me so as well. She knew my mother before she died. I had been hoping to speak with her about that, actually. That's where I'm going this morning."

"She is a delightful woman, from what I hear." Aunt Jane picked up her toast again. "Fortunately few people know of her inclinations. Take care not to spread it. From what I hear her family averted one scandal when she was young."

"Could she not go to the continent?" Regina asked.

"I'm sure that she could. It would be easier for her there. Something in England compels her to stay. From what I've heard, it's related to that business when she was younger."

Regina was burning with curiosity. "She did say that she was still in love with someone. The same person, for ten years."

"That would explain it." Aunt Jane gave a sympathetic sigh. "Love will make us do rather stupid things. It is a pity that she must struggle in this way."

Regina still didn't understand that. But she figured it wasn't her place to argue. "I will try and be home by dinner but I can't guarantee it. Miss Cora hosts friendly games of Whist and they can take up time. I quite lost track of the clock last night."

"So long as you have your wits about you, I am secure," Aunt Jane assured her. "And since your inclinations are towards men, allow me to remind you about them."

"I know, and I will guard myself against lies," Regina said. She had heard this lecture from Bridget and from Louisa many times over the years. She'd gotten abridged versions from various society matrons. And she'd gotten a sort-of lecture last night at dinner.

"I meant more that you guard yourself against pregnancy," Aunt Jane replied.

Regina dropped her fork.

It made a clattering sound and Aunt Jane laughed. "Oh, my dear. You really are adorable. Do what you will. Just be smart about it. Make sure no one will spread rumors, that the man will treat you with respect and keep it to himself, and that you do not end up with child. That's all.

"In fact, you might find it helpful. A few youthful romps will help prepare you for marriage. It'll make the whole affair seem less daunting. And your husband will be quite impressed with you."

Regna snatched her fork up again and hastily shoved some eggs into her mouth so she didn't have to talk. The world was far less straight-laced than she had been led to believe. She wasn't sure if she was excited or dismayed. Or some combination of both.

CHAPTER 19

When Regina knocked on the door that morning, a servant opened it.

Regina took a step back, instinctively on her guard. But the servant, a scullery maid by the looks of it, just curtsied. She didn't seem surprised to see Regina.

"Right this way Miss," the girl said. Her accent made her voice sound a little hoarse.

Regina followed the girl through the kitchen and up the back stairs, into the library. There, she found Lady Cora sitting.

Cora was reading a book in French. Regina had always struggled with the language herself. She couldn't even make out the title before Cora looked up and set the book aside.

"Good morning, Regina." She smiled warmly. "Come, have a seat. The fire is most inviting."

Regina sat down on the other end of the sofa. "What are you reading?"

"A French romance." Cora lowered her voice. "They're the best kind. Tell me," she added, "How do your sisters fare?"

Her tone was oddly light, as though she was trying to sound casual. Regina couldn't quite make out why. It felt like Cora was struggling to hide something.

"They're as well as can be expected."

Cora's gaze turned sharp. "What does that mean?"

Regina outlined what had happened to her family. She trusted Cora. Perhaps that was unwise of her but Cora had been childhood friends with Bridget. That was good enough for Regina. And the whole of England would know what her father had done soon enough. There was no use in hiding it.

The card game wasn't a matter of stopping the knowledge from getting out. It was fixing things before the knowledge did too much damage. It was winning everything back the same way it had been lost so that all honor was restored.

When Regina finished telling her, Cora was pale. "How is Bridget," she asked. Her voice was but a whisper and yet she sounded quite urgent. As though Bridget was badly ill. "How is she holding up?"

"She's weathering it better than the rest of us," Regina admitted. "Louisa is beside herself. She is convinced that she and Mr. Fairchild will never marry now. Bridget has done her best to console her."

"That would be Bridget," Cora said. She smiled, and there was something sad about that smile. Something Regina couldn't place. "She was always thinking of others before herself. Sometimes at her own expense."

"Elizabeth and Natalie object to it because they do not want to marry yet," Regina said.

"They're both of a marrying age," Cora replied. "As much as we sometimes try to deny it, our job as women is to marry. It's practically a business decision."

Her tone suggested that this was partially a joke, and Regina laughed. It was true, though. "I wish you would tell them that. Bridget gave them a fair tongue-lashing but they could always do with another."

"I am glad of it," Cora said fiercely. "They were the spoiled ones when we were children."

"They were?" Regina leaned in. "I must know what it was like when you knew them. I was barely eight when she died. I can hardly recall any of it."

Mostly she remembered reading indoors with Mother. She'd already shown a disinclination for the outdoors and other people. Instead she had read in her bedroom or with Mother nearby.

Then after Mother died, when everyone was filled with grief, Bridget had their governess teach her needlepoint. It would give her something to focus on besides her grief, Bridget had reasoned.

It had worked.

Cora thought for a moment. "Your mother was never overly strict," she said. "She always had love to spare. I loved her more than I love my own mother. If you think I ever have moments of hardness, that is where I get it. That woman was not born. She was carved from ice."

Cora's eyes took on a faraway look. "But your mother welcomed me in. Treated me like one of her own. I adored it. But she was firm when she needed to be. Louisa was a lot like you, when she was little. Your mother insisted she spend some time outdoors and with others. In time she grew to enjoy it."

"She's still more on the quiet side," Regina admitted, "But she handles social gatherings far better than I do. Everyone talks about how sweet she is."

"That's thanks to your mother. Bridget could have been like Natalie or Elizabeth had your mother let her. A flirt or too sharp of tongue, she had the potential for both inside of her, you know.

"But then when Natalie and Elizabeth came along... I think it was a little too much. Two daughters already. Then two more. All close in age.

"And your mother wasn't always in the best health. Her death of pneumonia from a rainstorm? That was horrible. But not unexpected. If everyone caught cold, she caught it the worst. In the summer she would get red itchy eyes and sneeze constantly.

"I think each pregnancy was harder than the last. I know that after you were born she was laid up for some time. Some time after she had recovered I overheard her talking to my mother. Your mother admitted she could not have any other children.

"Not that she didn't want more. Or that she was incapable of getting pregnant again. But if she were to get pregnant, it would kill her. It might also kill the baby. She couldn't risk that.

"And so I think that she got indulgent with Natalie and Elizabeth. Perhaps with you as well. She was tired and had the household and the children. A governess helps a lot but it's no complete substitute for a mother.

"As a result, Elizabeth and Natalie got a bit spoiled. Your father was the worst culprit. You spent most of your time inside, I recall. You were a voracious reader. I was not surprised when you said you still love to do it."

Cora smiled at her fondly, and Regina found herself smiling back. "I am glad that you told me of her. My sisters hardly talk about our mother. When they do it's as if she's a saint."

"She was a wonderful woman," Cora said. "A saint in many ways. But not even saints are perfect. Parenting takes its toll." Cora gave a small, rueful laugh. "Perhaps it is a good thing I shall never have children."

"Can't you marry a man and pretend?" Regina asked. "Many women marry men when they do not love them. And the other way around. Married men visit brothels and have affairs. Whether it's with a housemaid or a lady."

She had heard her sisters gossiping about such things.

She had overheard things at balls as well. Lord and Lady Morrison would openly discuss various affairs they'd heard of when they visited.

Bridget was always trying to protect Regina from hearing such things but she had heard enough. She knew that quite a lot went on behind closed doors. And sometimes things went on when doors were still open.

"Perhaps if I were not such a stubborn woman," Cora admitted. "Or if I possessed a meeker character. But I am quite stubborn. And I am far from meek. I could not submit to a husband. Not unless I loved him and knew he would treat me as an equal.

"Besides, I am a romantic. Perhaps it is my French blood. On my mother's side. But I want to marry for love. Therefore, I'm afraid, marrying a man is right out for me."

"You could go to the continent," Regina pointed out. "There are plenty of places there that are more tolerant. Or at least where you could hide better."

"I would like to go there someday," Cora said. "In fact I should like to live out the rest of my life there."

"Then why don't you go?" Regina asked. "What is holding you back? Is it the woman they mentioned last night?"

She didn't add that Aunt Jane had mentioned something of that sort as well. She had a feeling it would embarrass Cora. After all, it would certainly embarrass Regina if their roles were reversed. Regina wouldn't want her private business known to people she'd never even met.

Cora closed her eyes. When she opened them again, she looked away. Into the fire.

"Yes," she said softly. "I know that I'm a fool. I don't need my friends to tell me that. But I should like to know how I am any more foolish than they are. A black man who lets himself be treated with ridicule to please his father. Because he loves his father. A woman who gives up a year of her life, and risks destroying her reputation, to be with a dying man. Because she loves him.

"They act for love. Why shouldn't I? My pining is no more intense and no less foolish than their sins."

"I wouldn't say that acting for love is a sin," Regina said.

Cora gave a soft, pained laugh. "We are all sinners when it comes to love," she told her. "Because for love we will break all other vows. We will sacrifice all our principles."

Regina opened her mouth to argue—and then closed it.

Was she not sinning, in a way, for love? For her family, she was risking all.

"Is she married?" Regina asked. "Is that why you cannot be with her? Or does she not love you back?"

"She is not married," Cora replied. She was still gazing into the fire. "And she did love me once. I do not know if she still does."

"Then write to her. See if she will not run away with you." Perhaps run away was a strong word. But still.

Cora shook her head. "She had responsibilities. Family obligations. I could not impose upon her. Especially now."

"Surely everyone deserves the chance to seize their own happiness."

Cora looked up at her. "You truly are a sweet girl," she said. "I see your mother in you. But we can't always be selfish. We must think of our families as well. We must think of our friends.

"This woman has had to think of her family. She has had to take care of them. I could not ask her to abandon them. Not when they have needed her so. Perhaps, if things changed... if several things changed... if she was no longer beholden to her family..."

Cora nodded. "Yes. If her family no longer needed her. If she would be free to live her life without hurting them. Then I would write her. I would ask her if she still felt for me as I felt for her. If the promises we made back then were still true."

Regina could bear it no longer. Father, Bridget, Aunt Jane, Cora, Miss Eliza and Lord Mannis…

She burst out, "I don't understand!"

Cora looked at her. She seemed genuinely confused. "Whatever do you mean?"

"I don't understand," Regina admitted. "This love that you all talk about. The love that made my father turn to gambling after my mother died. The love Bridget still has for her childhood sweetheart. The love Miss Eliza and Lord Mannis have. The way Aunt Jane talks."

Cora had gone unusually pale about halfway through Regina's little speech. Still, she nodded her head encouragingly when Regina paused.

"I have never felt what you all feel. And I don't understand it. How can you be so willing to suffer for someone else? How can you cling to their memory so fiercely? How can one person bring you such happiness that you're willing to risk such pain?"

Cora looked at her. She seemed puzzled. "Do you not feel that way for Harrison?"

Oh no. Regina had forgotten about that. "I..." She found herself spluttering. "That is, I don't—I don't know."

"That's all right." Cora took Regina's hand. "Often we don't recognize how deep our love is until the person we love is taken away.

"You're young. This relationship with Harrison is new, yes?"

Regina nodded. That technically wasn't a lie.

"Then give it time. He's a charismatic man. If I could feel such things for men I should have fallen in love with him myself." Cora smiled. "You'll be head over heels for him soon enough."

"What if I don't want to be?" Regina asked.

"Then he is simply an older man providing you with an education?" Cora asked.

"In a way," Regina hedged.

"Well, there is nothing wrong with that. But even if it's not with him, I suspect someone will come along and sweep you off your feet. I do think it will be him, though." Cora shrugged. "Whatever you may say, there was something between you two last night. It reminded me of myself and my love."

"But what if I don't want that kind of love?" Regina asked. "All it seems to do is make people miserable. My father was miserable and now he's made us more miserable. Miss Eliza will be heartbroken once Lord Mannis dies. And you've been unhappy for ten years."

"Love, you will find, is worth it." Cora squeezed Regina's hand. "I cannot expect you to understand. It is something that you just can't understand until you feel it. But when you do, it will all make sense. That feeling will be worth all the pain that comes. I promise you that."

Part of Regina wanted to believe her. That scared her.

"What nonsense are you filling her head with?"

Regina jumped. She turned to see Harrison standing in the doorway. He was dressed casually once again. For some reason his appearance had her heart thumping wildly all over again.

"I'll have to start calling you Titania," Harrison said, addressing Cora.

"That makes no sense," Cora replied. "Titania and Oberon were fighting over a human boy. Not Puck."

"Technicalities," Harrison replied. "May I have my girl now?"

As he said that, he came to stand behind Regina. He put a hand on her shoulder. It caused his fingertips to rest on her collarbone.

It felt as though the fire in the fireplace had grown ten times in size. Regina's breath caught in her throat.

"Very well," Cora said. She stood up and took her book with her. "I shall be reading in the drawing room. Try not to stain any books if you start indulging."

She swept out before Regina could even begin to understand her sentence. Then she did understand the sentence and felt heat crawl up her neck and face. She must have been bright red from blushing.

"I hope she wasn't filling your head with too much nonsense," Harrison said. He came and sat down but kept his arm at such an angle that it came around her shoulders. It meant his hand was still on her shoulder.

"She was telling me about my mother," Regina said. "It was good to have an outside perspective. I learned a bit about my sisters as well."

"Then I take it all back," Harrison announced. "I'm glad that she spoke with you."

"She thinks that you're giving me an education," Regina said.

"I am," Harrison replied. "Or is that not what this whole arrangement is."

"No, I mean—well, she meant..." Regina lowered her voice. Even though lowering her voice was ridiculous because nobody else could hear them. "A sexual education."

"Ah." Harrison's cheeks got the tiniest bit pink at that. He cleared his throat. "Well, yes. But please know that I would never take advantage of you in that way. I want you to feel safe with me. Cora can serve as your escort, if you like, since you clearly do not trust the woman you are staying with to know where you are going."

"I do trust you, immensely," Regina said. "I know that perhaps it is not wise of me but I feel safe with you and I trust that you will help me in what I need to do.

"And it is not that I do not trust the woman I stay with. It's only that, well, you did not tell your friends the true reason why I am here. If she knows that I am going to visit you, then she will find out about the cards and our plan and she could let it slip to one of my sisters."

"Cora will not let it slip to anyone," Harrison promised her. "You will need to say that she is your escort should anyone ask, or else they will think of us as my friends did."

Regina nodded. "I will be sure to tell them. And Cora will be all right with it?"

Harrison nodded. "I am certain that she will be. She is a good and loyal friend in that way."

Regina smiled and relaxed a little. "Good."

"I was thinking," Harrison said, "Before we continue, that it would be good for us to show you some of the city. Cora and I can take you to some of the parks. I want you to get out a little more."

"What purpose would that serve?" Regina asked.

"It would serve to give you confidence, and you sorely need it if you are going to best Lord Pettifer," Harrison replied.

He stood up and offered a hand to help her. "Now. Let us fetch Cora and we'll give you a proper tour of the city."

CHAPTER 20

Regina really wasn't sure what all of this would accomplish. Going to a park? How on earth was that supposed to help her with winning against Lord Pettifer at cards?

Still, she supposed that Harrison had a point about her sense of self-worth. If she hated going out of doors and being around people then how could she possibly have the confidence to face down Lord Pettifer in what was essentially the Loo version of a duel at dawn?

They fetched Cora, who was more than happy to get some fresh air. "I have not been out in London in some time," she confessed. "My family does not even have a London home which is why I must stay with Harrison."

"Does your family not object to your staying with him without an escort?" Regina asked.

"My family, I think, hopes that I shall marry him and so they will finally secure a match for me," Cora replied. "I am getting older and soon will be considered an old maid. I am already a burden to them. In cases such as that, you will find, my family lets propriety fly out the window."

Regina could not understand a family that cared so little for each other. Even though Elizabeth and Natalie might not care to spend their company with her, Regina knew that in a heartbeat they would arrive if she called for their aid.

"I think that is enough depressing talk for one day," Harrison said. "Let us be off, shall we?"

He led them to a large local park known as the Regent's Park. "Our dear regent has had it named after himself," Harrison said.

"I could never have guessed that on my own," Regina replied.

Harrison laughed and Cora's eyes gleamed. "She is a rather quick one. Careful, Harrison, or you shall find yourself outmatched soon."

Regina blushed. "I say these things without thinking first," she admitted.

"They are clever things, I like them," Cora replied.

"I do think that you would do well to think before you speak," Harrison added, "But I also think that you tend to underestimate your wit."

"I've been told it comes from reading too many books," Regina said.

"Well that will never do," Harrison proclaimed. "If you start reading then you will start to think for yourself and we can't have that. There will be a full-scale rebellion on our hands."

Regina laughed. "Oh, didn't you know? It has already begun. We meet on Tuesdays."

"Laugh all you want, but I have heard of the unrest in France," Cora pointed out.

"I have not," Regina said. "That is, I have not heard much. It's not talked about in polite society."

"You might want to be kept abreast of current events," Harrison said. He paused, smiling self-deprecatingly. "Here I am, sounding like your father or something."

"I do not mind if you have suggestions for me," Regina

protested. "I know that I have been rather sheltered and that a part of it is my own fault. Indeed, this whole thing would be much easier for me if I possessed the talent of conversing easily with others."

She knew that Harrison would understand that by 'this whole thing' she referred to the planned card game. Cora, Regina hoped, would merely think that Regina was referring to life and society in general.

"Not necessarily," Harrison pointed out. "People that have things that come easily to them do not always appreciate them as they should. Playing cards always came easily to me but I did not appreciate my talent at it until I had to use it to earn my fortune back."

"If I could gain some confidence..." Regina let that sentence trail off. To gain some confidence in herself she would have to be a completely different person. Who she was now was not the kind of person who deserved confidence in herself.

"I see we are here," Cora said, pointing at the entrance to the park.

Regina had never been to a park before. They were novelties in her world. Country houses had their grounds and gardens that you could walk through. Otherwise there was just the English countryside itself.

The English countryside was beautiful. Regina could admit that. But it was beautiful when gazed at from inside a house window or a carriage rather than when one was riding or walking through it.

As for the gardens of a house, she liked those. They were pleasant and carefully cultivated. But their own house did not have grounds that were so pleasant. It was all hills surrounding them. And she did not get invitations to other houses often enough to be able to take advantage of their lovely grounds.

But this—this park, apparently, anyone could use it. Anyone could go in and walk about and then leave. So long as it was from sunrise until sunset, that is.

"It's like the gardens of a country house," Regina said, although that wasn't quite accurate. There was a different style to this.

"Yes, but it is for the masses," Harrison said. "I think that is nice. Everyone deserves a little green in their lives. In the city one does not often get it. It was the one downside to my city home. But now I can come here and relax and feel as though a part of the countryside has come back to me."

Regina let Cora take her arm and guide her around.

Cora was adventurous. She wanted to smell every flower and gaze up at every tree.

Harrison seemed amused by it all. "I see that you now have a puppet to drag around with you," he told Cora.

"Hush. Miss Regina here is far better company than you are," was Cora's reply.

She got to walk with Harrison as well. He asked her about what books she had been reading and actually listened when she talked about them. He never interrupted. He asked her questions with the intent to undersand more of her thought process.

"You cannot honestly be intrigued by all of this," she said at one point as they strolled up a lane. Cora was avidly talking to a groundskeeper about something regarding birds.

"I am," Harrison replied. "Part of it, I admit, is so that I can understand you and your thought process. That will help me in training you. But it is also because I genuinely like hearing you talk."

Regina gaped at him. Nobody had ever said that before. Nobody had ever seemed content to simply listen while she prattled on.

"Are you in jest, Oberon?" She said at last.

Harrison shook his head. "I am serious. I would never jest about something like that. To joke about something like that would mean I was insulting you and calling you boring. I would never do that."

"But I am boring," Regina protested. "I do needlework and read all day. I do not go riding and I hate balls."

"I know plenty of people who love to ride and go to balls and they are incredibly boring," Harrison replied. "It is not what activities you engage in that makes you interesting. It is how you think. It is how you engage with the world around you.

"You have worthwhile thoughts and so therefore you are interesting. If your head was filled with nothing, or if you thought only of what ribbon to put in your hair, then I would find you boring."

"You must never meet my sister Natalie," Regina said, infusing her voice with a great deal of solemnity.

Harrison laughed. "You see? Things like that. Those are the things that keep you from being boring."

Regina wanted to believe him but she was not sure that she could. But the walk through the park was far more pleasant than she had expected.

She kept making Harrison laugh, for one thing. Each

time it seemed startled out of him as though he couldn't believe that she was actually the one who was speaking.

He teased her, as well, but in such a gentle and loving way that she could not find it in herself to feel angry or put out. He would point out plants and such to her and explain what they were.

"Everyone knows that roses are for love," he explained, "But different colors signify different sorts. Pink is for young love, while yellow is for the love between friends."

"I would give you a black rose if such existed," Cora muttered.

"Sometimes I do not think your parents spanked you enough as a child," Harrison replied mildly.

"Then it would be possible to send someone a secret message using flowers, would it not?" Regina asked. "If certain kinds mean danger, or all hope is lost, or freedom?"

"They certainly could," Harrison agreed. "I rather like that idea, Puck, that's quite clever."

"Do not tell it to Eliza, or she will start doing it," Cora warned. "We'll all be getting bouquets as dinner invitations instead of cards."

Regina laughed. She was bent over a flower when it happened, a red rose that had been particularly gorgeous. She'd just had to take a sniff. The petals were soft and velvety against the pads of her fingers.

As she finished laughing, still bent over the flower, she looked up. Lord Harrison was staring at her. His jaw was slack and his eyes were a little wide. He was staring at her as if he had never seen her before.

It made a shiver shoot up Regina's spine, but not in an unpleasant way. She straightened up. "What?" She asked. "What is it?"

"You looked like a picture just then," Cora noted. "I should have liked to paint you if I had any talent at it."

"Does anybody have any real talent at it besides artists?" Regina asked. "I know that we are all supposed to learn drawing and such but I do not know a single lady who is actually accomplished at it who was not also pursuing it as a profession."

Harrison shook himself, as if he had been in a daze. "Yes, well. Perhaps it is time that we retire? I think that some tea will be in order and then we shall get started on the cards again."

"Cards again, Harrison, you will run the poor girl

ragged," Cora protested. "Is there not some other way that you two could occupy your time together?"

"Miss Regina asked me to teach her," Harrison replied. Was it just Regina's imagination or was his tone a little rougher than usual?

"Very well then," Cora said, giving in. "Lay on, MacDuff."

They walked back through the park. Harrison commented that he should like to make this a daily thing. They could go to the colleges and the art museums, and other places besides the park. But an outing, yes, an outing a day would be good for Regina, it was agreed.

Regina tried to figure out what had changed about him. It wasn't something that she could easily put a name to. It was simply as if, for a moment, a veil had been lifted. The veil was back in place now but the fact that she had seen it at all and now knew that it was there made her see him differently.

She shook herself. She was being ridiculous. What kind of flights of fancy was she giving herself over to? Time to focus back on the cards.

If only she could erase that one expression from her

mind: the moment when she had bent over the flower and had been laughing. The look on Harrison's face in that moment...

She could not forget it. No matter how hard she tried.

CHAPTER 21

Thomas braced himself against his dresser and tried very hard to remember the reasons that he was a good person.

He had never murdered anyone, that was a start. Otherwise he was having a hard time coming up with reasons.

He could not be falling for Regina. He could not.

For one thing, how could he possibly be falling for someone who was eight years younger than he was? Eight!

Yes, of course, he knew men all the time that had fallen for much younger women and married them. He knew of a gentleman of ten thousand a year who had recently married a woman seven years his junior. It was not at all uncommon.

But Thomas had never been fully comfortable with the idea, personally. It was part of why he had liked Bridget so much. Like. *Likes* her, present tense!

He liked that Bridget was much closer to his age. He had been surprised that nobody had managed to capture her attention yet. He was sure that there were plenty of eligible men who would make good partners that had shown an interest in her.

Still, one man's loss was another man's gain, and he had been eager to make himself known to her.

Regina, though... he was finding that he liked her more than he had ever liked any woman before. It concerned him, how much he enjoyed her company. He was happy when she was happy. Her unhappiness magnified his. It gnawed at him like an empty stomach when he hadn't eaten all day.

It was why he took her on long walks through the park and to the theatre. He knew that he didn't have to. It wasn't at all a part of their bargain.

He did it because he wanted to introduce her to the world. He wanted her to smile and to indulge in arts and culture and life. It was clear to him that despite the best intentions—for he knew that someone such as Bridget Hartfield could only have had the best of intentions—Regina had gotten the short end of the stick.

Someone like Regina needed to be introduced to people slowly and in intimate settings. The way to make her enjoy society was to take her to outings that piqued her interest such as the College of the Masters where people studied drawing.

Taking her to balls where she became easily overwhelmed did her more harm than good. It made her panic. She was either too overwhelmed to speak or blurted out the wrong thing.

Then to compound that, the natural gossip mill did its work. People spoke about her. They talked of how quiet she was or how awkward she was. And so Regina grew more afraid and more quiet in response.

It was a vicious cycle.

Thomas, however, had seen Regina blossom. She grew happier and more confident each day. He took her to Miss Eliza's house, or Lord Quentin's, and watched her converse easily.

She had firm opinions about the theatre and the plays they saw there. She was beginning to enjoy opera although that had taken some work. And she loved learning about art.

He was even getting her to enjoy their walks in the park. Regina had been right in protesting that she was not an outdoors sort of person. But the parks, Thomas had reasoned, were more contained and better kept than wild fields in the countryside.

He loved watching how she grew happier and more confident. It made him happy to see her.

But the more happy it made him, the more aware he became of their connection. He was more intimate with her than he should be. She relied on him too much.

It scared him, honestly. He had not truly given his heart to anyone since he had lost his parents—first his mother and then his father. He hadn't had time for one thing.

Now that his fortune was back and he could move about society freely, he knew that it was expected that he take a wife. And he had been planning to take one.

He had thought that he had found the perfect companion in Bridget. He had thought that he loved her. And now he was starting to realize that he'd had no idea what love was.

How could he have confused simple attraction and

regard for love? How could he have thought that his enjoyment of Bridget's company and his respect for her accomplishments were anything close to the intense pleasure that he felt when around Regina?

Regina, of course, must never find out. It would put her in a most cruel position. He wouldn't be accepting Bridget as payment of course. Now that he knew he did not love her then he could not propose to her. He would force neither of them into a loveless marriage.

But if Regina found out... she would feel beholden to him. He knew that she admired him and looked up to him. He knew that he must be as a brother or father to her. Regina's father hadn't, as far as he knew, been all that hands on with her.

It was a pity. The poor man was clearly entrapped by his addiction. Hopefully all of this would help to cure him of it. But it would take time and diligence.

Regina, though, had no real father as consequence. She had no real mother either but only Bridget as a substitute. It was natural that she would look up to Thomas when he was taking care of her and mentoring her like this.

If he told her about his feelings, she would feel as

though she had to marry him. It would be out of a sense of duty. For how could she love him?

How could she love a man who had accepted her sister's unwilling hand as payment for helping her? It was a cad move. A rake's move. And he had done it.

To say that he felt shame was like telling a dying man that he was feeling poorly. Not even having to play cards in order to win his family's fortune back had brought shame upon him in this manner.

No, Regina could not love him. But she was an honorable girl. She would marry him out of duty. And then where would they be? She would grow to hate him in time. He was certain of it.

She might even find another. She would find another and not be able to have them. He knew that Regina would never even think to cheat upon her spouse. She was loyal and followed the rules. The fact that she was skirting so close to disaster to save her family was eating her up inside. He could see it in her eyes.

No, he wouldn't trap her in a loveless marriage... loveless on her part, at least... and then keep her there, unhappy, resenting him.

But God, how he longed for her. He wanted to be able to kiss her hand. He wanted to tell her how he loved it when she opened up and teased him. He wanted to tell her that she looked beautiful.

He knew that Regina didn't think that she was beautiful. He could see why she had come to that conclusion. Her quiet personality and subdued posture meant that people did not immediately notice her. She tended to withdraw into herself around people.

But while Bridget was a beauty, and he had seen Natalie and Elizabeth and knew that they were also lovely, Regina could stand shoulder to shoulder with them and feel no shame. She actually looked a lot like Bridget, except for her eyes.

Regina had warm, solid brown eyes. They looked like the kind that you could just sink into. When you looked into them you knew that you could trust her.

Her pale skin and darling freckles only added to it. She looked decadently elfin. He loved it, far more than he had liked any other more statuesque beauties. And that included Bridget.

If only he could say the things to her that bubbled up in his chest. If only he could find a way to tell her that he would always keep her safe. That he would do any number of ridiculous things to make her smile.

He would keep taking her to the park and the museum

for the rest of his life if that was what would please her. He would buy her dresses and shower her with jewelry. But most of all he would make her feel confident.

Thomas wanted Regina to see herself as he saw her. And he wanted her to be able to walk into a room with her head held high because of it.

He wanted more intimate things as well of course. He especially wanted to show her the Ocean Room, the master bedroom. It was done up in blues all over and was so calming. He knew that Regina would love it. He wanted to kiss her everywhere and dance with her and hold her in his arms.

But above all of that, yes, he wanted her to have confidence.

Thomas stared at himself in the mirror above the dresser. His hair was in disarray from running his hands through it in frustration. He set about fixing it. He must look presentable.

If he could end this whole affair with Regina possessing the confidence that she deserved then he would be content. Would he be happy? No, he didn't think so.

He rather suspected that since it had taken love so long to come, it would take a long time in going away.

Perhaps an even longer time in coming back in a different form.

But it didn't matter about him. He didn't have to marry. Regina did. She would need to find someone.

With her newfound confidence, he was sure that she would. He hoped that she would. He wanted her to be happy even if that meant she wasn't by his side.

His Puck. Did she know that he truly meant it when he said that? That he meant *mine*? That he meant *stay by my side, little fairy*?

She could not. How could she? She saw nothing in him but a careful guardian and that was how it should be.

Yes, if he could end this with Regina confident in herself, then he would be content. Satisfied, even. He could watch her from the sidelines. And he'd find someone else in time, someone he could tolerate well enough who could bear him a child to continue the family line.

Now was the time for setting aside his torment. He was a man. Not some Gothic hero or the star of a play. He was a regular man and he did what was needed and he certainly did not waste his time pining over things that could not be.

Just as his father could not handle finances better. Just as his mother could not live longer. So Regina could not be his. It was simple. It was fact.

Crying over it wasn't going to solve anything, so why bother? Actions were what mattered.

He had bargained her sister for his aid and that had been wrong. Furthermore, Regina only saw him as a brother. Those two facts could not be denied so why bother with denying them?

Enough, now.

Thomas composed himself and left the room.

CHAPTER 22

Regina was starting to hate shuffling cards.

In fact, whoever had invented shuffling cards could be run over in a carriage accident and she would be perfectly happy.

As the deck once again spilled out of her hands, she let out a swear.

"Now where would a sweet girl like you learn a word like that?"

She startled, turning to find Harrison lounging in the doorway. He had changed into another pair of trousers and a shirt, although he still did away with his jacket and waistcoat.

"I can't seem to keep them from falling out of my hands," she admitted.

"It can be hard, with your smaller hands," Harrison admitted. He walked over and sat down next to her. "Here, I'll show you."

He took the cards and shuffled slowly, showing her how to hold them and how to use the wrists.

"If you get good enough, you can trick people with shuffling," he explained. "You can deal them bad cards and give yourself good ones. But you don't need to worry about that right now."

"What if someone at the table is doing that?" Regina asked.

She felt a little distracted by all the things she hadn't noticed about Harrison before. Or, to put it more accurately, the things she hadn't let herself notice:

The way that he smelled, heavy and masculine—the way it made her breath catch but also made her want to curl up against his side and breathe him in;

The darkness of his hair, and the way it curled slightly now that it was just the two of them alone together and he didn't have to tame it down;

The intensity and warmth in his eyes, the way they seemed to bore into her;

The skill of his hands, and how large they were, dwarfing hers...

So many things she hadn't consciously thought about. So many things she had dismissed, now all rushing to the forefront. She could remember noticing them before, and the rush of warmth inside of her, but she hadn't thought about it. Perhaps she hadn't let herself think about it.

Now she was thoroughly sunk. She wanted nothing more than to cross the distance between them and kiss him.

Harrison seemed as usual, however. There was no change in him. He treated her the same way that he always did, with casual warmth and teasing. He was obviously overall unaffected by what they'd done.

That hurt, a little, actually. Were all men like that? Could they all become overwhelmed in the moment and then act as though nothing had changed once it was over?

Still, nothing really had changed, had it? They were still the same. She was simply his pupil at cards. He was helping her to dig her family out of a precarious position. Nothing more.

Regina shook herself. This was ridiculous. She was proving herself to be the silly little girl that she'd always feared she was. She had no time to think about things like this. She had to focus on the cards.

"Lord Pettifer, for one, might be capable of that," Harrison said.

Regina realized that he was answering her question and that she had missed the good first half of his answer.

"But none of them would dare in a game such as Loo," Harrison went on.

"Do you know that for certain?" Regina wouldn't put it past Lord Pettifer to pull a stunt like that.

Harrison seemed to read her expression, because he gave a small chuckle. "Even the likes of Pettifer wouldn't dare. Loo is such a dangerous and popular game because of how much is up to chance. Your skill comes from how you're able to play the others around you."

"I thought it was about the cards."

"It is, I suppose, but if you truly want to be good at Loo, or any other game where it's about chance, you have to make the cards secondary. The cards serve the purpose of using the players."

"That's what you were trying to get me to understand when you brought your friends over that night," Regina said. "You wanted me to figure out that I should look at how they were playing and use that instead of relying entirely on my cards."

"Exactly." Harrison nodded. "I was hoping that you'd figure it out on your own, and you did."

He reached out and gently tucked her hair behind her ear, smiling proudly at her. Then his face grew more serious. "I haven't played Pettifer directly. I've heard plenty about him, of course. And I saw him play against your father. So I do have a very good idea. But I don't know his methods as well as I'd like."

"Then it will be all on me," Regina said, voicing her thoughts aloud. "I'll have to figure him out as we play."

She winced a little at the thought. Would she be able to fool him? A man who had made his living ruining others through cards? Could she keep up?

"No, none of that, now," Harrison said. He frowned. "You have to stop beating yourself up on the inside. Don't think I can't tell when you're doing it, you get this most put out look on your face. I'd say it's adorable but I think you'd take offense."

"I'm not—" Regina let out a huff of frustration. "It's perfectly reasonable of me to be nervous about my abilities, isn't it? I'm just a girl. I'm not even particularly sociable."

"You're intelligent and a quick learner," Harrison replied. "That's all you need to be. I'll help you figure out the rest. And you're a better liar than you think you are. You just need some coaching."

"That's so odd," Regina replied, putting on a thoughtful face, "Because I could have sworn someone who looked an awful lot like you telling me last night that my emotions could be read all over my face."

"Well, yes, that's true, but hiding is the part that I'll teach you. You've got the part where you go along with things down pat. In case you forgot the part where you didn't panic because my friends were rude teases and put you in an awful position.

"Lying isn't just hiding. That's the part you have to work on and I find that delightful, because that's what most people think it is."

Harrison started dealing out cards as he spoke, slowly, to show her how it was done. "You'll have to take a turn dealing so you should learn, even if you're not going to be using it to cheat. If you deal poorly, they'll pick up on it and see you as a weak player.

"But as I was saying, about the lying. Most people think that lying is just hiding the truth. They don't understand the other half of it, which is going along with things. It's redirection. Distraction."

Regina thought about that. "So I couldn't hide my emotions very well. But I was able to go along with it when we ended up having to pretend that we were a couple. And I could—hold my own, I suppose that you could say—with the others?"

"Yes, precisely." Harrison handed her a hand of cards. "You were able to engage them and keep up with them. Although we had to improvise and pretend that we were a couple, none of them suspected the full truth. And that's important."

"Because if you can just hide your emotions, people will know something is up even if they don't know what it is, or they won't want to engage with you because you'll be distant. I still want Lord Pettifer to engage with me."

"Precisely." Harrison smiled at her in a way she was beginning to realize meant he was proud of her. "He has to want to play you. You have to engage him and make him intrigued. He has to wonder who you are, and be convinced that he can beat you."

A thought occurred to Regina. Lord Pettifer had once made an advance towards Bridget. What man in England hadn't, she thought, but perhaps...

"Perhaps I should seduce him?" Regina asked. "Not truly, of course."

The very idea of kissing Lord Pettifer made her sick to her stomach.

"But perhaps, he is rather attracted to Bridget, after all. I am told I look the most like her, in that we both resemble our mother most closely. Maybe, if I were to play up the flirtation a little, that would intrigue him more? I would remind him of someone, but with my mask on he wouldn't know for certain who I was. It would appeal to him, I think, to be presented with a puzzle.

"Who knows, he might even believe that I am Bridget. That would certainly appeal to him. My sister appeals to everyone. And I wouldn't confirm it, of course, I wouldn't confirm anything about my identity but he could wonder. I could let him form his own theory and think that theory is true."

Harrison's brows drew together and his jaw clenched. He was unhappy, Regina realized.

"Did I say something wrong?" She asked.

Harrison shook his head. "No." He looked at her and his face gentled. "Oh, no, Puck, I didn't mean to scare you."

He ran his thumb over the line of her cheekbone, soothing her. Regina leaned into the touch, almost unconsciously. She liked it when he touched her, perhaps too much.

"It is a clever idea, I have to admit," he said, speaking quietly. "But I must also confess that I rather hate the idea of you appealing to him in any way."

"It's not me," Regina protested. "It's Bridget. Everyone wants Bridget. I would simply make it seem like I'm her."

"But it would still be you," Harrison countered. "You would be the one that he was looking at in that way, and he doesn't deserve it. Not a man like him.

"He doesn't deserve to look at Bridget or any other of your sisters that way either, of course. But I won't have you putting yourself in a position of vulnerability, even for a moment. If he thinks he has an invitation and then —in his rage after he loses..."

Harrison shook his head and Regina felt a sudden chill at what he was suggesting. What Lord Pettifer might try to demand from her as a way to humiliate and hurt her and sustain his own pride after she beat him.

"I would never want that to happen to you," Harrison said, his voice low and strained. "Part of my duty here is to keep you safe."

"What if he tries to do something like that, whether I seemingly encourage it or not?" Regina had never heard of anyone close to her experiencing such an act. But she had heard stories of others outside of her circle.

It wasn't something that people liked to talk about. The options were generally limited for the woman. Sometimes she was forced to marry her attacker.

Regina couldn't even begin to imagine being touched by a man in such a way. But she knew how much she generally disliked talking to people or having them touch her. She thought about how safe she felt with Harrison—and how easily it could go the opposite way with another man.

If she considered her discomfort in conversing or dancing at a ball and then multiplied it times ten... that began to give her a rough estimate.

She shuddered.

Harrison reached out and took her hand, squeezing it

gently. He had been doing that lately and Regina knew that it was wrong of her to allow it but she could not stop herself. It made her feel grounded and safe to have him touching her like that.

So often during all of this she felt as though she would float away. Or, even, that she was in some kind of awful dream and she was going to wake up if only she could remember how. When Harrison took one of her small hands in his it reminded her that this was real.

"I'll be there," he reminded her. "Pettifer's an ass, if you'll pardon the rough language. But he's also a coward. Why else would he strip men of their fortune through cards? Why else would he go out of his way to do people harm?"

"He feels small. He's a small man of little family and consequence. His lineage has been disgraced time and again."

"Your family was disgraced," Regina pointed out.

"Yes, and yet you don't see me taking other men down for it. He has felt deeply the blows from his peers. People will always find the wrong things to say about you.

"Instead of rising above it, he has decided to amass as much wealth and land as he can until they can't ignore him any longer. They will have to speak highly of him, because he will be so powerful they won't be able to afford not to."

"And he is doing it by hurting others that he feels look down on him because of his family's past scandals and his own reckless behavior," Regina added, showing that she understood. "But that will only make them hate him more."

"I do not think that he wants to be loved," Harrison mused. "I think that he merely wishes to be feared."

"Then I shall have to knock him down a peg or two, shall I not?" Regina replied. "Show him that even a small mousy girl isn't afraid to take him on."

"My darling, when will you believe me when I say nobody will think you mousy once this is all over?" Harrison asked.

A strange feeling formed in Regina's chest, weighing her down. It was hard not to believe Harrison when he said such encouraging things to her. He called her 'darling' while she was tucked against his side and it was so easy to believe that he truly meant it. That she was darling to him.

Regina shoved such thoughts aside. She'd been doing a lot of that lately.

Harrison seemed to like her and she appreciated that. He even saw fit to touch her, to show her pleasure so that she could find it for herself with a husband later on. She was grateful to him for it. But she must never let herself become confused.

This was all so that Harrison could be happy with Bridget. That was why he was doing this for her. Anything else must be a bonus to him, a diversion, something to entertain him.

It wasn't self-pity to say such things. It was merely the truth. She had to remember that.

"Now, enough about that odious man," Harrison said. His tone was light but he kept his arm around her. It was as if Lord Pettifer himself was somewhere about the room and Harrison felt he had to keep her close. "Let us turn to the cards."

Yes. The cards. That was what this was about.

If only she could concentrate on them.

CHAPTER 23

The rest of the afternoon was spent in dealing with the matter of cards. By the end of it, Regina felt that she better understood how the game worked. She still wasn't nearly as good at it as Harrison was.

"It will come through practice, never fear," Harrison said.

How he could tell that she was dangerously close to crying in frustration, Regina didn't know. He seemed to read her better than anyone. In some ways he read her even better than Bridget did, and Bridget had raised her.

"We have less time than we think we do," Regina replied. She did her best to keep her frustration in check and not let it bleed into her voice or face. "How am I supposed to become all of the things I must in order to defeat him?"

"All of the things you are supposed to become?" Harrison asked. He sounded genuinely confused.

Regina nodded. "Confident, and a good liar, and engaging, and witty, and an excellent card player, and an excellent judge of character, and sophisticated, and mysterious, and—and all of these things that I'm not. I'll have to become a chameleon at this rate."

Harrison looked at her for a moment, lips slightly parted as if he were about to speak. He blinked slowly, taking her in. Then he said, "Regina, you don't have to become anything."

"Of course I do," she scoffed. "I have to become a good card player, for one thing." She picked up a card and waved it in the air before letting it fall back onto the table. She partially wanted to set this entire deck of cards on fire.

"All right, I do admit, you will have to continue to gain confidence in that particular field," Harrison allowed. "But Regina, you don't have to be anything that you're not.

"You're already witty. And you're already sophisticated. Even if you don't see it in yourself. It's all in there. I

THE LADY'S GAMBLE   281

promise that, and I'm many things including possibly a horrible person but I'm not a liar."

"You're not a horrible person, either," Regina said automatically. She wondered what would make him think such a thing about himself.

"We'll get back to that," Harrison said dismissively. "The point here is that I'm not a liar. Therefore, you can trust me when I say that you already have all that you need. I'm merely letting you find a way to bring it out.

"I think it a great tragedy that you have four such accomplished sisters. Not that I think they are bad people. You know full well my admiration for your eldest sister. But they shine so brightly. They dazzle. And I think that has left you without the room you deserved to grow into your own.

"You are just as witty, and talented, and engaging, and sophisticated, as any of your sisters. But you're the youngest and I think—I think that you allowed them to hold the spotlight without even realizing that was what you were doing

"I think you've sold yourself terribly short. You have all that you need to walk into that card room and take that bastard—I'm sorry, pardon my language—for all that he's worth. You just don't know it yet. That's all."

Regina felt as though the room had become too hot and too small. And it wasn't in a pleasant way, like when she and Harrison were playing cards and she could feel every inch of her skin aflame, reminding her of how close he was and how alive they both were.

Instead it reminded her of when she was in a ballroom and it felt like there were too many people around her. All of them crowding around her and being loud. It stifled her and even frightened her.

She felt frightened now. Almost as though she couldn't get in any air, couldn't breathe properly.

She stood up abruptly, turning away from Harrison and breaking his hold around her. Literally, as his arm fell away from her shoulders. Perhaps metaphorically as well.

"I won't have you filling my head with pretty stories," she replied to him. She kept her back to him.

She felt like a silly child, on the verge of tears. She didn't want Harrison to see her in that way. She didn't want anyone to see her in that way anymore, she realized. She wanted to be taken seriously as an adult.

But how could she do that when she was about to burst into tears? And over something utterly ridiculous.

"They're not pretty stories—" Harrison began.

"I understand that you want to butter me up. That it will benefit me to go in there filled with confidence. But I will not be lied to. I want to go into that room knowing the truth about what I can and cannot accomplish and that means knowing the truth about myself."

She kept her back to him but she no longer felt like crying. That was good.

"I haven't spent my life being told that I'm one way to believe a man when he uses honeyed words to tell me I'm another. I know that I'm young. I know I might slip up and be childish.

"But I'm not unintelligent. I'm certainly not naïve. I understand who I am and how I am. And sophisticated, witty, those things—those things I certainly am not.

"Do you not think that, if I were, I would have shown some sign of them before now? That somebody, somewhere, would have seen them?

"Even Bridget—and I know that you care for her, and I don't mean to speak ill of her. You know that I adore her. She is the dearest person in the world to me. But even she, I think sometimes, I think she worries about me.

"I think that she doesn't think I'm quite up to herself or

my sisters either. As much as she doesn't mean to think it. And as much as it would hurt her to say it out loud because she would know that saying it would hurt me. But if even... if even my darling sister who I know loves me. And I know that she loves me—if even she thinks that of me...

"You can see how I know that you're flattering me. And I don't like it. It's part of why I don't like most men, they flatter you because they think every woman wants to be treated as a peacock. That women only want praise no matter how false it is.

"And maybe other women want that. Perhaps they would hear sweet nothings no matter how false those statements might be. I am not one of those women. I want the truth only.

"Society has been kind enough to give me the truth, if not to my face. You've said it yourself. You know what people have told you about me. I'm a mouse. I'm horribly rude when I do open my lips. I'm not at all fun to be around. I'm entertaining only in that it can be amusing to watch me stumble all over myself.

"I make myself and those around me uncomfortable. That's all I am. So you'll excuse me if I don't play the part of yet another ingénue who falls for your sweet words. I'm sure you've gotten many a girl with them.

"And I don't blame those girls! They're well-said words, very pretty, and who doesn't want to be told that they are special and valuable? I can understand why they like it so much. But I get enough fantasy from my books. I'm not one of those girls."

She heard the sofa creak slightly and the floorboards shift as Harrison stood up.

"You ridiculous, impossible creature," Harrison said quietly. "Why do you think that I chose to help you? Why I continue to help you even after my friends made it clear to me the danger that we are putting both of ourselves in by spending time with one another?

"The right thing to do—the proper thing to do—would be to send you home. No matter what you may wish to do to save your family, it cannot be worth the ruin that you risk bringing down upon yourself. Not only by playing cards but by spending time with me.

"Cora may be your escort but she is a tentative one. And we spend hours of every day together. It is suspect. It is more than suspect. If I were a truly honorable man I would give it all up and let you go.

"But I have faith in you. I know that you can pull this off. And may God forgive me but I actually enjoy your company, shocking a discovery though it may be to you.

"I am not the kind of man given over to flattering ladies who do not deserve it. Especially when it comes to something of this nature. You asked for my help. My help can only truly be helpful to you if I push you.

"As you are, you cannot win. But I know what you can be and if I push you, then you will become the kind of person who can beat Pettifer. But not if I simply flatter you.

"That is not how champions are made. That is not how anyone succeeds. One succeeds by being challenged. So if I tell you something—if I compliment you—then it is because you are genuinely worthy of that compliment.

"It is important that one sees one's self clearly. Especially when you are going to embark on a venture such as this one. That means you need to see your flaws, yes. But it also means that you need to see your virtues.

"You do have virtues, Regina," Harrison said. His voice gentled. "You have many of them. Please stop hurting yourself by claiming that you do not. It only hides the truly wonderful person that you are away from society. It teaches you to be ashamed of yourself when there is nothing to be ashamed of."

"And you claim that you are a horrible person," Regina said. "Yet you spend all of this time building me up."

She turned around and tentatively smiled at him.

"I am quite the rake," he warned her, "To let you behave in the way that you do. I'm encouraging your delinquency. A proper man would have sent you home."

"You're welcome to keep blaming me, if you like," Regina replied. Her voice was admittedly a little shaky.

Harrison laughed. "Impossible. By the end of this, you will have accomplished your goal of getting your family's land and money back.

"But I will have accomplished my own goal of making you value yourself. Have I made myself clear?"

Regina wasn't sure what to do with this—this strange conviction and faith that he had in her.

"I bet you say that to all the young ladies," she said. She didn't know what else to say or do so she fell up on humor.

"Only the ones who are worthy of it," Harrison replied.

He kissed her forehead gently.

And of course, that had to be the moment that Cora walked in.

CHAPTER 24

Regina stepped back. No, that wasn't right—she jumped back, as if branded with a hot poker.

She did, in fact, know what that felt like. It involved being a child with Elizabeth for an older sister.

The point was she jumped back, away from Harrison. As if Cora hadn't already thought that they were doing things together. Things like kissing and all the rest.

As if they were doing something shameful.

But they were—or at least, that was what she had been taught. This was the sort of thing that only husbands and wives did together. And they never did it where others could see them.

Sex and intimacy were private. Even something as simple as kissing your spouse was private. Bridget had been sure to plant that idea firmly in Regina's head.

"I never saw Mother and Father be affectionate around anyone," Bridget had told her once. "And they were devastatingly in love."

It was going to be difficult to get used to touching someone, even her husband, and be comfortable with others seeing. Never mind someone she would have been completely ostrasized for touching if she was seen by the wrong people.

"Oh, please, don't stop on my account," Cora said. "And by that I mean, please do stop, you two are disgusting."

"Oh dear, did we offend your delicate sensibilities?" Harrison asked, teasing. His tone was light but Regina could tell by the stiff way that he held himself that he felt thrown off-kilter as well.

"My sensibilities are far from delicate," Cora replied. "But you try watching two men kissing and then tell me how much it interests you. It's similar for me.

"Not to mention the last time I saw this girl was when she was a child all of eight years old or thereabouts. This is all very scarring for me."

Cora faked a swoon and fell gracefully into one of the chairs on either side of the sofa. How she managed to do that without falling on her back and looking like a fool, Regina didn't know.

She would have looked like a fool, had she tried a stunt like that. She wished some of Cora's sophisticated stature would rub off onto her.

"Any particular reason why you're boring us?" Harrison asked. Regina noted that there was an impatient tone to his voice.

As if to confirm this, Harrison slid an arm around Regina's waist. *We would like you to please go away, now,* his body language screamed.

Regina put a hand on his chest to soothe him. There was no reason for him to let himself get all worked up. She didn't mind Cora being there. Even if it did mean an end to the lovely romantic kisses he was scattering all over her.

She wondered what would happen if he would kiss her lower, on her breasts, even. Or her stomach.

All right, so maybe she could understand why Harrison didn't want Cora in the room.

"I thought that you were supposed to be educating her

about playing cards," Cora replied in a drawl. "I see that you're busy educating her on other things."

"Yes, and you've made your opinions on that quite clear," Harrison muttered.

Regina recalled the argument from the other night and dearly hoped there wasn't about to be a repeat of that.

"She does need to learn how to play cards, though, does she not? You seem rather determined to teach her, at any rate. I see you have them all laid out."

"Yes, she's expressed an interest in them. Seeing as how I earned my fortune back with them and all."

Cora arched an eyebrow at that. "Yes. That you did. It's healthy for a young woman to take an interest in the life of her partner, I suppose."

"Right. Yes." Harrison rolled his eyes. "Now if you could let us get back to it..."

"If that's how you teach cards, my dear, you haven't been doing it properly. It's a wonder you beat everyone else after all." Cora smiled, then winked at Regina.

Regina found herself blushing and had to duck her head a little.

"But anyway I thought that since I was dreadfully

bored, you might want to have me be an opponent for Miss Regina here. You can instruct her and I can be a sort of... practice player, as it were. You can't possibly be both an instructor and an opponent all at once, can you?"

"No," Harrison admitted. His body loosened up somewhat. Regina relaxed in turn, glad she wouldn't have to avert an argument.

Or physically plant herself in between them. That seemed like it might be a possibility if the two really started to go at it.

The respect and affection between Cora and Harrison ran deep. It must, for the way they spoke to each other, so frankly and with such fond teasing.

But Regina could tell that these were also two very strong-willed people. They could clash easily, she knew, and violently. She didn't fancy getting in the middle of that.

"Then why don't you let me help?" Cora asked. She gestured at the cards. "You know I'm quite a good player. Even if I'm not up to your exacting standards. I could handle any number of the men you play with on a regular basis."

"Then why don't you play?" Regina asked.

"I'm a woman," Cora replied. "I can't easily get away with doing that all the time, now can I? My reputation is in treacherous waters as it is."

"Oh, right, of course," Regina stumbled. She felt wrong-footed and as though she had said the wrong thing once again.

Cora made a clucking noise with her tongue. "Does she always retreat like that?" She asked. She was looking at Regina but directing the question to Harrison.

"Unfortunately," Harrison said. He gave Regina a kiss on the top of her head. "I'm doing my best to beat it out of her, I assure you."

"More like kiss it out of her," Cora muttered.

Regina felt her entire face heat up in embarrassment. "Perhaps we should play cards now?" She asked.

Harrison laughed fondly. "See, now, we've embarrassed her. Poor little Puck. However shall you survive suffering the indignities your Oberon must throw at you?"

"I think I can manage them quite well if you insist on being ridiculous yourself right afterwards," Regina replied.

Cora laughed so hard it almost sounded like a witch's

cackle. "Oh, dear, I do like her. Well chosen, Harrison, you've finally found a woman who isn't going to go all starry-eyed over you."

"Women go starry-eyed over him?" Regina couldn't quite believe it.

Well, that is, she could. She could easily believe it. Harrison was handsome. That otherworldliness that made her compare him to a fairy king could easily be a daring, adventurous lure for young women.

It had drawn her in, after all. Regina was many things but she wouldn't go so far as to label herself a hypocrite.

Yet from the way Miss Charlotte had spoken about him, Regina had thought that most women would want to stay away. Bridget had turned him down, after all.

A man with a mysterious past who took pains to keep it mysterious didn't seem like the sort of man that women would want to marry. Or should want to marry, she should say.

Women should be looking for husbands who were dependable. Husbands who had families that were well known and respected. Families that you could look back on and trace the genealogy. You wanted to be able to say, oh, Mr. Lane of the Hertfordshire Lanes? Yes, I knew his cousin, lovely young woman, she

married a man of five thousand a year if you can
believe it...

You wanted safety and security in a marriage. That was
what marriage was for, at least for a woman. Bridget had
always taught her that. Society had always taught
her that.

What good was a husband if you didn't know how much
he made a year? Or his family history? Or where his
money came from? Or who his friends were?

But perhaps Harrison's charms had been enough to win
women over despite all of that. They'd won her over,
after all.

Although those were for entirely different reasons. She
wasn't in love with him or anything. He was merely
someone that she could... use, so to speak.

If she wanted to use the cruel language that she had
used earlier, out loud to him.

But in any case, she wasn't in love with him. This was
simply an arrangement through which she could learn
how to properly play cards. He was getting something
out of this too. She couldn't allow his strange confidence
in her to blind her to the truth. He may have regard for
her, but his love was for Bridget.

"Spoken with such a tone of surprise," Harrison said. He put his hand over hers. That was the moment that Regina realized that her hand was still on his chest. She hadn't even realized.

"Miss Regina sounds rather too smart to go starry-eyed over anyone," Cora noted wryly. "But yes, my dear, you would be surprised how many people he's capable of charming if he wants to."

"Prostitutes don't count, they're paid to be charmed," Regina blurted out.

She never would have dared say such a thing normally and she was a bit appalled at herself. But how could she resist when everyone else last night had been making jokes in a similar vein?

She would have to school her tongue with extra rigor when she went back to her normal life. At this rate she'd be making remarks that offended everyone in the entire upper society.

Harrison laughed. "That wounds me deeply," he said.

"No, although I'm sure he's had his brush with those. Most men do. It's a part of their 'education'," Cora replied. "I mean the women he would run into while he was playing cards and rebuilding himself."

"I was never serious in my intentions," Harrison protested. "They had to have known that. A harmless flirt, that's all I intended to be."

"I think our dear lord here forgot that he was a man with a title, even if the land that title was attached to meant nothing for a while," Cora replied, addressing Regina.

"Women are bound to take any man's passing fancy as a reason to suspect he wishes to marry her," Regina added. "I think that is part of why Elizabeth is so harsh to them. She fears even being friendly will encourage them."

"I certainly don't blame any woman for thinking such," Harrison said. "Isn't marriage your most honorable and only profession? But I never intended to break hearts quite in the way that I did."

"You never made a promise that you then broke, and you never bedded them, so I see no reason to feel guilty," Cora replied to him. She then turned to look at Regina again.

"My point, Miss Regina, is that these women would go and fawn all over him. There was no subtlety to them. Far be it from any of them to dispute him.

"Yet here you are sparring with him. I find it most refereshing and something he is in dire need of, to boot.

I should think his ego far too large if it carried on for much longer without someone to prick it."

"I shall do my best to continue this honorable task," Regina said, speaking with great solemnity.

Harrison groaned. "All of the women in my life are turning against me. A sorry state indeed. How about we play cards now, as was the original intention?"

"You see, when the talk turns sour against him, then he's happy to play," Cora pointed out with a smile. "Very well then, let us see what we can do to spur along your little protégé."

They set themselves up. Regina and Cora each took a hand. Then they began to play while Harrison helped Regina along.

It was domestic, almost. Regina felt hopelessly nervous about the cards and was determined to do well. But aside from that, she found that she was enjoying this.

Cora was a fun person to play. She and Harrison would banter with one another almost constantly. At first Regina found it distracting until she realized that the card players when she faced Lord Pettifer would probably be doing the same thing. Cards were a social thing, after all.

Harrison was a patient teacher. He let her figure things out on her own most of the time. If he felt he could or should, he would gently nudge her in a certain direction. For the most part, however, he waited until she was feeling helpless and would turn to him, actively asking for his help.

"You mustn't get used to having me at your elbow," he told her at one point. "If I always assist you the second I see that you might need it, you'll never learn how to stand on your own two feet."

"Teach a man to fish and all that," Cora added, idly checking through her cards.

"I understand," Regina replied, and she did. She appreciated it. The one habit she knew she had to break herself off from was turning to Harrison when she needed help.

It was all right for now, of course. She was still a beginner. But when the time came she couldn't be instinctively looking around for her instructor. Nobody could help her.

"And what about hiding my emotions?" She asked, about halfway through the evening.

"We'll get to that," Harrison said. His tone was, as

always, a patient one. Regina had a feeling that she could scream at him and he wouldn't lose his cool.

In fact, the only time he seemed to lose any of his temper was when it came to protecting Regina. Or when Regina was getting down about her own sense of self-worth.

Well. Anyhow. She liked that she knew she could rail at him and he would never give her any reason to fear for herself. She appreciated that feeling of safety.

"You're waiting until I know the cards better?" She guessed.

"Very good," Harrison replied. "Yes. No sense in you trying to do too many things at once. Once you have the card playing down to a point where you're not spending all of your energy thinking about it, we can incorporate other things."

"Like how to carry yourself," Cora said. "Oh, Harrison, don't give me that look."

Regina turned and caught the tail end of Harrison shooting Cora a very sharp look indeed.

"It's not as though I'm attacking her. Good Lord, one would think you were her guard dog rather than her lover."

Regina instinctively blushed at the use of the word 'lover' to apply to her relationship with Harrison. Even though that was technically what they were now. Wasn't it?

Oh dear. This was all very complicated and embarrassing in her head.

"I apologize," Harrison said, although he spoke a bit stiffly. "I must admit that I am rather overprotective, yes."

"I can see why," Cora replied, winking at Regina. "She's clearly incapable of taking care of herself."

"Oh yes, I'm simply helpless all the time," Regina replied, joining in on the joke even though she did feel rather helpless for most of the time.

"I do think though—and do not jump down my throat about this Harrison or I shall have you drawn and quartered—that you could benefit from some lessons, my dear. Just simple ones in how to carry yourself."

"Bridget tried that. I inevitably forgot everything when I went to a ball."

"Well, if you're going to be mingling with the type of people that Harrison likes to mingle with, that simply won't do. And you're older now, aren't you? You can surely handle remembering how to carry yourself."

Cora then leaned in. "I'll let you in on a little secret. Nobody is as powerful as they portray themselves to be. But people will do as they say and treat them like a king if they carry themselves with the proper manner.

"If you make it seem as though you believe it, they will believe it as well. They'll have to. You'll convince them of it. Even if it isn't true."

"If you tell yourself something enough times and if you start to behave as though it were true, in time it will become true," Harrison added. "Or true enough."

Regina laughed. "So I can pretend to be a sophisticated woman. And eventually I will actually be sophisticated?"

"That's the theory," Cora said lightly. "In any case, Harrison, would you let me have her for an hour or so? Can you bear to be parted from her for that long each day?"

"I do have a life I have to attend to, you know," Harrison replied dryly. "I can take care of business. I won't be languishing if I'm not in her presence constantly, unlike certain lovebirds we know."

"I thought it best to check," Cora replied. "What with you being her guard dog and all."

So now she was to be taking elocution lessons, so to speak, from Cora.

It occurred to Regina that she was getting a great deal more out of this agreement with Harrison than she had originally thought possible.

CHAPTER 25

The days fell into a kind of pattern. Regina tried to stay cautious about it all. It wouldn't do for her to become complacent and then slip up and have the entire thing revealed to scandal.

But she couldn't help but notice that she had a routine now.

Every morning she would dine with Aunt Jane, who would ask her how things were going. She had never revealed to Aunt Jane anything that she was doing, although it made her feel terrible to lie in such a way to a woman who was so kind to her.

Aunt Jane would give her advice anyway.

Goodness only knew if the servants were listening in at

the crack of the door or the keyhole and could overhear her. Regina merely never confirmed anything.

She told Regina how to handle a snide remark at a ball, or regaled her with stories from when she was a young girl. Regina almost couldn't believe those stories. Aunt Jane still seemed so young, despite the fact that her daughter Lady Morrison was a woman grown and had been for some time.

After breakfast, she would go over to Harrison's house. Regina always wanted to get right to the work of gambling but Harrison would insist upon taking her to the park, or having Cora call upon friends with Regina in tow.

There were museums to go to as well, and showings, and the theatre. Regina felt as though she was getting a proper coming out rather than simply learning cards. She didn't see much point in it. After all, what good would any of this do when it came to playing her hand right?

Yet, Harrison insisted. He said that if she was going to be in London then she was going to take advantage of the London scene. The 'London scene' could apparently mean the art scene, the theatre scene, or the social scene. It depended upon the day and upon how Harrison was feeling.

She couldn't bring herself to mind these outings, not really. Cora was an excellent replacement for Bridget. No one could truly replace her sister, of course, but Cora was a close second.

They would go out together, the three of them, and Cora handled all situations with aplomb. Most people were intrigued by Lord Harrison, the mysterious Duke of Whitefern who had been all but missing from the social scene the last few years.

Between Harrison's reputation and Cora's social skills, people looked favorably upon Regina as well. She found that people spoke to her with respect and kindness. It was quite a new experience.

Of course, there was the guilty pleasure aspect of it all. She liked doing these activities and she gave into Harrison's insistence because she liked that he was doing things with her.

She liked his presence. She liked how he pointed things out to her in paintings or in plays that she wouldn't have otherwise noticed. She liked that he seemed to care for all of her. Not just the parts that were important for her to cultivate for learning how to play cards. All of her, all of her education and all of her confidence and all of her social life.

It felt a little like a fairy tale, only one of the nice ones with the more gruesome bits taken out for the small children. She got to explore and enter a world far different from the one she knew back home in her country house.

For once, she actually liked society. She liked the art and going for walks in the park. It was as if she hadn't truly known the world. The balls and people that she had grown up with were suddenly and truly just one aspect of a wide, wide world. And that wide world was now hers to explore.

Of course, the traitorous part of her wondered if she should like it half so well if she was doing all of this with someone other than Harrison. But that was the part of her that she ruthlessly ignored as best she could.

Afterwards they would return to the house and then they would focus on cards. Cora would come in at some point and steal Regina away.

Cora never seemed to have a set lesson in mind. Instead she would talk to Regina, filling her in on all the gossip. As she talked she would come up with something:

"I know it looks silly but I'm going to balance a book on your head."

"Now, notice how I'm sitting. See how I do this with my

legs? It shows men you're interested. Even if they don't realize that is what they're seeing and they only notice it subconsciously."

"Now, dear, you need to master the art of saying something cutting that people cannot call you out on. It's called passive aggressiveness and you ought to learn it now."

Regina wasn't entirely sure how all of this would come in handy. Why did she need to know how to insult someone without making it sound insulting?

She knew that Cora's answer was, "So they can't call you out on it and you get to be smug," but seriously. Why did she have to know these things?

More specifically, how were any of these things going to help her when she was playing a card game with several men?

She didn't protest, however. Partially because she knew that arguing with Cora was a fruitless task. Partially because she didn't know and it might actually come in handy.

After Cora was finished with her, they would play more cards. Cora would join them for a bit of it and play against her.

Regina had quickly found that Harrison was right when he said that Cora had been going easy on her the first night when they'd all played with his friends.

Cora was ruthless. Absolutely ruthless. She knew the game backwards and forwards. She was also fairly good at reading tells—and Regina was well aware that she was still hopeless at hiding her tells.

It took everything that Regina had in her to keep up with Cora in the game. Often times, it wasn't enough. Or at least that was how it was at first.

But as time went on, she found herself winning more and more. She had to look at Harrison less and less.

It started slowly, of course. She burst into tears of joy when she won her first game against Cora. Harrison had looked completely alarmed and had quickly pulled out a handkerchief for her to use, patting her shoulder awkwardly.

Cora had said something like, "For God's sake," and had found a servant to bring them all another round of tea and biscuits.

Of course, in order to find the servant, Cora had to leave the room. That must have been her design, Regina had realized later.

In the silence, she had continued to sit, feeling uncomfortable at her own outburst of emotion but safe in knowing that Harrison was not judging her for it.

"I haven't won anything before," she had admitted. Her voice had sounded soft and fragile. It had sounded like her voice when she was a small child.

It was more than that, of course. It was that she had never felt proud of herself for something before. It was that she had never been better than someone else at something. It was that she had never truly worked hard at something and earned it.

She had worked hard to learn how to read and to read well, and to do her needlepoint, yes. But those things were quiet, personal triumphs. No one had praised her needlework besides Bridget. And, well, Bridget praised nearly everything Regina did.

Nobody had been able to point at her and say, "Yes, you conquered this, and we have all seen it and cannot argue it."

Now it had finally happened, some kind of validation that she hadn't even known she was looking for, and she had been overwhelmed.

So she had found herself crying.

"I'm sorry," she had sniffled afterwards.

Whatever dignity she'd previously had was now in tatters. She had just cried into Harrison's handkerchief until it was soiled and wet. Like she was a child.

"What on earth are you apologizing for?" Harrison had asked. He had seemed bewildered.

At that moment, Cora had returned, leading a servant carrying a tea tray.

"You don't have to apologize to us," Harrison had said. He had indicated Cora as well. "We understand."

She had wanted to ask how they could understand. How could they possibly understand when she hadn't even said anything? Partially because she couldn't even have explained it if she'd tried. She hadn't had the words.

And yet—perhaps they had understood. Perhaps they had gone through something similar, whether it was with cards or something else. And so perhaps they had recognized it and understood, even though she hadn't explained her feelings to them.

Since that night, she had started to win more often. It had happened by degrees. One win per night. Then two per night. And so on.

It was slow going. Most of the time she was terribly

frustrated by it. Oftentimes Harrison or Cora had to be the one to remind her what time it was and that she should be getting home before Aunt Jane started to worry.

"I had no idea you were such a competitive one," Harrison commented one night.

Cora snorted. It was highly inelegant and unladylike. Regina was starting to realize that Cora was an odd mix of acting like the height of sophistication and acting like an uncouth man, often at the same time.

"She was raised by Bridget Hartfield," Cora said. "She has Elizabeth and Natalie for sisters. There was always a steel backbone somewhere in there."

Regina didn't know what to say to that. She was finding that she enjoyed the card playing more than she had originally thought she would. Perhaps it was because she was finally starting to get good at it.

Once she could be persuaded to stop and to go to bed and get some rest, she would return home. Aunt Jane would be up with some small snack of some kind and they would chat.

Aunt Jane would tell Regina about her day and the people that she saw and what they said. Regina would then write Bridget a letter, telling Bridget about these

things as though she had experienced them with
Aunt Jane.

She occasionally added in a small anecdote at the end.

I would like a man who makes me feel safe.

I would like a man with whom I can tease and banter.

I would like a man with large hands.

I would like a man with blue eyes.

She felt a little odd, writing those things in. It partially
felt as though she was confessing to Bridget, telling her,
in a way, of what she was getting up to.

But it wasn't all that bad, was it? Bridget had asked her
to figure out what she wanted in a husband. With
Harrison's help, Regina was slowly figuring it out.

That could only be a good thing, couldn't it?

If only it didn't remind her of all the things that she was
trying not to notice about Harrison. The very fact that
she was only calling him 'Harrison' in her head—even if
not out loud—told her how intimately she felt towards
him.

Every time she thought of what she wanted in a
husband because of something Harrison did or said, it
only solidified that what she really wanted... was him.

But she couldn't have that. How could she? Despite her growing confidence, she was well aware that she was still second fiddle to her sister. The bargain that she had struck hung over her head like an axe waiting to fall.

It didn't help that Cora thought that Regina and Harrison were already together. Her little comments, aimed to tease, only served to make the ache in Regina's chest.

Regina refused to name that ache. She refused to speak even to herself of what it meant. Only a short time ago, she had not understood why people were so willing to suffer for others.

Now that she was starting to understand, denying that she felt that way at all felt like the only thing that could save her.

She didn't want to end up like her father, miserable. She didn't want to be like Cora, pining for someone even years later. Even Bridget had a childhood sweetheart that she apparently still thought of.

Regina didn't want to be like them. She was selfish. She wanted a happy ending. She hadn't contemplated love before, not really. What place did love have in marriage when it came down to it?

Marriage was a business for women. A career. And so that was how she had thought of it.

The idea that it might also include love... well, if it was going to, then it was going to be a happy love. She would not be someone who pined or who went miserable or who signed herself up for loss and despair.

Let others do that. Let Miss Eliza risk her ruin by spending time with a man who was dying. Let Cora refuse to go to the continent for someone who might not even remember her. Let Father sign away his life for a deck of cards because of the loss of Mother.

Regina would not be like them. She would be stoic and pragmatic. So when she began to dwell upon the affection with which Harrison looked at her, she shoved it aside. When he touched her to guide her through the city or to get her attention, she shoved the bubbling warmth in her chest aside.

When it was just the two of them playing cards and it felt like there was no one else in the world that existed...

She shoved that aside as well.

It ate up more of her thoughts than she would have thought that it did, had someone asked her. Denial took quite a lot of discipline.

There was something else that bothered her, though.

Harrison was obviously very protective of her. She had noticed this in public and in private.

At the theatre, if someone jostled her, Harrison would insinuate himself between Regina and the offender. He would all but shove them back and then glare. It was like having a territorial puppy.

When Cora made remarks about what she thought the state of their relationship was, Harrison would respond with a cutting remark of his own and a look that would have melted bone.

But part and parcel with his protectiveness seemed to come a kind of... Regina couldn't find the right word. It wasn't condescension. But it was like he looked at her as though she was ten instead of eighteen.

She knew that she wasn't as old as some. She knew that Harrison had much more wisdom and experience than she did. But eighteen was considered quite a marriageable age. She had been out in society for two years, and she knew of many women her age who had married at sixteen or seventeen. Some of them were already mothers.

And while she might have many doubts about herself, Harrison was constantly reminding her of her intelligence and skills. So if he thought her so intelligent, then why did he insist on sometimes treating her like a child?

Her preoccupation was noticed by Cora at their daily lesson. Regina was starting to realize that there wasn't much that slipped by Cora.

"Regina," Cora said, having dropped the 'Miss' some time ago when Regina wasn't paying attention. "Dear, why do I get the distinct impression that you're not paying the slightest bit of attention to me?"

"I'm sorry," Regina replied at once, automatically.

Cora sighed. "What did we say about the constant apologizing?"

"Right. No constant apologizing. I know."

"Good." Cora smiled at her. "Now, honestly, is learning about the exchange rate that boring for you?"

"No!" Regina said quickly. "I need to know this."

"Simply because you need to know it does not mean that you enjoy learning it," Cora replied. "Although why you must learn the exchange rate, I'm sure I don't know."

"You know it," Regina pointed out.

"I am a horrible, unrepentant reprobate who might need

to depend upon herself someday," Cora replied. "You are a lovely young lady with many prospects ahead of you."

"Not anymore," Regina replied.

She had not forgotten the original reason that she was here. Time with Harrison and Cora might in a way feel like some kind of extended holiday but it couldn't hide the truth. Her family was in danger.

Cora grew quiet and serious. "Yes, I know. Have your sisters found husbands yet?"

Regina shook her head. Bridget's latest letter had detailed the updates. "Bridget told me that Elizabeth is apparently warming to Mr. Denny, or so she tells Bridget. Louisa and Mr. Fairchild are doing their best to work things out but they are still frozen until his aunt passes."

"And has Natalie selected someone?"

Regina pulled a face. It was something she would never have dared to do in polite society but around Cora such things came slipping out, as they did when she was with Bridget.

"She has managed to narrow it down. I believe Bridget is

finding the difficulty is in Natalie's ability to actually engage a man beyond the first flirtations."

"Ah, yes, actually discussing matters of substance and finding there is more to a potential marriage than subtle innuendos," Cora said. She gave a small smile, as though remembering flirtations of her own.

"I worry about her," Regina confessed. It felt odd, to worry about Natalie. Natalie had any number of suitors. Theroetically she should be fine.

Yet Regina couldn't quite shake the feeling of concern.

"As you should." Cora sighed and tossed aside her papers. It seemed she had realized they wouldn't get any further in her planned lesson that day.

"Natalie—well. Suffice to say, you're actually in a better position than she is."

"How do you mean? Everyone loves Natalie. Nobody even thinks about me."

Around Harrison and Cora, she had become used to speaking her words when she normally would only have thought them. They seemed to appreciate her speaking out.

"We want to know what exactly is going on in that pretty head of yours," Harrison had told her once.

Cora gave another little sigh. "Well. The thing is, you don't interact with many people, do you? You keep to yourself."

"Yes." Everybody knew that.

"But when you do interact, you make a point to know the person. You listen to them."

"That is only because I'm scared to talk to them."

"Perhaps. But it means that you do a great deal of listening, doesn't it?"

"Yes, I suppose," Regina admitted.

"And that means you get to know them rather well. People like to have that kind of validation. Especially men. They like it when they find a woman who will properly listen to them.

"I rather suspect that it's because they spend so much time talking over each other that most of what they want in a spouse is someone who will support them. Someone who they know is on their side and won't try to one-up them, so to speak.

"But in any case, you're a good listener. You never try to insult anybody."

"You cannot be serious. You've heard my big mouth."

"Yes, but you aren't trying to be rude. People can tell. You go an alarming shade of pink afterwards and they realize straightaway that you didn't mean it."

"That doesn't help me when it comes to society. They're quite willing to not forgive my faux pas."

"Yes, but I'm sure a man would be willing to forgive those more easily than Natalie's flirting," Cora pointed out. "Anyone who talks about you probably knows that underneath it all, you're a sweet girl. Not even underneath it all. Just in general."

Regina felt herself blushing and quickly ducked her head down. "Thank you," she said.

That was another thing that she was learning how to do: accept compliments. She was still inclined to believe that they weren't true but Harrison and Cora... all right, Harrison especially, was determined to rid her of the habit.

Cora reached over and gently took Regina's chin in her hands, lifting it up. "Now, Natalie, on the other hand, plays with men. She uses them to boost herself up. To make herself feel better.

"Men can sense that. You would be a loving wife. A devoted wife. You would validate them. That's all that we want. Someone who validates us and sees us for who we truly are. Natalie uses men for herself instead of truly learning about who they are.

"And because of that, no man will truly want to be interested in her. Not until she learns to actually care about them. Only then will they actually care about her."

Regina thought about that. "When I am playing cards," she said slowly, "In order to distract people, should I act like Natalie?"

"If you want them to know that you're only flirting and nothing more, yes," Cora replied. "Now, was that what was bothering you? Your family? How is Bridget?"

Cora was always especially concerned for Bridget. That made sense to Regina. Bridget had been Cora's childhood friend, not the others.

"Bridget seems to be holding up well. She has yet to choose a husband herself. I believe she is busy worrying over Natalie's state."

Regina failed to add that Bridget wouldn't get to choose a husband. Her husband had already been chosen for her. Regina wondered if she would ever stop feeling guilty over that.

"Then what troubles you? If it isn't that?"

Regina sighed. "I fear that shall sound like a child."

"Nonsense." Cora let out a huff. "I do not understand why you continue to see yourself as so young. I blame Harrison."

"He sees me as a child?" Regina asked.

"No, not exactly," Cora replied. "It is only that he is very protective of you and I think that you want to be taken seriously by him. Is that so?"

Regina nodded. She couldn't deny it when it was so blatantly the truth.

"Well, when we are with someone with whom we feel a little in awe, and we want to impress them, it's natural that we should always feel a bit childish. Especially if there is an age gap."

"I suppose," Regina replied. This was a nice side turn into the thing that had been preoccupying her. "I am a little in awe of him, I admit. I know that he is eight years older and that he has many experiences that I do not.

"But he also irks me. He treats me as a child at times and it frustrates me. He tells me on the one hand that I am intelligent and capable. Then, with the other hand, he handles me as though I am made of glass."

Cora gave a soft laugh. "It is because he cares for you."

"I know that I am as a sister to him—"

Cora had just reached for her cup of tea to take a sip. Right as Regina had said that, Cora had sipped, and upon hearing Regina's words she choked on her tea.

She coughed and spluttered in a most unladylike manner, before laughing again, harder this time. "You think that he thinks of you as a sister? After all—"

Regina could not take it anymore. "Cora, we are not together in that way. We never have been. We simply went along with the lie to hide the real reason for our acquaintance."

Cora stared at her. "And what is the real reason?"

Regina partially regretted her hasty words but it was too late to take them back now. She couldn't think of another lie that would suffice. And she was so tired of Cora's comments and her thinking that Regina was breaking even more of society's rules than she already was.

"You know of the unfortunate position that my sisters and I have been put into."

Cora nodded.

"Well, coming up soon Lord and Lady Morrison are hosting a masquerade ball. They have it every year.

People like to take advantage of the crowd and the masks to do things that they otherwise can't or shouldn't."

"Yes," Cora said, her lips twitching upwards. "I am well aware of the indulgences of the masquerade ball."

Regina took a deep breath. "Well, there are always card games there. And where there are card games, there is Lord Pettifer. I could not get away with it at any other time, but with my mask... I could play with the men. They do not know who I am. Everyone else is bending the rules."

"You mean to win your fortune back from him," Cora breathed out, her voice a mixture of shock and awe.

Regina nodded. "Yes. That is the plan. That is why I took the bold chance and wrote to Lord Harrison."

"That's why he's so obsessed with training you at cards." Cora made a scathing noise. "I am such a fool. To think that he was only training you for his own amusement. I should have known that there was a larger game afoot."

"We took care that nobody should know," Regina replied. "You are the only person who knows the truth now. Aside from Harrison and myself, of course."

"And you were willing to let all of us think you a fallen

woman rather than reveal the truth to us?" Cora seemed aghast.

"What else was I to do?" Regina replied. "If you and the others knew, then you might somehow let it slip to someone else. Then that someone else would let it slip, and so on. I could not dare risk Lord Pettifer finding out the truth."

"You risked everything of yourself, did you know that, Regina?" Cora said. "You could—if one of us had slipped up or someone else—there are so many ways that this could have gotten out. I mean, the wrong truth, the lie, could have gotten out."

"But that would have only ruined me!" Regina protested. "Don't you see? I would have been ruined. Me. Only me. If the truth of what I was doing got out, then Lord Pettifer would never play me. I would have no chance to save my family."

"You would risk yourself so that your family might have a chance. And you might not even win the card game."

"All my life I have done nothing. I have had no convictions. Finally I have something over which I feel strongly. Something that I know I can do. Something that makes me honestly want to get up in the mornings."

"It is something that you would destroy yourself over."

"And why do you not go to the continent?" Regina replied.

It was a bit of a low blow. Cora went pale.

Regina plowed onward.

"You could go to France. You would be quite welcome there. But you do not. You risk yourself as well, Cora. We all are willing to do stupid things for love.

"Perhaps my love is for my family and not for a lover. That I will allow. But does that make it any less strong or any less significant? Does that make it, in some way, less than? I do not think so."

"Miss Regina," Cora said slowly, "You have more of a backbone than most of the men that I know."

Regina blushed, curling into herself a little and looking away from Cora. She suddenly felt incredibly embarrassed by her outburst. This was why she was not fit for polite society.

"I apologize. My behavior just now was... rather uncalled for. I am sorry if I have offended you."

"Do not apologize," Cora said. Her voice was soft and understanding. "I am rather in awe of you and your choices. I do not know a half a dozen people who could be so brave as all that."

"It feels more foolhardy than brave," Regina admitted.

"Often times, I have found, they are the same thing." Cora smiled gently. "I don't blame you."

Then she straightened and stood up. "Harrison, however, is about to get an earful."

"What?" Regina sat up. "Oh, no, Cora, don't—"

It was too late. Cora was sweeping out the door and yelling for Harrison. Her tone clearly stated that he might not survive their encounter.

Regina, once again, wondered if the floor could just swallow her up.

CHAPTER 26

Regina sat by herself for some time after that, convinced that she was going to get up any minute and leave the house.

Yes. That was what she was going to do. It was the only proper course of action. Leave the house, and never come back. It was the only way to get over such embarrassment.

If only she could remind her body how to properly move.

After a time, wherein she found that she had apparently become a statue, Cora returned.

"Well," she said. "Harrison is ready to apologize to you."

"What on earth does he have to apologize to me for?" Regina asked.

Cora sighed. "He should have known that we would make the assumptions that we did about your relationship. He is the older adult here. And the man. It was his responsilbity—"

She cut herself off with a scathing noise. "Obviously his affection for you clouds his judgment. Now, off with you."

Cora waved Regina towards the library. Regina felt rather as though she was being used like a tennis ball, lobbied back and forth between Harrison and Cora. It reminded her a bit of how Natalie and Elizabeth could be.

But she rose anyway and went into the library.

Harrison was sitting and idly shuffling cards. He looked up as she entered and gave her a wry smile. "I've been told I am to apologize to you."

"Yes, I was told rather the same thing."

Harrison sighed and stood up. He motioned for Regina to sit down. "I do apologize. I was thinking only of covering up the truth. I forgot how deadly the lie could be."

"I should think the truth even more deadly."

"The truth is that you are a well-intentioned girl who is doing something very brave and very daring to save her family. The lie is that you are a reckless girl who is pursuing her own pleasure despite it leading to her ruin." Lord Harrison set the cards aside. "I think you underestimate the cruelty of society."

"I told Cora this, and I am telling you now, I do not care what society thinks of me. It already scorns me. Right now my entire family is under a cloud. I considered it an improvement if only I was under one."

"That is a fair assessment," Harrison replied. "I commend you for your self-sacrificing nature. But the fact remains that I should have planned for this. I should have spoken to my friends and made up a better cover for us.

"And I should not have allowed the misinterpretation of our relationship to continue for so long. Even if it was only Cora who was here to think so."

Regina bowed her head, accepting his apology. "I have a feeling that you will not stop until I simply say 'thank you' and agree to your wrongdoing."

"You would be correct." Harrison smiled at her for a moment. Then he sobered.

"I know that I am nothing of the sort, of course. But I cannot help but feel a sense of responsibility towards you. I find myself wishing to treat you as I would any young lady. Then I remember that I can't.

"You have put your faith in me and I find that makes me feel responsible towards you. If you were to find yourself in a position of danger or scandal it would be my fault. I feel that I must take care of you in that way.

"It's not because I feel that you are a child. I would feel this way, I think, even if you were older than I am. It is because rather of the position that we are in. Not our ages."

"I just want you to treat me as an equal," Regina replied. "You can look after me without coddling me. I appreciate how you treat me. I like that you are protective of me. I feel safe when I am with you.

"But I am a woman, and I wish to be treated as one. I know that there might be times when I am not always mature. I know that my age might create some barrier or moments of recklessness. I am certainly being reckless with this entire endeavor."

Harrison chuckled quietly, amused.

"But I am also an adult and any mistakes I make are the mistakes of an adult, not the mistakes of a child." Regina bit her lip. "Everyone always speaks of me as... as this mouse. As someone to be talked over and around. I do not wish to experience that from you."

"And I am sorry if I have made you feel that way," Harrison replied. "You are someone that I respect. Please do not doubt that. I will do my best to curb that behavior in the future."

"So are we at a truce?" Regina asked, teasing him. "I have accepted your apology and you have accepted my corrections?"

"Yes, truce." Harrison smiled. "Now, let us find Cora and avail her to play. There is not much time left and we must use all of it as best we can."

Regina nodded. "Yes."

Time was running out.

CHAPTER 27

They found Cora much in the same position that Regina had left her.

"Oh, my Lord, could you two look any more contrite." Cora announced her annoyance the moment they entered the sitting room. She was sitting and reading a book, looking thoroughly put out. "One would think that you two had killed one another's kittens or something from the looks on your faces."

"Perhaps I am merely basking in the first proper apology I have had to give in years," Harrison replied. "Contain your excitement, Cora, this does not mean I shall go about apologizing for anything else."

"Oh, of course, that would be too much to ask of you."

"Are you two certain that you are not related?" Regina asked. "Because you behave like siblings."

"Cora wishes that she was related to me, but alas," Harrison said dramatically, putting a hand over his heart, "Unless we stumbled into a Gothic romance when I wasn't looking and she is secretly my half-sister or somesuch, no. We are not."

Cora scoffed. "I thought that she was here to learn cards, hmm? Shall we go back to teaching her useful things?"

"Never mind her," Harrison said. "She uses her cruel sense of humor to show her affection. As I'm sure you have well figured out. Her jealousy is a petty thing next to her congratulations for you."

"She hides her congratulations well," Regina remarked, a little put out by Cora's attitude.

Cora sighed and set aside her book. "My sweet little one. I am quite happy for you. Although I must admit seeing your blissful faces does make my gut ache something fierce. So long as you do not flaunt it in my face overmuch, I see no reason to be anything but pleased for you. It is much better that you learn these things now, and snatch happiness where you can."

Happiness? Regina did not think this to be quite so much as happiness—was it? Certainly she felt contented. She felt blissful, her body sighing with the echoes of great pleasure. And she was most comfortable on Harrison's arm, at Harrison's side.

Was this happiness? And if so, was she so unused to feeling it that she could not properly recognize it when it hit her? The thought startled her.

"Cora does raise one good point," Harrison admitted. "We must turn to the cards. You are getting to be quite reliable in your talents, my Puck. Shall we?"

Regina nodded. Yes. To the cards.

They played again and again. Regina, her fears temporarily put aside by Harrison's reassurances in their relationship, was able to concentrate better than she had the last few days.

She entered a kind of zone, so to speak. It was like she was thinking, but not as hard as she had been. Or it was just as hard, but she didn't feel it. It was like she was coasting, almost, in her mind.

"It happens when you go riding for a long time as well," Harrison told her when she explained it to him. "When your body or mind is doing something for a great length of time, it begins to sort of enter this state where it's continuing to do it but without expending as much energy. It's strange but also a little addicting, isn't it?"

It was. Regina could understand why people went riding for so many hours. She had always imagined that it must be quite bothersome, getting knocked around on a horse and earning large bruises. But if they were entering the kind of state that she was, in their own way, then she could hardly blame them.

The next few days were very focused. Harrison and Cora let her be the dealer more and more often. In time her hands were able to go through the motions of shuffling and dealing without her looking at the cards as she did it.

She was winning more and more often, and it was getting harder for Thomas to beat her. She could see him struggling, even while Cora laughed at the both of them for their intensity and competitiveness.

"You two are a pair," she would declare. "Both of you stubborn as mules and refusing to back down. If this were an actual game you'd have both staked your entire fortunes and your first born children by now."

It was a joke, of course, but it struck Regina through the heart. Was this how her father was? Was she becoming a gambling addict as he was?

She brought it up to Thomas one night, after they had finished and she was preparing to be escorted home.

"You seem thoughtful, my Puck," he noted as he put away the cards. "Is something amiss?"

Regina sighed. "It is merely that I worry that I am turning into my father. The way that Cora describes us —how competitive we are with one another—and how determined I am to win. The way I love... I am ashamed, I admit, of the way that I love how my mind gets when we are deep in a game. I fear that is how my father is and that after this game, I still will not be able to stop playing. That I will bring my family to disgrace and ruin, as he did."

Harrison sat down next to her. "Miss Regina Hartfield. Listen to me. You are becoming good at something. I think, perhaps, that this is the first thing that you have truly worked for in the company of others where you can show off your skill. Is that true?"

Regina nodded.

"Then it is only natural that you should be a bit competitive. If you were used to doing activities with others, such as riding, I think it would not strike you so hard to be the best. When we are deprived of something, such as praise or recognition, to finally see the chance to obtain it is tempting indeed.

"But do you think of the cards as you lie in bed? Do you

wake up with only one longing in your chest: to play again?"

Regina shook her head. It was only when she was in the middle of playing that she felt that strong determination to win. In those moments it was as if someone had wrapped a string around her stomach and pulled, and she was compelled to follow that string.

But the rest of the day? No. She was easily distracted, by Cora and Aunt Jane and letters from her sisters and so on. Thomas himself was most distracting as well.

She shook her head again, for emphasis.

"Tell me, then, what you think of when you sit down to play."

Regina thought about that. "I think of my family," she admitted at last. "It feels foolish to say, I know. But that is what I think on. I remember that this is the only way to save them. I remind myself that I must be the best, and if I do not best you, how can I hope to best Lord Pettifer?"

Harrison nodded. "That is good. That is as it should be. If you thought only of how you enjoyed playing and how you wanted to win, then I should be concerned. But your goal is still firm in hand and your senses are about you.

"It's all right, you know, to enjoy this a bit. I should hope that learning how to play hasn't been a trial for you and that you should find some joy in it. If you were miserable every game, I would feel quite awful, I must admit.

"But you do not have to worry. I have been watching you, as I must, to help you to improve. I have seen no sign of addiction about you. And why should I? There is no hole in your life that you are trying to fill."

"It seems that there is," Regina admitted. She could feel her cheeks burning with shame as she spoke, revealing herself in such a way. How Harrison had the ability to make her feel so young and small and stupid, she didn't know.

"I feel as though my entire life has been empty up until now, and that in some ways it is still empty, and that once this is over it will be empty all over again. Only it will be more painful this time, because I will know more of myself.

"I will know that I have been clever, and accomplished, and useful. Even if it was with something that I am not supposed to know of, even if it is something I cannot share with others. Even though I can never tell my family of what I did. I know. That is what matters.

"But after I defeat Lord Pettifer, if I defeat him, then it's gone. And I don't know what I shall do after that. My sisters will marry soon, even after this dark cloud is lifted. They all wish to marry and of course they must. And then it will only be me.

"I know that no man will have me. And so there is nothing for me. I have no friends."

"You have my friends," Harrison cut in. "They are your friends now as well. They all like you. Cora certainly likes you. I believe that she views you as a younger sister such as she never had."

Regina blinked rapidly to hide her tears. It had not occurred to her that Cora or any of Harrison's other friends would wish to continue to see her. But of course...

"You will forgive my impudence, but I feel compelled to remind you that your friends are not always the sort that are welcome in everyone's homes."

"That is true," Harrison allowed, "But they are always welcome in mine. And you are welcome in mine as well, and must be, for when I marry your sister I know she will hardly bear to be parted from you for any length of time."

"I confess that I feel I have grown somewhat in her absence," Regina replied.

"That is natural. She is as a mother to you. All children must grow a little away from their parents."

Regina thought of some of the things that Cora had said. She wondered if perhaps even Bridget didn't see all that Regina was and could be. Perhaps her sister, in her love, had coddled Regina just a little bit.

"Well, then, I shall have you and your friends," Regina said. "Although of course I must share you with Bridget."

"Of course."

Regina ignored the sudden pang in her heart at the thought. Thomas was never hers, not truly. How could she be sad to lose him, or share him, rather?

Their card games and their time with one another could not continue after things returned to normal and Bridget married him. It was foolish to think so.

But oh, she would miss it. She would miss having Harrison's full attention. No. Lord Harrison. She must remember to think of him that way again. She must put distance between them, even if it was only in her head.

She would miss knowing that he was taking time out of

his day simply to be with her. She would miss having his gaze upon her, looking at her like she was the only person in the room—in the whole world.

She shook herself out of such thoughts. Thomas was only behaving this way because it would get him Bridget. Regina knew that he cared for her, of course. He would not be so kind to her if he did not. But to think he looked at her as though she were the only person in the room?

What a childish fool, to think of such things.

"I cannot have a social circle that only includes you all, of course," Regina went on. "And I fear going back into ballrooms on my own."

"Perhaps," Lord Harrison said, speaking slowly, "This masked ball may be an opportunity in more ways than one, then."

"What do you mean?"

"I mean that while you do have a habit of speaking out of turn, you are not so awful as you fear. With your mask on, nobody will know you. You can move freely.

"I think that, before the card game starts and after it is finished, it would be good for you to roam the ball. Dance with some gentlemen. Chat with some ladies.

"After all is said and done, I believe that you will find they embrace you. I truly believe that you will discover you have more to offer than you think you do. Furthermore, I think that you will enjoy yourself more than you anticipate. All that is needed is to free yourself from the burdens of what you feel others expect and believe of you."

Regina did not quite believe him, but she was willing to give it a try. If only to prove him wrong.

"Very well. Another little bargain between us. I shall move about the ball and engage others in conversation and dance. If they embrace me as they have embraced my sisters in the past, then you are right. If they reject me, then I am proven right and the fault lies entirely within myself."

"I have found that so rarely does the fault lie entirely with one person." Harrison's lips twitched in amusement. "But we shall see in the end who has the right of it."

Regina smiled at him, looking forward, almost, to winning. Yet at the same time hoping she lost. She was never going to be a social butterfly but she did want to discover that she could discourse with others.

She wanted to prove herself as more than she had always thought she was.

"Again, Regina, if I may return to the subject of your father—if I thought you in danger of developing an addiction, I promise you I should not have continued in your training.

"You are a lady, and as such cannot play outside of this masked ball. Even if you were a man, I would not allow you to play if you were addicted to it. It's a dangerous thing and always only ever leads to ruination.

"Many a man has thought that he could use it. Rather, the addiction uses him. He will not stop while he is ahead. If he gains a large win, he loses it the next day in another game. No man can win every time. Not with the cards such as they are.

"And yet men try. They try. And they try. And they try again. And for every win there are only heavier losses to follow."

Thomas's eyes were glinting in the firelight. It made him look otherworldly once again. As always, it drew Regina in. Even though she knew that it probably should have done the opposite.

"Trust me, my Puck, I would not have let you throw yourself away on such a hopeless endeavor."

"I suppose I ought to thank you, then, Your Majesty," Regina replied. She allowed herself to tease a little, fearing that she had made the mood too somber with her childish fears.

"I would be an irresponsible mentor if I did not take such care," Thomas replied. "And do not beat yourself up about this, Regina. You do enough of that already. It is a legitimate fear and I am glad that you are aware of it as a potential pitfall."

He rose, holding his hands together behind his back. "Now, I think it is best that we retire. These next few days will be the most intense. The ball is only a week away. Therefore, we must prepare as much as we can."

The ball. Yes. Only a week away. It startled her at how fast the time had flown. And yet, it felt like ages ago since she had been in her own home.

Had it only been a month since she had been so blissfully unaware of how her father's sins would ruin them all? Had it been so short a time since she had last been idle? Had she not seen her sisters in such a time?

Soon it would all come to a head. There were only the next few days to focus on card playing. Then, the last details must be hammered out for attending the ball:

how best to approach the game, how to avoid anyone recognizing her, and so on.

Then it would be the day of the ball itself. And there would be the game.

Regina's stomach twisted with worry and anticipation. On that day, she had to be her best. There was simply no other option. Her feelings for Lord Harrison, any esteem she had for him, her fears, her misgivings, their silly bet about her social skills. All of it must fall away.

There could only be the game.

CHAPTER 28

The next few days were an absolute flurry.

Regina arranged for Aunt Jane and Cora to meet. The two women took to one another immediately. They cited various mutual acquaintances. Aunt Jane made a remark about Cora's mother that was not permitted in most polite society, which sent Cora off into peals of delighted laughter.

"The fastest way to form friends, my dear," Aunt Jane said after seeing Regina's aghast expression, "Is to find things that you mutually and vehemently dislike."

That seemed rather backwards to Regina. But since Aunt Jane and Cora were getting along so well, who was she to question it?

Aunt Jane and Cora worked together and went with Regina to select what she would wear to the masquerade ball.

The plan was that Regina would have two outfits.

The first would be an outfit done in such a fashion that anyone looking at it should instantly know that it was her. It was rather simple in style and done up in a dark, muted blue. It went well with her eyes, or so she was told by a cooing Aunt Jane and a beaming Cora.

While the fabric was lovely, the style of the dress was just far enough behind in fashion that it fit with the rest of Regina's style. She wasn't much into shopping and was the youngest, so she was forever a step behind in the latest fashions.

The muted color, the modest cut, and the slight laziness in style would tell anyone who cared to look that it was Regina Hartfield wearing that dress.

Furthermore, her chosen mask was a simple one and did not cover much of her face. It was her eyes that were mostly obscured. If the dress was not enough for someone then the almost entire reveal of her face would soon set things to rights.

Regina would arrive at the ball in this first outfit. She would meet up with her sisters there, with Aunt Jane serving as her escort. After catching up she would do a few dances and chat around so that people would know that she was there.

This way, someone could say, "Why yes, Regina Hartfield? She was just right here. I wonder where she went. Perhaps try the dining room?"

Everyone would know that she was about somewhere. The masquerade ball was a large one. In fact it was the largest one that Lord and Lady Morrison hosted all year. It wasn't unusual for someone to get swallowed up by the crowd.

Once she had established herself as present, Regina would slip away. Cora would find her, and then help her to get undressed and put on the second dress.

The second dress was much more daring than the first. It was the latest fashion, from Paris. It was entirely white, which would stand out at the masquerade ball. Perhaps it was the nature of the ball or what those in attendance tended to do during it, but most people wore darker clothing.

Putting on a white dress, with such expensive fabric, in such a fashion forward style, would all help Regina to stand out. Cora would have a trusted handmaid upon attendance who would take Regina's hair and put it in a different style.

Finally, there would be her mask. The second mask was a lovely piece of white lace, but it covered almost her entire face. It even had feathers sticking out of it that folded back and covered some of her hair.

"You look almost like a bride," Cora noted.

"You look absolutely ravishing, my dear," Aunt Jane added.

Regina did not care what she looked like so long as she was not recognizable. She wanted to appear before the card players as a mysterious and worldly woman. She needed them to be in awe of her. Her joining them at their table should be something that they enjoyed and wanted despite the taboo.

If this second outfit helped to accomplish that, then so be it.

When she was not handling the issues of dress, she was working with Harrison on cards. Or she was taking lessons on accents from Lord Quentin. He had been fetched by Harrison so that he might teach her the accent of his mother's people.

"Nobody will realize that is what you sound like," he

said. "They will only know that you speak with an accent not from here. It will make you seem exotic. They will be more curious about you."

When Aunt Jane asked why Regina needed a second dress, or why Lord Quentin was teaching her an accent, Regina only told her that she wanted to enjoy the ball without the pressure of her sisters breathing down her neck.

"I also have a little friendly wager going, between Lady Cora and I," Regina added. "Lady Cora feels that I underappreciate myself. She says that if I go through the masquerade ball and interact with others through dancing and conversation I should find that I am not such a bother as I fear."

"And what do you think?" Aunt Jane asked.

"I think that whether they know me or not they should find me a bore at best and an impudent girl at worst," Regina admitted. "But mostly I fear they shall find me a small nuisance."

She did not think she was so bad as all that to mortally offend anyone. No matter what might come flying out of her mouth at a moment's notice.

Aunt Jane let out a little sigh. "I am afraid I must be

with Lady Cora on this one, Regina. You undervalue yourself."

"So everyone seems determined to keep telling me."

"And when will you begin to believe it then, hmm?"

When Lord Harrison sees that— Regina cut herself off before the thought could continue.

She had been having the most disturbing thoughts lately in regards to her mentor. She knew, of course, that she would form an attachment to him. He had helped her so much in this time of trials and need.

He had agreed to help her, although it must put himself at risk. He had been kind, a friend to her, someone who bolstered her spirits and comforted her without letting her give into the power of her fears. Of course she should feel something for him.

But this... this was deeper, and it scared her.

It was jealousy, and frustration, and sadness. Such an aching sadness, one that she had never known before.

How could Lord Harrison, she thought, love Bridget when he had only spoken to her a few times? How could he love a woman he hardly knew, and not the woman he knew intimately? They had shared so much time together. Was she not good enough for him?

It scared her that she could be jealous, hoarding her remaining time with Lord Harrison like a dragon clutching at his jewels and gold.

She was jealous of Bridget, even. That horrified her even more. To be jealous of someone who had done her wrong or who she did not know was bad enough. To be jealous of someone who had shown her kindness and friendship was worse. But to be jealous of the woman who had raised Regina as her child? The woman who had often put aside her own desires and needs in order to give to Regina?

It made her feel like a traitor to her sister. First she had all but sold Bridget off like so much property. Now she was jealous of what her sister would have: Lord Harrison.

This could not go on. Regina tried to think of ways that she could dismiss her mentor from her thoughts. It was difficult, when so much time was spent with him.

Lord Harrison seemed determined—no, more than determined. He seemed obsessed with her winning. It was as though he was a jockey and she the horse, and they could see the finish line in sight. Now that it was so close he was pushing her as never before.

It felt as though nothing she did was good enough.

Regina came close to crying more than once over it. She steeled herself, though. She was not a child anymore. She couldn't hide. If she could not handle the man she had come to trust, then how could she handle such sternness from the strangers who would be gathered around the card table?

It was up to her to have a strong backbone. She would not tolerate weakness in herself. If Lord Harrison chose to be a perfectionist about these things then that was up to him. She could understand it, even appreciate it a little. How could he sit back and relax if he was not safe in the knowledge that he had trained her as well as he could and pushed her as far as she could go?

Her limits were tested, again and again. He tried to think of ways to distract her while she was playing. He played in as many different ways as he could, to throw her off.

It wasn't easy. There were times when she wanted to burst into tears. There were other times still when she wanted to throw down her cards and leave. She wanted to rail at him until he understood how awful he was being.

Could he not see that she was doing her best? Why must he push her so?

But it had to be. She knew that. There was only one chance. Everything hung on this one game. She was never going to be good enough to beat Lord Pettifer unless she was stretched beyond her limits.

Regina was determined not to fail. Cora had to make her sleep and Aunt Jane had to remind her to eat. It felt as though she was no longer existing on earth but in some kind of limbo, an in-between space.

She had to win this. It had always felt real, of course, and some days it had felt more real than others. But now it felt unbearably real. This was her family's only chance.

The others had all noticed. She could feel them being more gentle with her—well, Cora, Aunt Jane, and Lord Quentin were. Lord Harrison, on the other hand…

It was fair not to expect any mercy from Lord Harrison. She needed to be the best and that was what he was pushing her to be. She had literally asked for this. She couldn't be angry with him.

Still, it hurt a little. These were their last few days together and it was as though her friend, her mentor, her Oberon, had disappeared. In his place was this other man who pushed her. He was going to help her win the card game, of course he was. But he wasn't her friend.

It made her sad. She had been hoping for more... Well, she didn't know what. It was all jumbled up with the strange feelings within her.

Every time she felt that strange urge to reach out and touch him or beg him for—she didn't even know what— she stamped it down. And yet fear gripped her. Fear at how she must now lose him.

Lose him to Bridget, of all people. And she had orchestrated this. How could she be so upset? She wasn't losing anything. Lord Harrison had never been hers to begin with.

It was all her fault, really. It was her fault for being a young and foolish girl. She was growing... or she had grown... attached on a deeper level.

Lord Harrison was kind to her. He teased her. He called her his Puck. But all of these could be just as easily interpreted as the kindness of a friend, soon to be brother.

She told herself that she looked forward to having him as her brother. She told herself that worked. That was fine. She could have him in her life and she would be happy for it.

But she couldn't bring herself. Instead it only made her sadder.

Regina did her best to keep these feelings to herself. It wouldn't help anyone to share them. How could it? There was nothing that they could do. They couldn't make this intense sadness and sense of loss go away.

Indeed, to say it out loud would be to make it more real. It would, in fact, give these feelings a name. She did not dare to do that. Giving it a name made it real and making it real gave it a name, a name that she hadn't wanted, something that had terrified her and only brought sadness to the people she loved.

She did not want that sadness for herself.

She didn't want to be like Cora. She didn't want to be like Bridget. She didn't want to be like Louisa. And she definitely didn't want to be like her father.

If she said all of her feelings out loud to anyone, they would know. They would say it out loud. They would make it real. And then there would be no denying anymore how she felt. She'd have to accept it.

Perhaps she had grown bolder over the course of this. She was no longer as afraid to speak. Her opinion of herself was no longer quite so low. She now knew that she was intelligent and capable of becoming skilled and respected at something. Even if she never played cards again, not even as a friendly game in her own home, nobody could take that away from her. And she could find other ways to showcase that intelligence and skill.

But there was one way, she realized, in which she was a coward, and that was in the matter of her heart.

She would rather never say anything then talk to someone and risk all of these feelings bubbling up to the surface completely. They would ruin her. They would cut through her heart and destroy her. She'd never felt anything so strong as this pull.

Lord Harrison made her feel safe. He made her feel valued and intelligent. She enjoyed teasing him and being teased in return. She liked just being in his presence. She wanted to go on more walks through the park with him. She wanted to read her way through his library and discuss all of the books with him.

And she wanted him for her very own. Not sharing him with a wife. Even if that wife was her beloved Bridget.

It was all she could do not to find a dark corner and sob.

No, she told herself. She wasn't a child. She wasn't going to cry and make a fuss over this.

She would handle these feelings with dignity and in silence. The way that Bridget handled the loss of her childhood sweetheart. Regina would be just like that—make it so that no one would suspect how she truly felt.

Perhaps she had been a child about things before but she wasn't going to be a child now. She was going to carry herself forth with dignity, as an adult would.

To the world, she would appear only as she always had. And to Lord Harrison, to Cora, to the others who knew what time she had been spending with him—she would seem only as a dear friend. A devoted sister.

Nobody needed to know the truth.

Nobody *could* know the truth. Not even Regina, not really. She couldn't speak it even to herself.

That way lay ruin.

CHAPTER 29

The day of the masquerade dawned like any other. Regina almost wondered if she didn't have the date wrong. A part of her had expected the day to dawn with thunderclouds and rain, some sort of signal of the danger and last chance she was throwing herself into.

Instead, however, the day began as usual, with sunlight streaming in through the windows. Regina rose and took breakfast with Aunt Jane.

She didn't go over to Lord Harrison's, however. There was no time for a last card game, so much as she might want there to be. She and Aunt Jane had to ride all the way to Lord and Lady Morrison's, and there she must meet up with her sisters and prepare for the ball.

Cora would take her own carriage to the Morrison lands. She would take with her Regina's second dress and accessories and have them in her own chambers until the time was right.

The night before, Lord Harrison had stopped her just before she went out the door to return home.

"A few last words," he had said. The moonlight from the door and the firelight from the grate had warred on his face. The duality had reminded her of their first meeting and how he had taken her outside.

Would she always be partially entranced by him, she had wondered. Would she ever truly know him, know his heart, or would there always be a part of him that was bathed in shadow and unknowable to her?

Not that she had a right to think such things. Regina reminded herself that she was not his bride.

"Tomorrow you will be afraid," Lord Harrison had told her. "Ah, do not protest. I would be more worried if you were not afraid. It would mean that you are overestimating yourself. It would mean that you were forgetting the importance of what you are doing.

"But I want to remind you that even though you are afraid, you do not have to let it own you. You are capable of doing this. You have the ability to defeat

Lord Pettifier. I know that, from the bottom of
my soul.

"I do not praise lightly. I've tried to avoid praising you,
because I have not wanted you to slack off in your work
or to fill your head with overconfidence. But I believe in
you. And I will be there, even if I cannot help you
directly. I will not leave the room, and if things should
turn ugly, I will be at your side in an instant. You will
be safe."

Of course she would be safe, she had wanted to say. So
long as Lord Harrison was there with her she felt as
though she could take on a dragon, because if it looked
like the dragon might eat her he'd jump in to help her—
even if he wouldn't interfere until that point.

She appreciated that. She could slay this dragon on her
own. Or at least, she hoped that she could.

With Lord Harrison's encouragement ringing in her
ears, she started the day with Aunt Jane. She wouldn't
see him until after she had changed into her second
dress with Cora and prepared to enter the card room.
She missed him already, like a limb.

She did so hate these ridiculous feelings.

Aunt Jane did not know the full story but she was not an
ignorant woman. She knew that something was afoot.

"Are you quite all right, my dear?" She asked. "You seem rather quiet this morning."

Regina wanted to laugh. She had not realized that she had become talkative. Her sisters would think nothing of her being silent at the breakfast table. In fact, with all of their chatter, they would not even notice. They might not even know if she came down at all.

"This will be my first ball in some time," Regina answered. "I am nervous for it. Especially since I have promised myself and Lady Cora to try out being more social and seeing where that shall lead."

"I think that you will find yourself surprised at your own abilities," Aunt Jane replied.

They ate, retired to change and to pack, and then were loaded up into their carriage to begin the journey.

Regina had to admit that her thoughts were somewhere other than the rolling hills and green woods that they passed through. It was all rather lovely and at any other time she would have enjoyed it. The peace and quiet and the view were all together quite something. She could see why poets waxed poetic about the English countryside.

And yet, she almost couldn't see any of it. She kept picturing in her mind's eye all the times she had seen

Lord Harrison. It was as if, after this, she would not be allowed to daydream on him, and so she must get it all done at once.

"You seem rather distracted," Aunt Jane noted.

Regina could not offer up an explanation. Fortunately she did not need to, for Aunt Jane continued to speak.

"You know, my poor husband—may he rest in peace—had quite a time of it in wooing me."

"Oh?" Regina asked. She was not sure where this direction of conversation was going, but she did owe Aunt Jane much. The woman had let her into her home and had allowed Regina to spend time with a man with an escort that Aunt Jane hardly knew. It was skirting propriety, and yet Aunt Jane had never complained.

"Yes. Harold—for that was his name—Harold had to practically fling himself at my feet to show me that he cared for me. When he proposed, most ladies would see that as a sign of affection. Men generally care for their wives when they choose them, even if they are not passionately in love with them.

"But that was not enough for me. I was convinced that he had proposed because of my good breeding and my looks. It honestly did not occur to me that he should choose me because he had fallen in love with me. What was I? I thought.

"In my mind, you see, I was a poor imitation of a proper woman. I had never been good at needlepoint or the piano. I could not draw. I loved to dance but I fear I was not very good at it.

"And I did not have the habit of conversing easily with those I did not know. I learned, in time, but that was later. At the time of his proposal I was quite inadequate at the dinner table for talk.

"Yet, somehow, he loved me. He had seen things in me that I did not see even in myself. I loved him, of course. He was so handsome. Do not tell my daughter this but she takes her good looks from him. She has always been convinced that she looks after me and I cannot bring myself to tell her that her father was always more handsome than I.

"But in any case. I did love him. He was gentle and kind, witty, and excellent at riding and dancing. I couldn't fathom that a man such as that could love me in return. I resigned myself, therefore, to simply be content to be his wife and to have him near me, even if I did not have his love.

"And you know, the man seemed determined to prove

me wrong. He would arrange for my favorite flowers to be sent to me. He would purchase me gifts when he went out, little ribbons and baubles and such. He consulted me about all matters and seemed to truly value my opinion. When he was away he would write me such long letters—the whole bundle of them seemed to weigh a pound!

"After about a year of this, my poor suffering husband came home, and presents me with this beautiful pearl necklace. I was quite astonished, for I knew that it must have cost him dear and should make me quite the envy of all the ladies at the next ball.

"I burst into tears." Aunt Jane chuckled at herself, shaking her head. "You see my father was a good man in many respects but he was not faithful to my mother. Oh, we all knew it, though no one spoke of it. Every time he broke one of his marriage vows he would gift her with some truly astonishing jewelry. It was his way of absolving his guilt.

"So when my Harold brought me the necklace, I was sure that it meant he had strayed. I could not bear it, for though I knew he did not return my love I had also thought that he was a good man who would stay faithful.

"The idea of him betraying our marriage broke me, and I simply cried my eyes out. The poor man was so confused! He asked if I did not like pearls, if I was with child and therefore temperamental, if I was sick and needed care.

"Finally I got round to telling him why I was so upset. You should have seen his face!" Aunt Jane laughed heartily. "I had never seen the man more surprised!"

Aunt Jane sobered up. "More than that, though, my dear, he was appalled. I could see it in his eyes.

"He knelt before me and took my hand. I shall never forget that moment. He looked at me—and for the first time I saw it. I suppose that he had been looking at me like that the entire time but I hadn't seen it until that moment.

"He looked up at me and said, 'Darling'. He called me that you know but I had never heard it with such reverence. 'Darling', he said, 'How is it that you can doubt my utter devotion to you?'

"I responded that his devotion to a wife he did not love must naturally be suspect. A man's loyalty to a wife he loves is one thing. Loyalty to a woman he has married for the sanctity of marriage, a wife he respects well enough but does not love—what can be expected of him then?

"My husband was appalled, and rightly so. I don't think

it had occurred to him in that moment that I did not know that he loved me. I had certainly never voiced my thoughts aloud. It was not my place and it was, or so I supposed, so obvious that there was no point in speaking of it.

"He took me into his arms and—well. I won't tell you what he said or did in that moment. I must have some secrets." Aunt Jane winked at her. "But I remember realizing, oh. He is in love with me, as I am in love with him. What a fool I was not to see it."

Aunt Jane reached over to a small red velvet box that she had been carrying with some of her luggage. She placed her hand over it and Regina knew without a moment's doubt that the pearl necklace was inside.

"Will you be wearing it tonight?" She asked.

Aunt Jane nodded. "I always wear it on special occasions. I get out so rarely now. Whenever I do, I feel as though he is with me."

Regina supposed that was why Aunt Jane had told her that story. She was feeling nostalgic and missing her husband. If only Regina should be so lucky as to find someone who loved her in that way.

Aunt Jane sighed, as though she had fired an arrow and it had missed its mark. Then she perked up, peering through the window. "Oh! Lovely sight, is it not? I always feel my heart swell when I see it. Of course that is largely because I know my daughter resides within."

Regina peered through the window as well and saw indeed that they were approaching the Morrison estate. There was no turning back now. In a few short hours, she would be seated at the card table.

Time to shove all thoughts of romance and Lord Harrison and daydreams out of her head. She could not be Regina the girl right now.

She had to be Regina the card player.

CHAPTER 30

The moment Regina stepped out of the carriage she was assaulted.

"She is here!" Natalie cried out.

All at once Regina was being picked up and swung around, causing her to let out a shriek. "This is quite undignified!" She protested. They were not children, after all.

"I shall greet my darling sister however I please," Bridget said, setting Regina down.

Regina could not contain her joy. It suddenly felt as though her heart would burst. "Bridget!"

Her eldest sister smiled down at her, eyes wet and smile wide and warm. "My darling."

They hugged fiercely, and Regina had to admit that she clung to her sister a little more tightly than usual. Unlike Bridget, she knew how this evening was going to end: with her sister engaged to Lord Harrison.

When they pulled back Regina was tugged from behind and turned to be pulled right into the arms of Louisa. "And how are you, Regina?" Louisa asked, her voice as gentle as ever.

Regina hugged her back. She hadn't realized how much she missed her other sister and her gentle presence until that moment. "I am quite well. I hope it is the same with you."

"As well as can be expected," Louisa said, pulling back with a smile.

Regina took in her sister's wan appearance. She then looked at all of her other sisters.

Natalie looked as though she had not slept in some time. It was the same with Bridget. Louisa seemed pale. Elizabeth seemed healthy, but her mouth was drawn into a tight, unhappy line.

"Has there been more ill news?" Regina asked.

The sisters all looked at one another, and then shook their heads.

"None that we did not anticipate," Bridget said. "Come. Walk with me."

They turned to take a small turn about the drive, Bridget's arm linked with Regina's.

The other three turned to help Aunt Jane out of the carriage and then lead her up to the house, where Regina could see the Morrisons waiting with open arms.

"Mr. Denny has proposed to Elizabeth," Bridget said quietly.

"Does she care for him? Or was it out of necessity?"

"She does care for him. I think that she has rather surprised herself with the force of her affection. Once she was forced to spend time with him I think she found that she liked him rather more than she had expected, and that she had formed ill judgment on him based on presumptions."

"Yet she does not seem happy."

"She is worried for the rest of us. She was with Louisa when Louisa was discussing things with Mr. Fairchild."

"And what was the end result?"

Bridget sighed. "He cannot marry her, as we suspected. The original understanding that they must wait until his aunt dies still holds. From what Elizabeth has told me, Louisa tried to break off the engagement."

"But why?"

"To save him. She loves him and wanted him to find a woman he did not have to wait to marry, a woman who is not furthermore marred by family scandal."

"And what did Mr. Fairchild say to that?"

"He refused." Bridget's mouth twisted up into a grimace. "He protested that if she no longer loved him he would take their breaking off in good grace but he would not allow her to make a martyr of herself to save him. He stood by her."

"That is well for Mr. Fairchild. It speaks to his character."

"Yes, I suppose so. Louisa is not happy. She fears that she will bring ruin to him and that their engagement will be discovered and he shall lose everything."

"It's not an unfair conclusion at which to arrive," Regina pointed out.

"I know. But I think that they would only make

themselves more miserable in breaking things off. There is still time yet. Mr. Denny and Elizabeth have been arranging things for the wedding. Hopefully her marriage to him will make the path more clear and smooth for Mr. Fairchild and Louisa."

"And what of you and Natalie?"

"I am choosing tonight, as I have told you all previously."

"And do you have someone in mind?"

Bridget did not answer that. They walked in silence for a moment, and when she spoke again, it was of Natalie.

"Our middle sister is finding that she does not have the gift of conversing seriously with a man."

"No man has chosen her, then."

Bridget nodded. "It is a blow. To think that you are beloved by all and then to find that when you spend a great deal of time with them they do not want you after all... it is a hard pill to swallow. I think that some self-improvement is in her future."

"But will she be able to? With our futures such as they are?"

"Two of her sisters will be married," Bridget pointed out. "And Louisa's future will be secure once we are well off. Natalie will have time to come to herself, I think."

"That sounds like rather wishful thinking, sister," Regina replied.

Bridget gave a sad, tiny laugh. "I have nothing but wishful thinking Regina. The men that have previously made their interests known to me might have moved on after all, you know. My position is precarious as well. But what can I do? We must remain hopeful or there is nothing for us."

Regina laid her head on her sister's shoulder and strengthened her resolve. She would make things right. After tonight, her sisters would no longer have to fear for themselves and for their future. All would be well again.

Anger burned, hot and fierce, within her chest. She would utterly vanquish Lord Pettifier for this. She would. She had to.

"And what of you, my sweet darling?" Bridget asked. "I hope that city life has improved you somewhat."

"I have found some confidence," Regina admitted. "And made acquaintences. I believe you will see some of them tonight. If they allow you to recognize them, of course. There is a Lady Cora Dunhill, who has been my escort on many occasions."

Bridet stumbled. Regina helped her to continue walking. The pathway was really quite old, with cobblestones that stuck up at odd places.

"I have also made the acquaintance of Lord Harrison, Duke of Whitefern." There was no time like the present and she must make Bridget amenable to his proposal when it came.

"He is quite a gentleman, Bridget. Of course I cannot presume to know your mind but you said that he expressed an interest in you in the past.

"I've found him to be a worthy man. I know that you must choose someone tonight as you have promised. And he has been such a kindness to me. He has helped to introduce me in London and given me great instruction on improving myself. He has been as a brother to me."

That last part was a lie, for in her heart Regina could not see him as a brother and had not imagined that was how it was between them. But that was how it was to his mind, she was certain. Furthermore it was how he would be to her once he and Bridget married. Best to start thinking of him that way now.

And who knew? Maybe if she said it out loud enough times it would become true to her.

Bridget gave a thoughtful hum. "I see. Well, I am glad to hear of it. Having a gentleman on your side can be quite helpful when moving about in social circles. It discourages rakes, for one thing."

"I only speak because I fear that you held a rather low opinion of him, and I think that opinion to be unfair."

"I appreciate you informing me," Bridget said. She turned and looked to see that the others had all retreated back into the house. "Let us join the others, shall we? We will have to start getting ready soon."

Regina nodded and allowed herself to be led into the house.

Lord and Lady Morrison were as delightful as usual. Regina was eager to embrace them and to learn of all that they had been up to.

Everyone was eager to hear about Regina and all that she had got up to on her own. She had not expected that everyone would care so much about her escapades in

London. She had thought that only Bridget would ask after her.

To her surprise, however, all her sisters wished to know.

"Our little sister, off on her own and about in London society," Elizabeth teased. "I do hope that you have some good gossip."

Regina found that lying to them went more easily than she had anticipated. She shared stories that she had heard from Cora and the others. She talked about the people that Aunt Jane had met with as if she had been there. She described balls that she had only heard about.

"I most loved walking about in the many parks," she confessed.

"You? Enjoying a walk?" Natalie laughed, but not in a mean spirited fashion. She sounded genuinely surprised. "Well, knock me down with a feather. I had thought you would spend the entire time wrapped up in your needle and thread."

"I found that when one has the right company, walks can be calming and invigorating," Regina admitted. "And I like the tame nature of the parks better than the wild lands about our country house."

Her sisters were all eager to meet Aunt Jane and

thanked her profusely for looking after Regina in London.

"Oh, the thanks must go to Lady Dunhill," Aunt Jane said modestly. "She was Regina's escort in going out. I fear that after calling in the morning I am far too tired to go out to balls anymore."

"Lady Dunhill? As in Lady Cora Dunhill?" Louisa smiled. "I recall her being a frequent visitor to our house when we were children."

"Indeed. She remembered my birth and sought to look after me as a sister," Regina said. "Her kindness I cannot overstate."

"We shall have to thank her in some way," Louisa said, turning to Bridget.

Bridget, in uncharacteristic silence, simply nodded her agreement.

After the greetings had finished and the catching up had been done, and tea had been taken, it was time to get ready.

Regina had never before actively participated in getting ready for a ball. She had always waited until the last moment in the hopes that she could get out of it. Then she had been quickly done up by her maid and by

Bridget, and bundled into the carriage without ceremony.

Now, however, she was getting ready with the others. She was looking forward to this ball, although not for the reasons that her sisters knew.

"London has done you well, sister," Elizabeth said as Regina helped her to do up her corset. "It has finally made you properly sociable."

"When do you announce your engagement?" Regina asked, in order to change the subject.

"It shall be announced next week," Elizabeth said. "We must then allow for some months of engagement before the actual wedding day. We do not want to seem too hasty."

"But then everyone shall hear of our disgrace before you are married," Regina pointed out.

"There is little thatcan be done about that," Bridget said. "If they marry now everyone will either suspect that Elizabeth is in the family way, or they shall assume the marriage was only because of the loss of our fortune."

"Which it is," Natalie cut in.

"I should not marry a man I did not esteem, and I esteem Mr. Denny in the highest," Elizabeth shot back.

She was obviously ready to go to war with her sister over this matter.

"Natalie, do not let bitterness have a hold on you," Bridget scolded. She turned back to Regina. "This way will only assure everyone that the marriage is done out of affection and mutual respect. It will do a credit to Mr. Denny to be seen as standing by Elizabeth in such trying times. It can only benefit everyone's estimation of his character."

Regina nodded. She trusted Bridget's judgment in the matter. And it wasn't as if Mr. Denny was going in blind. He had been there when their father had fallen.

Hopefully, however, none of this would matter. Hopefully by the end of tonight, their fortunes would be restored.

Everything was a flurry around her, sisters yelling and calling out to one another for help.

"Did you see my shoes?"

"Where on earth has my feather got to."

"Elizabeth, darling, you must choose one of the three masks. You cannot use all three."

"Would someone help me with my stays?"

"Natalie, can you do my corest up even tighter, please?"

It was all a whirlwind, but Regina found that she enjoyed it. It saddened her that she would not be able to enjoy it for much longer. Before long all of them would be married off. Or at the very least, Elizabeth and Bridget would be.

Once that happened, they would not all be together again, getting ready like this. Regina felt a pang of regret. She felt as though she had not appreciated her sisters as she should have. She could have had so many more of these moments if she had.

Louisa seemed to sense her inner distress, for she came over and helped Regina into her dress, her hands and face soft and loving.

"This is a lovely dress that you have chosen," Louisa said kindly, helping Regina to do up her buttons.

"Thank you. Lady Cora and Aunt Jane—for that is how she instructed me to call her—were most kind in helping me to select the fabric and style."

"It is a bit behind the times," Louisa admitted, "But it suits you. The modest style is quite fitting to your character."

If only her sister knew how immodest Regina was about to be.

"Thank you."

Louisa turned her around, smiling at her. "You know, I fear that we have not appreciated you as we should have. Our baby sister. You do know that you are loved by us, don't you?"

Regina nodded. She could feel it now as she never had before. She'd always known that Bridget loved her dearly. And she knew that Louisa loved her for Louisa was a gentle soul and incapable of disliking anybody.

Elizabeth and Natalie she had doubted. They loved her as family but Regina had not been sure of their affection for her as an individual.

But now she could feel it. Perhaps their being away from their sister had led them to appreciate her more, just as her being away from her sisters had led her to appreciate them.

Well, weddings or no weddings, she sensed that this was a new step in her relationships with her sisters. They were all crossing thresholds now, in their own ways. She felt certain that, in the future, they would all be closer.

She wished she could find it in her heart to be grateful for the calamity that had brought them together in sisterly affection. She couldn't, but it was, at least, a silver lining.

Natalie had been the first ready and had vanished from the room at one point. Bridget, who had been helping everybody, was barely dressed. Regina and Louisa were helping Bridget to finish up when Natalie burst back into the room.

"The guests are arriving for dinner!" She announced. "We must put on our masks and hurry down!"

"Wait but a moment, I'm almost finished with the laces," Louisa said, referring to Bridget's dress.

Fear gripped Regina. She was to begin, now.

She steeled herself. What was the point of fear? It would do her no good. It could only hinder her and cause her to fail. No, she was better than this. She was going to walk down there, head held high, and she was going to establish her alibi so that she could enter the card room and defeat that rake that had destroyed her family.

Regina reached into herself and pulled on the anger that arose whenever she thought of Lord Pettifer. She held onto it and stoked it. It grew in her chest until she thought that she could feel it trembling inside every inch of her.

She was not a timid mouse. She was not a forgotten sister. She was more than anyone thought of her. She was a woman, and hell had no fury like that which burned inside of her.

She was Regina Hartfield. She was a gentleman's daughter.

And she was going to take back what had been stolen from her family.

CHAPTER 31

Regina made her way downstairs with the rest of her sisters. Despite her mask, it was evident when the guests saw five redheaded sisters who all of them were.

Elizabeth wore a red dress, a daring color given her hair, but it worked for her. Louisa wore a soft yellow. Natalie was in green, her signature color. Bridget was in purple. It was Cora's favorite color, perhaps because it was regal, and Regina had to agree it suited her most regal of sisters well.

Regina, of course, was in her dark blue.

They must have made quite a sight, all descending the stairs with their almost-matching hair and their rich, colorful dresses. Regina had to duck her head to hide her smile. For once, she didn't mind if people stared at her. She felt as though, standing side by side with her sisters, she was worthy of being stared at.

She did not see Cora or Lord Harrison among the crowd. But then, she might not have recognized them if she had. Lord Harrison she wouldn't see until she entered the card room. Even then they must pretend to be strangers. No one could suspect that he had tutored her.

Cora she wouldn't see until she grabbed her to change her dress. It wouldn't do to be seen together either just in case someone noticed them both missing at the same time and made the connection between Regina and the mysterious red-haired woman in white.

It was appropriate, Regina thought, that she would be wearing that color. White was for spirits and the otherworldly. She would be like that to Lord Pettifer: a woman with no name and no title and no background. A woman that was there in front of him and yet did not exist.

It was rather poetic.

Remembering her bet with Lord Harrison, Regina made her way through dinner and the first few dances. She conversed with everyone that she could. At first she stuck close to her sisters but as time went on she drifted farther away from them.

Part of this was necessity. They couldn't notice the moment that she vanished. Part of this was just how the ball was. It was large, and more people, scads of them, were arriving after the dinner. It was easy to get separated in a mob such as this.

But part of it was that Regina didn't mind being separated from her sisters. She actually felt as though she could hold her own without them. She didn't need them for a safety net.

It was a liberating and giddy feeling. She could do this, she thought. She *was* doing this. Never had she been so happy to lose a bet.

People spoke with her. Most of them obviously guessed who she was given their inquiries after the health of her family, 'especially her elder sisters'. And yet none of them scorned her.

Her time with Lord Harrison and Cora, it seemed, had in fact emboldened her. She talked gaily and freely. There were times when she had to stop herself from making a misstep or when she found herself at a loss for words. And there were certainly times when she felt it was all too much and she had to retreat outside to get some fresh air and calm her nerves.

But people welcomed her. It was more than she could have anticipated. She was not the mouse that she had thought she was, and it seemed that once she knew it, everyone else knew it as well.

Society was a fickle thing. She had seen how it praised her mother on one side and then gossiped about her possible affair on the other. She had seen people express sympathy for her father and then turn around and take advantage of his addiction.

But in this, society's fickleness was in her favor. She stood up boldly and all but announced that she should be taken seriously, that she did in fact know how to dance and to converse.

And once she did that, they believed her. It was as though she had never been timid or embarrassed in the first place.

After an hour or two had passed, she felt a hand on her elbow. She turned, and found herself staring into the face of a woman in a black dress.

Regina smiled. Only Lady Cora would dare to wear a black dress, even at a masquerade ball.

"And just what are you mourning?" Regina asked.

Lady Cora laughed. "The death of my sanity. Or perhaps the death of your former self, Miss Regina. You are quite changed since I first saw you. Now we see what the power of real friendship can do for a woman."

She offered her arm to Regina. "Come. They have just begun to set up to play. We must get you ready."

Regina took her arm and allowed herself to be led off from the main hall and up the steps to one of the bedrooms.

Inside sat a maid, ready to assist. Lady Cora threw off her mask so that she might see clearly and help Regina. "Turn around. We must make haste."

Regina allowed herself to be quickly undressed, and then redressed in her second gown. The maid undid all of Bridget's hard work on Regina's hair and then did it up again in a different fashion. She even added small white pearls to it so that her hair seemed to have a nest of stars in it.

"Why on earth are there so many buttons," Cora grumbled, doing up Regina's dress.

"It is only to vex you, I am certain," Regina replied teasingly.

Then the mask was settled upon her face and there was nothing else for it.

Cora stepped back. "You are a wonder," she admitted. "I think you would quite steal the ball away from the other women if they saw you."

"There will be time for that later," Regina replied. "We have to go to the game."

Cora nodded. She took Regina's arm yet again and guided her out of the bedroom, down the hall, and around several times until Regina felt herself quite lost.

"They are in here," Cora said, indicating a study on the ground floor which they had got to by the back way.

Cora turned and placed her hands on Regina's shoulders. "Now, my dear, do not be afraid. They are merely men. You are more."

Then she opened the door.

Regina took a deep breath.

And she entered.

CHAPTER 32

The assembled men were talking quietly and amicably amongst themselves. They were scattered about the room, twenty of them, all dressed in their finest and wearing their masks.

All talk ceased the moment they saw her.

For a moment, all was still. The men stared at Regina. Regina stared back at them. She resolved to not be the first to break the silence.

Part of that might have been due to her not being able to breathe properly. She was here now. Here, with the men, with a mask on. She could still technically flee the room if she wished. There was still time for that.

But she couldn't. She felt frozen still, pinned like a

butterfly to that spot in the floor. Her heart fluttered in her chest, which felt oddly tight. She was breathing— she knew that she must be—yet it felt like she couldn't draw enough air.

She had to calm down. Regina sucked in a greath breath and forced herself to hold it. Then she slowly let it out. She did it again. The frozen, lightheaded feeling began to fade. It began to feel like she could breathe properly again.

Regina took a moment to have a proper look about the room. She could not recognize most of the men with their masks on but she did recognize Lord Harrison. It had been foolish of her, she thought, to suppose that she would not know him. Something as simple as a paper mask could not hide him from her.

She knew his bearing. She knew his hair color. She knew the shape of his jaw and the bow of his lips. She knew his preferred style of dress. And she knew his eyes, blue and warm and piercing, staring at her like he could read her soul.

He was over to the side, talking to a shorter man. Regina thought that the other man might be Mr. Denny but she could not be certain.

She also knew Lord Pettifer.

He was seated at the card table of course. But it was his smile that she remembered. It was the same awful, predatory smile he had shown when he had bested her father. It was the smile of a predator who had has just eaten until it cannot even move and then licks the blood off its maw.

Regina's anger flared up. She wished to smack him.

"How can I help you, Miss?"

It was Lord Morrison. Regina recognized his voice. And of course, as the host, he must come forward.

For a moment she completely forgot what to say or how to say it. She almost let out a kind of squeak. Then she remembered herself.

"I am here to play," Regina said. Her voice carried the accent that Lord Quentin had taught her.

All the men glanced at one another. It was plain to see that they did not know what to do with her.

"She can't," one man said.

"And why not?" Someone else added. "It's the masquerade. Anything goes, and all of that, wasn't that what you said earlier Daniels?"

Some of the men nodded, looking at one another with a

gleam in their eyes that their masks could not hide. Regina drew herself up. She would not be seen as an easy target by them.

Not all of the men seemed convinced by their compatriot's argument, however. They looked at Regina suspiciously. Regina could see the fingers twitching on one or two of them. She wondered if they were going to stride forward and yank off her mask, exposing her, sending her away for being a foolish, rebellious girl.

"I say that we let her play as well," Lord Pettifer said. He was smirking. He thought that he had found easy prey.

The other men shuffled their feet and looked at one another. Regina could read the nervousness in their twitching mouths and their stiff limbs. None of them wanted to contradict Lord Pettifer, it seemed. Regina wondered how many of them owed Lord Pettifer in some way, same as her father did.

When no one contradicted Lord Pettifer, his smirk broadened. He looked at Regina with a gleam in his eyes. Already he was overconfident. That was good.

Regina focused on her anger in order to keep the smile off of her face. Yes. She would play. And she would destroy him.

Lord Morrison seemed torn for a moment. It was still his house and ultimately still his word on what was allowed and what was not. He looked at her, and for a moment, Regina thought he might recognize her. The Morrisons had been great friends of her family for years. If she could recognize Lord Harrison even with his mask, surely it was not impossible for Lord Morrison to recognize the girl whose family he had been entertaining for so many years.

Regina felt that lightheaded feeling returning. Lord Morrison looked her up and down. Would he know her? Would he turn her away if he did? Escort her out? Expose her?

Regina forced herself to look him in the eye. She met his gaze and did not flinch when he looked directly into her face. He looked a little resigned but not angry or surprised.

Then, with a sigh, he stepped back. "If someone would bring a chair for the lady?"

Regina had to remind herself to stay upright and proper and not to slump down in relief. He had not recognized her. She could play.

She sat down in the proferred chair and settled herself. She could feel that everyone was watching her now. She actually wanted them to. She wanted everyone to bear witness to what was about to happen.

For a wild moment, then, panic seized her. It was like someone had dumped a bucket of cold water on her head. What was she doing? How could she possibly pull this off? She was about to disgrace herself beyond reason and lose everything.

Then she got a hold of herself. This was no way to act. She had to win this and she was not going to let the fear have its way with her. She remembered what Cora had said. These were just men, really. Just men.

Lord Pettifer was the dealer to start with. Regina did not recognize any of the other men. Had their faces been exposed, Lord Harrison had told her, he should have warned her how each man played. But with her unable to recognize them, she would have to rely upon her ability to read them while they played.

There were eight of them to start out with: Regina, Lord Pettifer, and then six others. It was a good number for playing a game of loo with large stakes. For ruining Lord Pettifer, not so much. Regina would have to find a way to get the others out of the card game while keeping Lord Pettifer in and not losing it all herself.

Lord Pettifer shuffled the cards and dealt them out. Regina looked at her cards and breathed slowly.

She looked around at the card players. She would play it safe this first hand so that she could get a feel for how they all operated and then she would start to get more aggressive.

Regina focused on her breathing as they began to play. She could do this. She could do this. She could do this.

And then she found out—she could.

In the first round she played it safe. She watched the others as they played—that one gentleman, two to the left from Lord Pettifer, would tap his middle finger nervously when he had a bad hand.

The player directly on her left, he was raising immediately, putting too much money into the pot. She could see the strain around his eyes—he was bluffing.

None of these men, Regina thought, were as good as Lord Harrison. They weren't even as good as Cora. All right then.

She knew this. She understood what was going on. She could read the players by their nervous ticks and the way their eyes moved and the expressions on their faces.

She understood the cards and the different hands and possibilities and how to bet.

The one thing she wasn't sure that she knew was if she could bluff.

It was something that Lord Harrison had often told her she needed to work on. Cora had noted it as well. Regina was not good at lying. If she had a bad hand at the end and she was up against Lord Pettifer...

No, she would not think about that. If she thought about how she failed, she reminded herself, then she would fail. She had to fake her confidence, Cora had often instructed her. If she acted confident, then others would believe it, and eventually it would become true.

She played, and played, and played. One gentleman, she saw, was playing it too safe. She would have to draw him out by increasing the pot to the point where he could no longer safely bet. Another was chewing his lip when he had a good hand—he was nervous the tide would turn against him. It was an odd tick, as much men showed their nerves when they had a bad hand but Regina was able to figure it out.

Regina affected a nervous habit of her own. She stroked the back of her cards when she had a good hand. When she had a bad one, she rolled her shoulders, just slightly.

It might not be enough to throw off the less experienced players. But then, she would throw those players off herself. It was the better players who would notice and throw themselves on the pyre by ministerpreting her.

The other men began dropping out. It was Loo, but with an unlimited pot. Regina could hardly believe the amount of money exchanging hands. It was flowing back and forth like a river that kept changing course. Regina had cash, given to her by Lord Harrison, that she used to play with. It would all be returned to him at the end of the night of course—provided that she was able to win it all back.

She could practically hear his voice in her head, telling her what to do. Her back was to him but she could feel his eyes upon her as surely as if his gaze were the touch of his hand. It made her feel safe, to know that he was there and silently encouraging her.

As the pot grew, some men became reckless. They bet when they should have folded. They continued on when they should have walked away. For the first time Regina could see first-hand the fever of gambling upon them.

It was terrifying in a way. It was almost as if these men were seized by some spirit that took a hold of them and made them play. They were men possessed.

Regina just tried to focus on her own cards and on her end goal. Some men, she noticed, were just doing this for the thrill of the gamble. They didn't care about the cards, not really, and they didn't care about playing well. But others were good. They wanted to win and they enjoyed the skill of the game, such as it was, although there was always a fair bit of luck involved in a game such as Loo.

Was this what her father had been like when he had played? She could see the tightness in the lines of the men's faces—what of their faces she could see, anyway. There was a wild look in their eyes.

It made her want to get out of the way, like she was standing in the path of a runaway horse. Instead, she kept playing.

If she could just keep her head while everyone else was losing theirs, she'd be fine. But it was harder than she had anticipated not to get caught up in the fervor of it.

Everyone was so intense in a way that Lord Harrison and Cora simply could not replicate. Regina could all but taste the desperation in the air. It was a struggle to stay calm when everyone around her seemed to be the opposite.

The men standing around and watching didn't help.

They were constantly muttering to one another and making whispered observations. Their enthusiasm in watching and their predictions only added to the intensity and risk of the game.

Focus, Regina reminded herself. *None of them matter. Only Lord Pettifer.*

She squared her shoulders and imagined there was a book balanced on her head, the way that Cora had made her practice nearly all of one afternoon. She was confident. She knew what she was doing. If she said it, if she believed it, these men around her would as well.

Time seemed to both drag on and to have no meaning at all. There didn't appear to be any clocks in the room and if there were she couldn't see them from where she was sitting. She didn't even really bother to look up. All of her attention was on the men around her and the cards in front of her.

Mostly it was on Lord Pettifer.

It was clear that he thought her an amusement at best. He didn't consider her a very serious competitor. At least, not at first.

Then she started winning.

There were three men left besides herself and Lord

Pettifer when she looked down at her cards—and then had to keep herself from alarmingly looking over at Lord Harrison out of habit.

She had a good hand. In fact, going by everyone's tells, she had the best hand.

When she played her cards and raked in her part of the pot for that round, she had to keep herself from screaming. Whether it was in fear or delight, she couldn't tell. She had the most out of all of them, she was—she was winning.

Regina had to hold in her gasp as she realized that she was actually doing better than all of the other men. She wasn't just doing better than some of them. She was the current best player, at least going by the pot.

She felt torn between yelling with triumph and running out the door to hide for a few hours. Days. Weeks. But she certainly couldn't do anything like that.

Now that she was winning, she had to use it to bait Lord Pettifer. She had to finish eliminating the other men and then get Lord Pettifer to overextend himself.

To her surprise, it actually took a while for the men to notice that she was winning. They hadn't thought for even a moment that she could be a serious threat to them. When she started to take their money they actually didn't seem to even really see it. It just... went over their heads, almost.

But they couldn't avoid the truth forever, no matter how uncomfortable of a truth it was for them. Eventually, they saw. They saw that they were getting thoroughly beaten by a young and mysterious woman whose name they didn't even know.

And then they went after her.

Regina could sense the tide turning against her and knew that the men by unspoken agreement were trying to oust her from the table. She could not let that happen.

She fought, tooth and nail. She could read them better than they could read her. She just had to keep herself blank. She thought of Natalie and how Natalie behaved around men, and that was how she acted. She wasn't Regina, she thought, she was Natalie. That was all.

Soon the tension in the room was palpable. Regina felt as though if she took out a knife she could cut herself a slice of it. Everyone was watching her. No, more than watching her. Waiting. Waiting for her to fail.

She would not fail.

You have to lie, she thought. You have to lie as you have

never lied before. You can do this. You are more than you think you are.

She had to give Lord Harrison and Cora a reason not to doubt her. She had to win back her family's fortune and honor.

The men eventually seemed to see that it was a lost cause—or at least most of them did. One by one they left the table. One by one, they vanished, leaving their lost money in the middle.

Until it was only her and Lord Pettifer.

Regina and Lord Harrison had been right. His pride was pricked and he was eager to taste her defeat. He wanted to take all that she had and he wanted to prove that he was still the man to beat. He would not be bested by a mere slip of a girl, oh no.

With just the two of them at the table, Regina knew that time was up. There was no further she could go. She would win this hand, or she would lose, and lose all.

One more deep breath.

Lie, she thought. Lie as you have never before lied in your life. Lie with your heart and every fiber of your being. Lie with your soul. Lie until even you believe that lie. Believe that you are a stupid girl with no chance who

has gotten this far on luck. Believe it and he will
believe it.

"It appears that I have no more cash upon me," Lord
Pettifer said. He smirked at her. "And what of you,
dear lady?"

Lie. Lie with everything you have.

"I suppose that I do have some lands that I could put
down a signage for." Regina spoke casually using the
accent, and shrugged one of her shoulders. "I suppose
that you do as well?"

She paused, as if considering. "Wait. Perhaps, sir, I
know you. Are you not the man who they say took the
Hartfield estate in a game not a month ago?"

Lord Pettifer smiled. Of course he would be proud at
being caught out, rather than defensive and contrite
as he ought to be. He spread his arms wide. "I
am he."

"I have long admired those lands. Perhaps you shall
wager those while I wager mine."

"A fine bargain," Lord Pettifer said. "I shall win more
lands with lands I have already won previously."

"Careful Pettifer," one of the other men said in a low
voice. "You have already written several notes of debt. If

she wins, your coffers are empty and the Hartfield lands are all that you have."

"Nonsense." Lord Pettifer's tone was scathing. "You say that as if I do not have the winning hand."

Regina said nothing. She merely gestured for a quill and paper.

Lord Pettifer copied her, and paper and writing utensils were produced for the both of them. Regina's heart was in her throat as she wrote out the name for an imaginary estate up in the north. Lord Harrison had at one point suggested that they use Whitefern, but Regina had refused. He was already giving her so much, she would not let him risk even more for her.

Once everything had been written down, they placed their papers in the pot in the middle. The game resumed, but not for long. With such high stakes and only the two of them in, it would soon be time to show their hands.

Regina looked down at her cards. She had good cards and—she looked at Lord Pettifer. He was overextending himself. He was narrowing his eyes, the way he did when his hand was not as good as he would have liked and he was contemplating if he thought his hand was better than hers.

She rolled her shoulders slightly and saw Lord Pettifer's lip go stiff as he tried not to smirk. He'd bought into her fake tell. He thought she had a worse hand than she did.

But was her hand high enough to beat his? Her cards meant that currently, she would Loo. But if he also Loo'd...

There was nothing for it. Cards was a gambling game, after all. Regina could only play it safe for so long. Eventually she would have to take a risk, take a leap of faith.

So she called him.

'Calling' was the term which meant that she was essentially forcing Lord Pettifer to show his hand. Then she would show hers, and they would know who had won.

The air seemed to sweep out of the room. Everyone was poised, watching. She could feel Lord Harrison's gaze on her like a brand.

"I call, sir," Regina repeated.

With a smirk, Lord Pettifer set down his cards.

Relief filled her. Pure, sweet relief, such that she had never before tasted.

She had suspected for some time that Lord Pettifer's cards were only middling. She had faked a tell early on, a nervous tap of her finger, that would make him think she used when she had a bad hand. She had noticed that Lord Pettifer would blow his hands out of proportion, acting as though they were better then they actually were in order to fool others into folding.

Personally Regina would have thought it better if he faked having poorer hands in order to trick his opponents into thinking he was doing more badly than he actually was. That way they would bet more and be overconfident.

But that was too smart for Lord Pettifer, at least in Regina's opinion. Now she was going to take advantage of his foolishness.

Regina set down her cards.

She had loo'd. She'd won the hand.

For a moment, everyone just stared. It all sank in gradually, the realization of what had happened.

A woman, and an unknown woman at that, had just beaten the biggest card shark and rake in the country. More than beaten him, in fact. She had taken everything that he had.

There was a moment of silence.

Then—well, the room did not erupt. These were gentlemen, after all, and it would not do to yell and make a scene. They were English, not French or, God forbid, Spanish.

But there was a sudden outburst of murmuring. Everyone was muttering to everyone else. People were outright staring at her. They stared at Lord Pettifer as well.

Lord Pettifer sat there for a moment longer. It was as though he could not truly believe what had just happened to him. Then, in a rush, he stood up—so violently, in fact, that he knocked over his chair.

"You little snake," he hissed. His face had gone an alarming shade of red. "You must have cheated. How did you do it?"

"She did not cheat, sir," Lord Morrison said. "We all watched both of you with much scrutiny. And you were the dealer more often than she was. If you wish to blame anyone for cheating perhaps it should be yourself."

Lord Pettifer pointed an accusing finger at her. "Do not think that I shall forget this. I will find out your identity and there shall be no escape for you then. I will—"

"You will leave her alone, or the consquences upon your person will be far more dire than a loss of fortune."

Regina stood up abruptly, caught by surprise. She turned, her skin tingling at his presence. Lord Harrison.

He stood just behind her, and even with the mask on his face was thunderous. It was the fire that she had seen directed at Cora before, and now it was burning even hotter when directed at Lord Pettifer.

Cora was a friend, Regina realized. Of course Lord Harrison's anger, although fierce, had been somewhat tempered when directed at her. He had known that her intentions were pure.

Lord Pettifer, on the other hand, was an enemy. A dangerous one. There would be no quarter or withholding from Lord Harrison against this opponent.

Regina's heart beat rapidly. She could feel the heat off his body and smell him, masculine and oddly calming. She was safe. He wouldn't let Lord Pettifer do anything to her.

"Are you protecting this lady?" Lord Pettifer scoffed.

"One month ago you took all that a man had," Lord Harrison replied. "I was there, Pettifer. I saw it. You showed no mercy. When he protested you mocked him, even though he had five unmarried daughters.

"And now that you are in his shoes you seek revenge? You think that you have any moral ground to stand upon? If you forced that man to honor his debts then you must be put to paid to honor yours.

"If you do not—if you lay any harm upon, of all people, a woman—she is not even a man, Pettifer. And yet you would threaten violence upon her? Shameful, even for a man such as you.

"The first person that shows his hypocrisy and violence and dares to raise a hand against this woman will have that hand cut off. I am also available for a duel, if someone wishes to settle the score in that manner."

Regina's blood ran cold at the thought of Lord Harrison putting himself in the path of a gun. But none of the men looked liable to take him up on his challenge.

Many of them, in fact, were looking at Lord Pettifer with disdain. Regina could read it in their eyes even though their faces were mostly obscured.

They were on her side, she realized. Her father could not have been the only person that Lord Pettifer had ruined. He must have quarreled and treated ill dozens of men by this time to claw his way into the sort of social position that he occupied.

Regina squared her shoulders and drew herself up. She was in the right—and the men knew it. Lord Harrison was at her back and the room was with her rather than against her.

She saw the moment that Lord Pettifer realized that the tide was against him. He shifted, his rat face growing tight and his eyes darting about.

Finally, Regina gave into her anger completely and allowed a sardonic smile to grace her lips. She remembered the darker side to Puck, the side that played with mortals and men and left them gasping and humiliated.

"I will not stand for this," Lord Pettifer said, but his words sounded weak and desperate.

Regina let her smile grow. "Thou coward, thou art bragging to the stars."

She flicked her gaze over to Lord Harrison and saw that he, too, was smiling.

CHAPTER 33

Regina gathered up her winnings with the help of Lord Morrison. It still wouldn't do for anyone to see Lord Harrison with her. They could still get in trouble if someone realized that he had coached her.

"That was a fine thing you did," Lord Morrison told her. "I hope that you will give those lands back to the family to which they rightly belong."

"I shall certainly do so. I have fortune enough," Regina replied.

Lord Morrison smiled at her, then gave a small bow and walked over to speak with some other men.

Regina had her winnings, and so she left the room. The gossip would take care of itself. She was sure that Lord

Morrison, a good friend of her family, would ensure that everyone who had heard of her father's loss also heard of how the woman who had beat Lord Pettifer had restored the Hartfield lands to their rightful family.

She didn't know if any of the men would go back to playing cards after such a spectacle, nor did she care. She did not, however, expect Lord Harrison to exit the room shortly after she did.

Regina paused and allowed him to catch up to her.

"I must return, so as to avoid suspicion," he said. "But I wish for you to know, that was magnificent. You did well, my Puck. That was a game for the ages."

"I feared I could not bluff well enough," Regina confessed. "You know that I am horrible at lying."

"When there is enough at stake, I have found that people are capable of things that they never imagined," Lord Harrison observed.

He looked at her with such naked affection that it made Regina's heart feel as though it had taken up residence in her mouth. She swallowed.

"I had not thought him so easy to beat," she added. She needed something, anything, to break this strange tension she was feeling. "Lord, what fools these mortals be."

Lord Harrison chuckled. "Yes, indeed."

"You should return," she added. She felt oddly breathless. Perhaps it was just that this would be the last time they would be alone together. After this he would belong to Bridget, and Bridget to him.

It would never be just the two of them again.

"I should," Lord Harrison agreed. He looked as though he might say something more for a moment—his lips parted and his eyes warmed.

But then the moment passed. He shook his head, as if to himself, and then made to return.

"Lord Harrison?"

He paused.

"I must thank you, one last time." Regina passed him her winnings, keeping only the deed that would allow her family home to be restored. "Here. You lent me money so that I might play. You must take it."

Lord Harrison held up a hand. "No. They are your winnings, fair and square. Pay me back what I lent you but do not offer me more than that. What you won is ten times, twenty times, what I lent you. Use the extra to pay off your father's debts and restore his finances."

"You are too kind."

Lord Harrison gave an odd laugh. It sounded almost strangled. "No. I am not all that kind at all."

He then vanished into the card room before she could say anything more.

"And just how ridiculous are the two of you being this time?" Cora asked.

Regina whipped around. Cora was just turning the corner, and so Regina relaxed. She did not think that the other woman had heard the conversation.

"I must find Bridget," she said. She did not have time for Cora's teasing. The bargain must be carried out. Bridget had to marry Lord Harrison now.

"Yes, you must tell her the good news." Cora paused. "Or is it bad news? Why, child. You look like you are about to cry."

Regina hadn't realized that was the truth until Cora said it, and only then did she notice the tears stinging her eyes and clouding her vision. "It is nothing."

"Did you lose?" Cora asked. She looked past Regina, at

the closed card room door. "Harrison will fix it. You will see. He will not let you come to ruin."

"No, I won," Regina protested. She held up her bag of winnings and opened it up so that Cora might look inside. "I earned back twenty times what Lord Harrison lent me to play with. I got the deed back to my home. Lord Pettifer is utterly ruined."

"That is marvelous!" Cora burst out. Then she sobered. "But why do you cry? Come now."

She gently untied Regina's mask and pulled out a handkerchief, dabbing at Regina's cheeks to wipe the tears away.

"It is stupid," Regina said. "Really, it does not even bear speaking about."

"Nothing involving such tender emotion is stupid," Cora replied. "I should know. I have ofter been mafe to feel ashamed of how I feel. I will not have it for myself and I will not have it for you. Now. Tell me what troubles you."

"It is nothing."

"Is it your feelings for Lord Harrison?"

Regina gaped at her, and Cora sighed. "My darling girl. You are intelligent. But when it comes to the matters of your heart, you are almost willfully ignorant. Anyone could see that you were falling in love with him. Why do you think that your Aunt Jane told you that story about her husband earlier?"

"You knew about that?"

"She told me when we were all assembled at the ball that she had told you and she had hoped that her words had rung true for you."

"I do not understand."

Cora smiled patiently. "She did not think that her husband loved her, although she loved him desperately. Does that not sound like anyone that you know?"

"But..." Regina was woefully confused. "But Lord Harrison does not love me. He loves Bridget. Her hand in marriage was his price for helping me."

Cora raised an eyebrow. "I shall be giving him an earful about that later. But sweet. I think that he stopped being in love with Bridget a long time ago. Have you not seen how he looks at you? How protective of you he is? He fairly well bit my head off that one night and he's hardly let you out of his sight."

"That cannot be."

Cora sighed in exasperation. "Now listen here. I know

that I am no lover of romance. I can be a bitter old maid when I wish it. But I care for you as a sister and for Lord Harrison as a brother. I want both of you to be happy.

"So listen closely to me now. I know Harrison and I know you. The only one who does not realize that you are in love with him is him! Your sister Bridget, the one that you think he loves, she noticed it even."

"What?" Regina was filled with horror at being so easily read.

"Yes. She tracked me down during the ball while you were playing cards. She did not even stop to re-make my acquaintance after so many years apart. Her questions were all about Lord Harrison's intentions towards you, for your speaking of him and your praise had led her to understand your regard for him."

"I was only praising him so that she would accept his proposal!" Regina protested.

"If you wish to tell yourself that to ease your own nerves, you may," Cora replied promptly.

Regina wanted the ground to swallow her up. So now she was to be humiliated.

"Come, come, darling, none of that." Cora gently hooked two fingers underneath Regina's chin and raised it up so that Cora could look her in the eye. "He loves you too. Just as he is the only one who does not know how you feel, so you are the only one who does not know how he feels.

"He loves you, Regina. Go downstairs. Do not speak to Bridget. Dance and be merry. In time he will come to you."

"How do you know that?"

Cora smiled. "I just do. I have been on this earth longer than you have, remember?"

Regina took a deep breath. She had trusted Cora so far and had not been led astray. Perhaps she could trust her with this one last thing. "All right."

"Good girl."

Cora took her hand and led her back to the chamber where she had changed. She and her maid helped Regina to get back to her original hairstyle and dress and placed the first mask back on Regina's face.

Part of Regina was sad that she could not show off her dress more. Perhaps at another ball. But at this one, she could not afford to be discovered as the woman who had gambled. Even the bent rules of the masquerade only extended so far.

But perhaps—just perhaps—she was just enough as she was. Regina Hartfield. Not the mysterious woman in white. Just as herself.

Cora finished tying her mask firmly upon her face, then smiled at her. "I shall deal with what little matters are left. Now go, my darling, and dazzle them all."

CHAPTER 34

Regina felt another pang of panic as she stood at the top of the stairs.

She felt like a completely different person after everything that had happened. Yet at the same time it felt as though what had gone on in the card room was something out of a dream. It hadn't really happened.

But it had. She had won back her family's fortune and honor. Her sisters were safe.

They would all find that out soon enough. Cora had said she would handle it. She would make sure that they all found out about their reversal and return to honor.

Louisa could marry. Elizabeth could marry without it

being under a cloud. Bridget could take her time. Natalie could grow in substance.

It would all be all right now.

And what of her? What would happen to her now that it was all over?

She would find another man. She did not know if she could love him as she loved Lord Harrison, but she could find someone with whom she felt safe and who she knew respected her.

Love. She had said it to Cora, or rather had it called out to her by Cora. It was real now. She loved Lord Thomas Harrison, Duke of Whitefern.

It made her want to curl up into a ball in the darkest corner and cry until she was spent and could no longer feel a single emotion.

But no. She was stronger than that.

Regina held her head up high and descended the stairs.

It was no grand entrance. Everyone was busy chatting or dancing. The masquerade was still in full swing, after all. She descended into a sea of color that swallowed her up almost at once.

She found, for once, that she didn't mind. She wanted to be swallowed up and forgotten, just a little.

Regina moved through the crowds of people. Natalie was out on the dance floor, but appeared for once to be listening to her partner rather than talking over him.

Elizabeth was seated with Louisa. It seemed that the two had grown closer after spending time together, just the two of them, while Elizabeth was courted by Mr. Denny.

Mr. Denny himself, apparently, was hovering nearby. Regina suspected that it would surprise no one when the engagement was announced.

She could not see Bridget, but it didn't matter. She had time to tell her about the deal and what she had done.

Despite Cora's words, Regina could not believe that Lord Harrison had moved on from Bridget. Regina was coming to understand that she was more than she had previously thought, but enough to outshine her eldest sister?

No. Nobody could outshine Bridget. Regina, even at her best, couldn't compare to her.

It was probably why she couldn't see Bridget right now, actually. She was certain that Lord Harrison would want to break the news to her himself. Regina wasn't sure which would be right. She was the one who'd agreed to the bargain, after all, but Lord Harrison had been the one who had expressed a desire for Bridget's hand.

Regina watched the dancers for a while, when a young man approached her. "If I may have the next dance?"

She nodded. She might as well distract herself while she could.

Dancing wasn't so bad when you needed to avoid thinking about something. Her partner was engaging and it took quite a lot of thinking to stay true to the steps while also conversing. After that dance, she found another partner. And another.

This would be all right. She was more confident than she had been before and therefore she was more comfortable. She could do this, dancing and going to balls. Eventually she would find someone.

If only it didn't feel so empty.

She danced, and danced, and danced, until when her last dance was over and she turned around only to hear a very familiar voice say, "May I have the next dance, Miss Hartfield?"

Regina turned.

Lord Harrison was standing in front of her. His blue eyes were warm and welcoming, looking at her with that affection that she had told herself she only imagined. He wore a small, enigmatic smile on his face.

"My sister is Miss Hartfield, if you wish to be proper," she responded, slipping into her natural teasing with him.

"If my understanding is correct, in a short time your middle sister will be the proper Miss Hartfield," Lord Harrison replied.

"Oh. Yes. Bridget will be marrying you."

Lord Harrison shook her head. "Bridget, I suspect, will be going to the Continent for quite some time."

Before Regina could even begin to figure out what that meant, Lord Harrison indicated the dance floor with his hand. "The next dance is beginning. May I?"

She allowed him to lead her out onto the floor.

As the dance began, so did Lord Harrison. "I was recently drawn into a corner by a friend and informed of what an unmitigated fool I am."

"Is that so? I had a similar experience most recently."

"Indeed." Lord Harrison smiled at her.

For the first time, Regina understood why people could be so enamored with dancing. In dancing with Lord Harrison she was no longer simply enjoying herself with a partner along with a dozen others.

Instead, it was as if none of the others existed.

She could have been alone in the room with Lord Harrison for all that she took notice of the people around her.

"This friend told me that I had been a fool not to notice that my affections for a certain young lady were returned, and I was encouraged to inform that young lady of how my regard for her had turned into something much deeper."

Regina's breath caught in her throat and for a wild moment she thought that her heart would stop beating. He wasn't—was he?

"You see, I started out thinking that I was in love with this young lady's eldest sister. And I do have quite a high regard for that sister. She is a remarkable young woman and very accomplished.

"However, when I spent more time in the company of

this young lady, I found that... that even her remarkable elder sister paled in comparision to her.

"I struggled to hide my feelings, for I was certain that they could never be returned. How could they, when I had agreed to marry the lady's sister in a move that was, I realized, selfish and unfair to both the lady and her sister?

"I had treated the elder sister like property and taken advantage of the family's dire straits. Surely this woman could not fail to realize this and would hate me in her heart.

"So, I resolved that I would not say anything. I was so certain that this woman could not love me in return. Everything spoke to me only as a testament to that fact. I was a source of learning for her. I was a safe place. I was a mentor, a tutor, nothing more.

"After all, when one is desperate for a way out, one will take any escape offered, even if that escape is made by a man one should not esteem."

"How could I not esteem you?" Regina cut in. "You cannot have such a low opinion of yourself. If you may sink into despair for your actions regarding our agreement, then you must allow me to hate myself as well, for I offered up my own sister."

"No. No you were desperate, you had no choice. I should have been magnanimous—"

"Are you saying that you love me?" Regina blurted out.

Never before had she been so grateful for how crowded and noisy balls were. Nobody heard her. Nobody marked what she said. The entire swell of people didn't stop and stare at her for being so bold.

Instead, everyone just carried on.

She and Lord Harrison even continued to dance.

But now they just looked into one another's eyes, not speaking. Just staring.

What she saw in his eyes then was devastating. "Yes," he managed to whisper, his voice hoarse. "Yes, I have—I have come to be devoted to you. I wish nothing but for your happiness.

"If I thought that you might allow me to be by your side I would in a heartbeat. I would not spare a single coin or moment if I could invest it in your happiness. I want to spend every day proving to you that you are worth so much more than you believe you are.

"I know that you have already started to believe it. But you don't yet understand—you cannot know—"

"I never should have thought that I would see you at a loss for words," Regina said, her voice soft and awed.

Lord Harrison laughed. "Yes. Well. You rather take the words right out of my chest."

The dance finished and they began another without asking, unwilling to be parted.

"I suppose what I am asking, then," Lord Harrison said, "Now that we have understood one another, is if I can dare to hope. Our mutual friend led me to believe but I cannot... I must hear it from you."

"You may do more than hope," Regina assured him. "You may presume as much as you would like."

"And dare I ask if you would join your sisters in entering into an engagement?" He asked. "Bridget will be settled on the Continent. Miss Elizabeth and Miss Louisa are engaged. I should not think it too impudent if the youngest sister then entered into an engagement of her own."

Regina felt sad for Natalie for a moment. She would be the only unmarried one—or uncommitted one, she added to herself, thinking of her eldest sister. But she would find someone in time.

After all, Regina had found someone, and she hadn't even been looking.

"Are you asking me for my hand?" She asked. "Because I must tell you, sir, that to do so without my father's permission and in a crowded ballroom is most unconventional."

"Using a masquerade ball to steal into a man's card game and strip a rake of his fortune is also most unconventional." Lord Harrison smiled. "It appears we are a match, Puck."

"Oberon."

The second dance ended. Lord Harrison directed his head towards some doors that led outside. "Shall we?"

As they walked through the crowd, Regina finally caught sight of Bridget. She was standing next to Cora, and their arms were linked. Bridget was smiling, smiling as Regina had never seen her smile, and Cora—

Oh, she realized.

She smiled to herself and allowed Lord Harrison to lead her just outside, where they might take in the fresh air.

"Consider this a promise," he said. "I must speak with your father, of course. I must obtain his blessing. But I wish to have your agreement first."

"You have everything of me," Regina confessed. She laughed, giddy. This felt unreal. "Let us strike another deal."

"Oh?" Lord Harrison smiled down at her, infinitely amused. "What sort of deal?"

"A deal that you will obtain my father's blessing and we shall be married."

"In that case, I had better make this official." He took her hand in his. "Regina Hartfield. Puck. My... my everything. Will you marry me?"

Regina nodded quickly. Her heart felt so full that she was sure it would burst. She might start crying as well. "Yes."

"Our last deal was signed with a handshake. How shall we seal this one?"

"This deal..." Regina smiled at him, letting him draw her closer. In the darkness of the balcony, nobody could see them if they engaged in this one last impropriety. "This deal shall be sealed with a kiss."

He took her face gently in his hands and lifted her face up, and did just that.

It was everything that she had dreamed it would be, back when they had almost kissed to fool and appease his friends. His lips were warm and gentle as they worked against hers, and she sighed into it. She hadn't known there was happiness such as this in the world.

"I love you," he whispered against her lips.

Regina could only smile and reply in kind.

THE EXTENDED EPILOGUE
FALLING FOR THE GOVERNESS

I am humbled you finished reading my novel **The Lady's Gamble**, till the end!

Are you aching to know what happens to our lovebirds?

Click on the image or one of the links below to connect to a more personal level and as a BONUS, **I will send you the Extended Epilogue of this Book!**

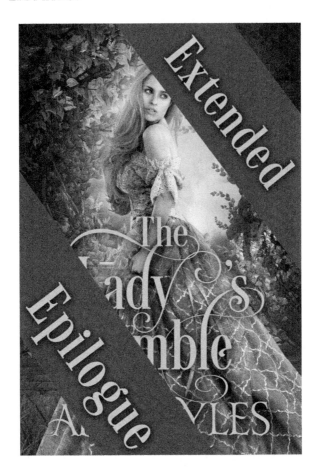

or click here

BookHip.com/FZWDXG

With Love

Historical Romance Author

DO YOU WANT MORE HISTORICAL ROMANCE?

Turn on the next page to read the first chapters of my best-selling novel: Falling for the Governess

FALLING FOR THE GOVERNESS

PREFACE

My dearest Louisa,

I fear my heart is broken. It is with the saddest news I find myself writing to you today. Just yesterday I received a visit from Mr. Jenkins, my father's lawyer.

As you know, my father was on a ship set for Cayman Island in relation to his import business. As I had mentioned a few times at our last meeting, I was becoming exceedingly concerned since his vessel had not yet returned. Without any ill news, I hoped that they had only been delayed by poor wind and calm waters.

Unfortunately, this is not the case. While in the tropics, father contracted a most dreadful fever. His most experienced sailors fell ill.

To prevent the sickness from spreading, the ill were to be left behind to recover and return home aboard another vessel. My father was too prominent of a figure to just leave behind, and the MHS Poseidon decided to stay in Cayman Island for a fortnight to allow him to recover.

I am told the fever passed. For that I am grateful, but why did my stubborn father have to push himself? I don't know how to feel. You are aware of how much I disliked him going on these journeys to begin with.

Having gained his strength back, father sailed Poseidon homeward bound, but his health took a turn for the worse.

The ship's surgeon did all he could to help, but in the end, it was not enough. My father passed away a little over a month ago in the middle of the Atlantic Ocean. There's nothing I could have done, and I resent myself for that.

Mr. Jenkins, having been informed himself just last night upon the arrival of the ship, came to bear me the sorrowful news this morning. He assured me that my father had the most lavished and honorable burial at sea that could be mustered for the situation.

I am so overcome with confusion and sorrow, it is a wonder that I can even compose myself to scribe such a letter to you.

Though father was always very busy with his business

and adventures, he was a loving and attentive man. I feel my life vastly emptier without the assured knowledge that though he may be away, he will always return home here to Rosewater house.

Mr. Jenkins has also informed me that I will need to come to his offices on the morrow to discuss my father's estate and I suppose, to some effect, what is to become of me.

I cannot even imagine being able to subject myself to conversations of financial and worldly status when my heart is so full of turmoil.

It is for this reason that I must offer my deepest regrets to inform you that I will not be able to accompany your excellent mother to tea. Please tell Lady Gilchrist that I send my deepest regrets.

I hope that I will see you very soon, my dear Louisa, so that I may receive comfort from the words of wisdom you always seem to use so deftly.

With humble heart,

Isabella

The next evening Isabella received a return letter from Lady Lydia in the five o'clock post.

My Dearest Isabella,

It is with the heaviest of hearts that I give you my deepest condolences on your loss.

I have informed her Ladyship of your necessity for absence from her humble event tomorrow afternoon. Though you will be greatly missed by not only my mother but all those who are to attend, we all understand your need for time to quietly reflect and compose yourself.

Please do not fear for your well-being. Your father was a good man, and I am confident that he will provide for you even after the untimely event of his death.

As soon as you are able, please come to call so that I may be able to comfort my dearest friend in her time of need.

Your humble friend,

Louisa

CHAPTER 1

Isabella's eyes wandered lazily as she sat in Louisa's comfortable drawing room. It was the smaller drawing room of her dear friend's London residence, used for the entertaining of very intimate friends of the ladies of the house.

Isabella was struggling to collect her thoughts or even know where to begin after the events that had transpired over the last two days. She did her best to keep her trembling hands clasped in the lap of her dark black cotton dress.

Her hand rattled the teacup just slightly when she took it from Louisa's loving hands. Isabella was happy for the privacy such an intimate setting provided. She wasn't sure if she would be able to hold her composure as she retold Louisa all that transpired.

"I scarcely know where to begin," she said after taking a small sip of courage.

She didn't have much appetite at the moment but felt the tea might help to clear her head. The last few nights had been restless and anything but rejuvenating.

"Start with when you arrived at Mr. Jenkins' offices yesterday. I am quite sure we will find a way to untangle any mess you may now find yourself in," Louisa responded calmly.

She was just two years older than Isabella but not the slightest in comparison to physical beauty. Where Isabella had rich, shiny black locks and emerald-green eyes, Louisa had mouse-brown hair, which rarely plaited as it should, and ordinary brown eyes.

It did not prevent them from finding an inseparable bond as young girls at the prestigious Mrs. Mason's School for Exceptional Young Ladies.

Louisa had always been a quiet child who often kept to herself. Isabella, on the other hand, was openly pleasant to be around and was commonly found at the center of the conversation, entertaining the other ladies of the school with wild tales heard from her father's adventures.

Louisa, at first, had listened quietly to her tales, but Isabella saw more to Louisa than her shy exterior. Much as Isabella had expected, Louisa was the most kind and giving young lady she had ever met. Her friendship and confidante was something she treasured all through her youth and young adulthood.

"I suppose you're right," Isabella responded with a steadying breath before setting the tea down.

"I arrived at Mr. Jenkins office yesterday morning. I was surprised when I was shown in to find Mr. Smith already there."

"Mr. Smith? Your father's horrid business partner," Louisa clarified, and Isabella nodded in agreement.

"I had done my best to avoid him at all costs since that dreadful event four years ago. It gave me quite a shock as it had not been mentioned to me that he would be there.

Though now looking back on it, it was certainly reasonable that he should be there as we discussed my father's estate."

"Of course, you are not expected to have the clearest of

minds in such a time," Louisa said attempting to erase any guilt Isabella might feel on her state of propriety.

"That awful man," Isabella stated, now with her green eyes full of anger. "He didn't even stand at my entrance, and in truth, I didn't see him at all from his chair at the back of the office till Mr. Jenkins motioned to him during the conversation."

Isabella thought back to that horrible meeting four years earlier. She had been barely seventeen at the time, having completed her schooling and finished her first season out among society.

It was a small dinner party that her father was having at their very own Rosewater house. She had been all aglow with the excitement of her season and the joy of having her father momentarily home with her.

Mr. Smith was there, of course, since he was Baron Leinster's closest friend and business partner. Isabella had not paid him much attention as he was even older than her father and she could never imagine him having interest in such a young girl.

As the evening transpired, however, Mr. Smith found a chance to enter into a private conversation with Isabella. It was then that he requested that she consider him a suitor and accept his proposal of marriage.

Isabella was so shocked by the declaration that all she managed to say was 'but you are so old.' It was probably not the most polite thing for her to say, but so often when she was shocked, she tended to speak truths without thinking.

Isabella was young and full of spirit. She had received much attention from various social gatherings of the season. She was not so conceited enough to think she was above those outside the peerage. Isabella had always assumed that with her father's honorary title she would find herself a gentleman in the society she had been raised to be a part of.

Of course, having affection for her future husband was a necessity for her, his status had not been. Even so, she would never have imagined marrying such an older, coarse man at such a young age.

She did her best to regain her composure and thank Mr. Smith but politely decline. He became enraged by her very respectable but negative answer and made quite a scene of it.

From that day on, Isabella had done everything in her power to not be in the company of Mr. Smith. It was not always an easy task when he had such close financial relationships with her father.

"Mr. Jenkins informed me that my father had left his import and export business to Mr. Smith."

"I suppose that seems reasonable enough," Louisa said. "After all, as partner, it would only be right that he inherit the whole of the business. And I suppose you are to be left Rosewater house and a living?"

"That is the worst of it. Mr. Jenkins informed me that all of my father's estates had been specifically put in the charge of Mr. Smith, having no other male family member. He then informed me that my father had also collected a large sum of debts," she lowered her voice, "gambling."

"Oh dear. Had you any idea of these debts?"

"I was aware of his enjoyment of gentlemanly horse races. I suspected the thrill of it was much like that of a boy crossing the sea. But I had no idea that he was in such a poor situation."

"What does this mean?" Louisa asked with fear in her soft doe eyes.

"Well, Mr. Jenkins said that he had been in conference with Mr. Smith all morning and had made several arrangements."

That moment, when she finally looked over her

shoulder to find Mr. Smith sitting behind her would most likely haunt her the rest of her days.

He had stood then and walked forward, wholly unearthing himself from the morning shadows the windowless office provided.

He was much older now than would be expected for the four years that had passed since his proposition. His hair was long and straggly on the sides and completely missing on top. Instead of choosing to wear a wig, he tied the straggled strands back with a ribbon.

His face was worn and marked by the years he, himself, had spent as captain on a merchant ship before striking business with Baron Leinster.

Though his clothes were of a gentlemanly style, they were worn and soiled badly. The edges of his coat were stained with dirt.

Undoubtedly, his lifelong bachelorhood had led to the inferior care of his outward appearance. He smiled smugly, showing his blackened tooth, something she remembered quite clearly from her first encounter with him.

Quite awkwardly Mr. Jenkins had fiddled with some paperwork on his desk. He was a rather young man for his position, only recently taken on by her father. Her interactions with him, however few, had always been enjoyable ones.

Usually, he had a jolly expression to his eyes, especially since the birth of his first child.

Isabella wasn't sure she had ever seen Mr. Jenkins so uncomfortable, even when he had informed her of her father's passing.

"As the benefactor of your father's estate, Mr. Smith here has decided to sell all assets in order to pay off the debts incurred, including Rosewater house and everything in it."

"But that is my home!" Isabella said with a raised voice. "Where am I to live?"

Isabella could not bear to take her eyes off Mr. Jenkins to turn to the scoundrel behind her. Most certainly he was enjoying the destitute situation he had put her in.

"I have spoken of this very concern with Mr. Smith at length," Mr. Jenkins replied, obviously understanding her fear. "He feels, as sole proprietor, he is, and I rightly agree, responsible for your safety and security."

Isabella stood up from her spot, forgetting all dignity, "I won't marry him!"

Mr. Jenkins looked at her apologetically, whether from

the necessity of marriage between a senior man and a young lady of one and twenty years or other less favorable options she wasn't sure.

"Though I suggested such an arrangement, for the sake of your comfort, I was informed that such arrangements were no longer…no longer…" he hesitated to try to find the words, "no longer a possibility unless…" Mr. Jenkins gave a horribly painful sigh. "He would like you to ask him to take you in."

"Absolutely not," Isabella stated still standing, trembling with fear and embarrassment.

She could hear a tisk of disgust behind her but refused to turn to look at him.

"Before you speak Miss Isabella, I encourage you to consider your situation. Mr. Smith does intend to sell all valuable possessions. Even so, it will just barely cover your father's debts. Without such an arrangement I cannot imagine how you will see to your comfortable lifestyle.

"Then I shan't live as I have thus far. I am not above being more frugal with my life. Am I not allowed some sort of income from my father's business?"

"I did discuss such matters with Mr. Smith in the event that you did not want to…um…abide to his requirements. He agreed a yearly income was only fair since, after all, he was named your protector. The sum he agreed on was...well...it was fifty pounds a year."

"Fifty pounds a year?" Isabella now turned to face Mr. Smith.

"It is half his yearly wage, though you wouldn't know it by the way he lived, and is quite generous considering I will most likely need to take on another partner," Mr. Smith spit back indignantly.

He had quite the smug look on his face as he rocked back and forth on his heels, hands pleasantly clasped in front of him. What was torturous to say for the lawyer, and unbelievable to hear for Isabella, was quite enjoyable for this horrible man.

He had positively backed her into a corner. With such a small amount, there was no possible way for Isabella to live alone. It wouldn't even support a house staff of just one or two servants. He had meant it to force her to beg before him for that which she had denied him all those years ago.

"Good heavens, Izzy, what did you do?" Louisa asked as she listened, horrified and enraptured by the retelling.

"Well, I refused to give in to his boorish demands. I told him I would find a way to settle on such low income and that was the end of that. I will starve to death before I give that man the benefit of seeing me grovel at his feet.

"But Izzy- without a home or any possessions of your own, how will you do it?"

"Well, after I announced I would not give in to the wretched blackguard, Mr. Smith stormed out of the room, slamming the door quite loudly behind him. Mr. Jenkins, the poor man, began apologizing profusely, saying that if there were anything he could do to help me, he would."

"Well, what is there to be done, Izzy?"

"I thought on this fact for the better part of last night. I have come to one conclusion. I will need to find myself some sort of employment."

"Certainly not?" Louisa asked with surprise, though Isabella could already see the wheels turning in her head that this was the likely alternative.

"I think we both know that this is how it must be," Isabella said with a defeated tone.

"It is either that or giving in to Mr. Smith. My pride, however sinful to keep, will not allow such a thing. I will not be offended at all if at such a declaration you find yourself unable to keep my company."

"Absolutely not!" Louisa said using a firm tone.

"You are my dearest friend. You were the only one who cared to spend time with me when we were together at school. I would never abandon you, no matter the cost."

"Not even if I am a lowly scullery maid?" Isabella asked, tears welling in her eyes.

In all honesty, she had spent the whole of her night not just thinking about a life of employment but terrified of the fact that she had no idea what employable skills she had.

Though she may have been born on the lower side of the peerage, her father had never spared her a comfort, and she feared she could not even dress on her own, let alone take on tasks.

"You will be no such thing," Louisa said firmly. She placed her own small, delicate hands in Isabella's lap and began to ponder.

"I understand now why you have come to me. We will most certainly find something that would be suitable for your position."

"But I don't have a position; I am free of status now and completely destitute, without any skills at hand."

"Of course you have skills," Louisa encouraged. "Why,

you were always one of the top performers in our school! Do you not remember? Mrs. Mason would have you stand and recite your French lessons before prospective students. Why, that is it!" Louisa said with the light of a plan. "You could easily find employment as a governess."

Isabella thought this new idea over for a bit. She unquestionably had loved school and took to it quickly.

She was accomplished enough in her educational knowledge as well as music and other various genteel talents. She could certainly teach such things to young lords and ladies.

Of course, it was a definite step down from being one of the peerages to serving and educating them. It was not as low as the serving class but somewhere in between.

Between her employment and her small allowance, Isabella would most certainly be able to manage on her own.

"Do you think I would be hired as such? Mr. Jenkins did offer to help me find employment when I found myself in need of it."

"Of course. I am quite sure that Mrs. Mason would also be happy to give you a shining reference. You could most likely find a home here in London to instruct pupils at and we could still be close friends."

"Oh, my dear Louisa, I fear wishing so much good fortune to happen at this time in my life is much like wishing to catch a star. I will be quite satisfied with any position and your continued friendship, even if through correspondence only."

"Have faith, Izzy," Louisa said, reaching across the small table of tea and taking Isabella's hands.

"We will find a way to overcome this hurdle together. Certainly, it isn't something to worry about now. The Season is almost upon us. Mr. Smith certainly won't put you out till after. It will give you an opportunity to more earnestly search a match and perhaps escape all the necessity for such talk."

"I hope you're right, Louisa," Isabella responded, giving her a grateful squeeze of the hand in return.

"I was frightened by his rage upon my declaration not to heed his request. I am almost certain he will do everything in his power to hinder my progress at every turn."

CHAPTER 2

The following week, Isabella made her way back to Mr. Jenkins's office after receiving a note that he had found a suitable position for her. She had been reassured by Louisa that she would have at least the season to see if she could come up with a better course of action before settling on being a governess.

It was not to be the case.

Sadly, no more than a week after finding out about her father's untimely death, Mr. Smith had visited Rosewater house. There he had informed Miss Isabella that she would have a month only to collect items and vacate her home.

He then proceeded to boldly go through the house,

solicitor in tow, informing her of what things he planned to sell.

Isabella hadn't informed the servants yet of the impending liquidation of her father's estates. Mr. Smith even went boldly into Isabella's own room and rifled through her belongings. Mr. Smith announced he would be procuring all her belongings including dresses and jewelry.

The solicitor, embarrassed, hastily suggested that such tactics were not necessary to the closing of the amount owed.

Mr. Smith reluctantly allowed Isabella to keep her clothing but still required all jewelry be turned over to him for selling. She didn't have much in the way of fancy jewelry.

Therefore, she didn't care much for giving it up if it meant not allowing Mr. Smith the satisfaction of seeing her beg him for marriage.

Her hardest items to part with were the silver comb her father had stated her mother wore on their wedding day, the small gold band that was her mother's wedding ring, and a silver chain with a locket of her mother's hair which she wore around her neck always. It had been a gift from her father on her sixteenth birthday.

Having never met her mother, for she had passed in childbirth, any stories or items her father shared with her were cherished.

After taking all belongings worth selling on the spot, including the ring and comb, and informing Isabella that they would be back in a month, for the third time, to take possession of the house, Mr. Smith set his evil eyes on the locket around her neck.

Isabella defiantly clasped her hand around it. This was one thing Isabella would not allow to be taken from her.

Would Mr. Smith really stoop to such a level of evil?

Luckily the solicitor interjected, "I believe we should allow Miss Watts to collect herself. I am sure it has been a very tiring day for her. We can always come back to collect any other items upon the sale of the establishment."

Mr. Smith had reluctantly agreed and left. Not a minute after the front door shut on the two men, Isabella crumpled to the hall floor in a heap of sorrowful tears.

Her kind maid, who must have also been beside herself to learn that she would be without a situation in a month's time, helped Isabella up to her room to lay down.

It was clear that she would not have time to find a better end to her situation. The next day, Isabella inquired of Mrs. Mason for a letter of character reference and delivered it to Mr. Jenkins that same day.

She wrung her hands for the next week, waiting for word from Mr. Jenkins. She had no idea if anyone would ever accept a governess at her age without any prior employment references.

Mr. Jenkins had assured her that he would do everything in his power to see her well settled. She had felt so blessed to have such a willing friend to help her in her time of need.

The time had come when a letter arrived stating that Mr. Jenkins had found her a station of employment. She made it to his office the following day in haste.

Isabella was dreading and desperate to know what establishment she would be employed at for the remainder of her days.

Would she find herself teaching in a girls' establishment just as she, herself, had attended? Or would some member of her peerage take pity on her and take her on for the benefit of his children's private education.

She sat nervously across from Mr. Jenkins.

"I must confess I had a harder time finding a situation for you than expected. You see, most of the lady schools in London were well staffed. Mrs. Mason did express in her letter, had she the room, she would have happily taken you on."

It was something that Isabella had expected. There were often more ladies seeking employment than available opportunities for suitable work.

A part of her wanted to feel slightly shocked or betrayed that not one of those in her acquaintance here in London had tried to take her on for employment. She was no longer a member of that society, however, and would not be seen as someone to have around.

"I am sorry to say that the situation I found for you is far outside of London. I know you had expected to stay in the area, and I did my very best to do so but..." he trailed off.

"It is quite alright. I know you did your very best, Mr. Jenkins, and I am very appreciative of all your efforts. I am sure that no matter the location, I will find my situation quite adequate."

"I am glad to hear your brave words. The position is for the Duke of Wintercrest. He has taken on a small ward over the last year, a young woman I believe, and is seeking a governess for her. He specifically asked for a lady of London breeding to prepare her for society, as well as provide her with a strong understanding of the French language."

Isabella, of course, knew of the Duke and Duchess of Wintercrest, though she had never had the honor of making their acquaintance. She was aware that they were relatively older in age with children of their own, and therefore questioned who this young ward might be. Perhaps a relation they willingly took on.

"It seems that it might be an ideal position for me."

"Just as I thought when I was told of it. The Duke is also willing to give a much more significant pay than often given for a governess, forty pounds a year. I had assumed that you would be willing to take the position since they were in need fairly soon. I took the liberty to tell them that you would accept the position. I hope that is fine?"

"It is quite alright. I suspect it is more than I could otherwise hope for and I thank you for all your hard work on my behalf."

"I am glad to hear it," Mr. Jenkins said relaxing into his normally happy face. "As I said, they are in need of a governess right away and have made transportation for you. You will travel by public coach in two days' time. I must warn you to pack relatively lightly as there is not much room in such situations, and dress comfortably, for that matter. You will be spending two nights on the road during your travels."

"A three-day travel? Forgive me, but where exactly do the Duke and Duchess of Wintercrest live."

"Yes, that. It is quite far north. Just a day's ride south of Edinburgh."

"Is it in Scotland, then?" Isabella asked, a little shocked. She had not dared to hope that she would stay in her beloved London, but to leave England altogether seemed terrifying to her.

"No, not quite. Just short of it. I do believe the vast lands of Wintercrest come into contact with the country, but the manor itself is still on English soil."

"I see," Isabella said trying to accustom herself to her new lot in life. "I thank you again, Mr. Jenkins, for not only your work with my father but for the help you have given to me and your continued friendship. I will hurry home now and begin my preparations for travel."

Isabella did just that. She did her best to pack a minimal amount of clothing into her chest and prepared anything she might want to keep safely tucked inside.

Luckily, her maid, Sally, was there to help her with the work. All the time she wondered how she was going to make do on her own.

Her last step was that of utter defiance. The night before she was set to leave she took her small sewing kit and sewed her silver locket into the hem of her dress.

She certainly couldn't be seen leaving the house wearing it, for Mr. Smith might come after her, demanding the property. That would be no way to start her new life.

At the same time, she refused to leave it behind in the house that was once her home, for that wretched man to handle so roughly and sell like nothing more than a worthless trinket. She hoped that by the time Mr. Smith learned of her deceit she would be far away and out of his reach.

If there was one good thing about having to travel so far away from the city she loved, it was that she would also be far away from the man who sought to destroy her life at every turn.

Her three-day journey up north was not entirely uneventful. She was very uncomfortable having been placed inside a carriage with five other people. There was scarcely room to sit let alone adjust one's position.

She had to count herself lucky, though. After all, the

fare was paid by her employer, and he had given her the kindness of a seat inside the carriage. There had been two who could only afford to sit on the roof of the carriage out in the elements.

Many of those in the carriage were friendly enough and made small talk. As the days progressed, each got off in their turn till she was left alone with one other man.

She noticed quite quickly that the scene outside her window changed from the warm sunshine of spring air to dark and gloomy clouds as she progressed northward.

The final morning, just before he took his leave, Isabella asked the portly gentleman across from her if grey weather was the norm in the north.

"My dear Miss Watts," he said with a gruff, mustache filled voice, "I have lived here my whole life and can only boast of seeing full sunshine a handful of times each year. You are lucky that you have come for spring and summer first. It will help you acclimate before the harsh winter falls. I, myself, choose to stay in town for the dreary months, now that I am able, and only return for these warmer seasons."

Isabella looked out her window again and contemplated how he could have possibly counted her view outside as a warmer season. She had decided to wear her simple light brown traveling dress. It was relatively without frill, which also meant it wouldn't show wrinkles as much in her travels.

Though there was beautiful, lush green land as far as she could see, the sky had been nothing but grey. A hard, bitter wind bit back against the carriage and, from time to time, it even drizzled down on them.

Isabella had also learned from her companions on the ride that she would be staying just east of Northumberland along the coast. From the description of the estate, it sounded astonishing. Isabella supposed she would just have to get used to not only coastal fresh air and beautiful greenery, but also grey skies and damp weather.

Finally, as dusk was beginning to settle on the third day, Isabella saw a long stone wall along the road. The driver had informed her earlier that this was the edge of Wintercrest estates and when they came to it, he knocked on the roof to silently point it out to her.

Her excitement reached its limit as the driver slowed to a stop before the main gates. She got out and took a moment to stretch her limbs. The driver was already down and removing her trunk. Watching him struggle with it, she wondered if she had perhaps packed more then she should have.

He set it down on the ground next to her at the gate and dusted his hands off, looking up at the expanse of the property. Isabella followed his gaze and admired it as well.

Turning back to the driver, she was surprised to see him retaking his place on top of the carriage.

"But wait," she called out. "Please sir, what shall I do now?"

"Can't say, Miss Watts. All I am to do is drop ye right here."

With a flip of his reins, he made his way onward, leaving Miss Isabella Watts utterly alone and confused at the threshold of Wintercrest Manor.

CHAPTER 3

Isabella looked down the way leading to the manor house. She couldn't say for sure, however, since she could see nothing in the dimming light but the road before her. She tugged at her trunk, unable to lift it from its grassy resting place.

She supposed that most seeking employment here only brought the clothes on their back and another outfit for Sunday attire. If the six gowns she had foolishly packed weren't too much, then the books from her father's small library surely were.

She had convinced herself that she could use these beloved stories as part of her pupil's education. Of course, the Duke of Wintercrest had enough of a library on his own that bringing books of her own was a silly, selfish move on her part.

A cold wind whipped at her and she tightened the simple shawl she had wrapped around herself. Isabella suddenly wished that she had thought to bring a pelisse in her chest. Certainly, they knew she would be arriving today. She waited a few moments considering that the coachman that was to meet her was just a bit late.

After a period of ten minutes, she was convinced that at least a footman would eventually come to fetch her. Finally, as her ability to see in the cloudy, dim light was almost impossible she determined that no one was coming and began to drag her trunk down the road.

Had she been in the right frame of mind, she might have left her chest at the gate and walked on only to have it fetched at another time by someone more capable. She, however, was not in a good state of mind. She was shivering with cold and had no idea what she was to expect or have expected of her in her new lot in life.

Luckily, the moon was full, and as clouds parted, she was able to get brief views of the way forward. When clouds obscured her only illumination, though, she did her best not to panic as she could only see a few feet in front of her. Hopefully, the lights from the house would begin to show in a parting of the hedge trees that ran along the road.

Finally, in a glimpse of momentary light from above, she saw a gentlemanly figure walking toward her up the road. He stopped upon also spotting her form.

"Oh, thank heavens," she called out, assuming it to be a servant sent to receive her. "I feared I was all forgotten about. Please, would you kindly help me with my portmanteau."

She straightened from her crouched, pulling position. The figure across from her, no more than ten feet ahead, didn't seem to move. She couldn't make out his features in such dark lighting but assumed that no one but a footman would be out at such a late hour.

"Certainly," a sure, deep voice called back to her. The hurried figured met her and bent down to pick up her chest.

"Pray, do tell me though, why exactly are you dragging a chest down this road so late at night," the man asked as he began to walk forward easily with chest in hand.

"Oh, forgive me. I thought you were the footman sent to retrieve me. I am Miss Isabella Watts. I have been employed as governess for His Grace. I do not mean to impose on you if your intention was not to come fetch me," she added quickly.

"Well, I don't think I could leave you here to continue dragging such a large item," he said, smoothly shifting the weight in his hand.

"I just assumed. You looked from a distance to be a footman by your stature, sir," she hesitated on her last word, pointing out that he had yet to give his own name.

"Beg your pardon, Miss Watts. I am Captain Grant. I had just stepped outside for a walk in the fresh air. Sometimes things can get quite stifling inside."

"Captain. Well, no wonder you have the stature of a footman," Isabella said, realizing it might be quite forward of her.

"I just mean, my father was a sailor as well. I suppose I found kinship with your nautical air."

"Was he also in the Royal Navy?" Captain Grant asked as they continued on their way. He seemed to know the direction by heart and walked at a steady pace through the now almost complete darkness.

"No, he was on a merchant ship as a boy, and had his own set of vessels later in life. He had quite a taste for the adventurous sea life," she added with a bit of nostalgia.

"Pray, what was his name? Perhaps I met him on my journeys."

Isabella was quite unsure of what name to give- his Christian name or his title. Certainly, to have a titled gentleman's daughter in the house might raise some animosity when it came to fitting in with other servants.

Since Captain Grant was unquestionably a guest and not a member of the staff, Isabella risked the chance of giving her father's proper title, as he would have liked.

"My father was Baron Leinister. He unfortunately passed a few months back."

"I am so sorry to hear that," the gentleman looked down at her in the little light and held a tone of sincere sorrow. "My deepest condolences."

Isabella gave her thanks for his kindness, and they walked on a few more minutes in silence. She was about to ask him about his service in the Royal Navy, hoping to make a good transition in the conversation, when she saw the lights of the manor up ahead.

She gave a grateful sigh of relief. She had done her best to hide it, but her thin traveling dress and shawl had not been much to protect her from the wind that sliced between the hedge trees. She noticed immediately that her companion made his way to the head of the house.

"Oh, if you please, Captain Grant, I would find it more appropriate for me to find my way to the servant's entrance. If you could just point me in the right direction, I would happily part company with you with my full thanks for your service."

Captain Grant seemed to hesitate a minute.

"I couldn't possibly leave you to take the portemanteau yourself," he finally said. "I am certain the household will find you a welcome guest."

As much as Isabella would have liked to enter the vast manor in front as a guest, she knew that was no longer her station in life. It was time for her to divide the line from who she had been to who she was now.

"I appreciate your kindness, but I am quite sure the housekeeper will expect me."

"Alright then," Captain Grant seemed to resolve to her reasoning, "I shall escort you there. You are lucky you came upon me, for I know the servant's entrance well."

"You do?" Isabella asked, surprised.

"Yes," he replied with a soft chuckle. "I lived here in my

youth, and as a young boy I was quite gangly and always in want of something to eat. Usually sweets," he continued with that same flow of storytelling that Isabella had so enjoyed from her father.

She smiled and wondered to herself if all seamen were expert folk-tellers. "I would often make my way through into the kitchen by way of the service entrance to sneak a sweet cake from under the cook's nose. She, of course, knew exactly what I was doing and kindly turned a blind eye to it."

"She sounds like a very considerate chef."

"She is that, not to mention the best in all of the county."

"How fortunate His Grace must feel to have her here under his roof."

They had finally arrived at the side entrance door, and moving the trunk to one hand, Captain Grant unceremoniously opened it and gestured for her to enter. Isabella was startled, when she entered the room, to find a well-lit hall with three long tables all filled with servants, no doubt eating their evening meal. They all stared at her in silent shock until the Captain entered the room behind her. Instantly, the whole hall stood up.

An older woman with a tight-fitted blonde bun and keys

jingling at her waist came rushing forward. Isabella had no doubt that she was the housekeeper of the manor.

"Lord Bellfourd, can I be of service to you, sir?"

She was frantically looking between the new lady stranger and the Marquess of Bellfourd, son of the Duke of Wintercrest.

"Mrs. Peterson, please let me introduce Miss Watts, our new governess. I was out on an evening stroll when I found her in some distress."

Immediately, at Mrs. Peterson's request, a groomsman came forward and took the portmanteau away. He left the room with it, Isabella hoped to her own room. She, however, noticed that Mrs. Peterson had not addressed her or even looked at her directly.

"I do apologize for your inconvenience, Lord Bellfourd. The governess was meant to arrive much earlier in the evening. Mr. Larson and I were just discussing sending out someone to inquire after her only a few moments ago."

It was a little irritating to Isabella that she was being treated like a child and discussed without any acknowledgment of her presence.

"I was left at the entrance, Mrs. Peterson, with no one to

see me to the house," Isabella chimed in, tired of being ignored.

Mrs. Peterson looked at her in shock, like she had just noticed her for the first time. Finally, she turned back to the Marquess.

"Thank you again, Lord Bellfourd. Is there anything else I can get for you before you return upstairs?"

Isabella could see his countenance sink at the mention of his proper place above the servants' quarters. The situation was confusing enough on its own, but why had he given her a false name? Why hadn't he told her that he was the Duke of Wintercrest's son?

She may not have been entirely well-versed in all the peerage, but she had certainly done her research before leaving and had learned that the Marquess of Bellfourd was the oldest son and heir to the Duke of Wintercrest.

Lord Bellfourd turned to her and, giving a slight bow, began to bid her goodnight, probably something he should not have done. His eyes stopped at her feet though, maybe coming to his senses she thought, and looked up at her questioningly.

"Miss Watts, there seems to be something coming out of the hem of your gown."

Isabella looked down in fear to see the chain of her locket sticking out and dragging along the ground.

"Oh dear," Isabella said, crimson with shame.

She pushed her skirt with her folded hands in front of her, as if the act would hide the charm dangling below. It was bad enough that she had obviously made a fool of herself, calling the Marquess a footman, but now she had the added shame of showing the jewelry she had sown into her dress for safe keeping.

No doubt, in the short time they had been together he had surmised she was not only naive and rude, but also very odd.

"It is very dear to me and I feared to lose it in traveling," she stammered, most embarrassed.

Much to her horror, and the horror of everyone in the room, Lord Bellfourd bent down and removed the last of the chain from her hem. He stood and held it out for her to take. Without looking him in the eye, for fear of crying, she let the chain fall into her gloved hand.

"Thank you, Lord Bellfourd," she said softly, with the most profound curtsy she could manage.

"I will bid you goodnight, then," Lord Bellfourd

responded, not wanting to make the young Miss Watts any more embarrassed. "Good evening, Mrs. Peterson."

The whole room waited till he was out of the hall before resuming their seats and whispering amongst themselves.

Isabella finally met the gaze of the housekeeper, who seemed to be measuring her, once the room went back to hushed speaking and clanking of dishes. Without so much as a word, she turned on her heels, pausing only once to beckon, in an irritated fashion, for Isabella to follow.

Utterly put in her place, Isabella did her best not to look at the side glances around her as she followed Mrs. Peterson out of the servant dining hall.

CHAPTER 4

Isabella listened silently on her hastened tour from Mrs. Peterson, the weight of her locket heavy in her hand. Mrs. Peterson insisted that the trip must not? be a quick one since she had arrived much later than expected.

She cared not for the fact that Isabella had been left on the side of the road with no help getting to the manor.

"You will be situated in the west wing of the manor in the extra servants quarters in the attic. Your student's room, nursery, and school room are also located on that side of the manor. There is no reason for you to venture outside that wing without express permission, is that clear?"

"Yes, of course," Isabella responded, now leaving the

lower levels of the servants' quarters and up to the main floor. Not stopping on the main floor, Mrs. Peterson immediately turned and went up the second set of stairs, then a third, and finally, a fourth.

By the fourth set of stairs, the ascension was steep and narrow. The final floor was, no doubt, the attic space used for overflow staffing. The ceiling was scarcely tall enough not to rub against Mrs. Peterson's high bun.

She walked two doors over and bade Isabella enter. The room was unquestionably smaller than the one she had at home, but not at all displeasing to look at.

The footman had kindly deposited her trunk at the end of a small, but comfortable looking bed. It was dressed in a simple quilt decorated with embroidered flowers.

The footman had also been kind enough to light a fire in the small fireplace that was to the right of the bed. To the left of it was a little, round port window in the pointed arch of a spire.

In front sat a small table and one plush, but ragged looking, chair. No doubt, it had been moved up when no longer suitable for the main house.

Aside from that, the only other furniture was a small table, for basin and water pitcher, and a petite cabinet closet. Though none of the furniture matched and the walls were only a pure whitewash, the room was warmed by the fire and cozy.

Isabella was grateful to see the space she could call her own after the long trip with such close quarters.

Mrs. Peterson waited, arms folded in front, while Isabella inspected the room. When Isabella turned back to her, she didn't have a moment to speak before Mrs. Peterson began.

"Your breakfast and basin of water will be brought to you every morning. You will eat your breakfast here, luncheon and tea will be served with Miss Jaqueline and her nurse, and dinner will be brought up to you here, promptly at nine o'clock."

"I won't be taking my meals downstairs?" Isabella asked, a little surprised that she would be expected to hole up in her room any time she was not with her student.

"Of course not. You are not one of the staff, you are the governess. Your meals will be taken here, where it is good and proper."

It was easy to see that Mrs. Peterson found propriety very important.

"I was told that your father was Baron Leinister," she continued.

Isabella was slightly disappointed that her upbringing was already well known.

"Yes," was her simple reply.

"Well, I am sure you understand that things are different now. You are not a guest of His Grace, but a paid worker. You are expected to do your job and to do it to the best of your ability. You will not have a lady's maid. I trust you expected this and can take care of yourself." It was more of a statement than a question.

"Of course, I would never have presumed otherwise."

"Very well, then. As I said, warm water and your breakfast tray will be brought to you in the morning at seven and seven-thirty, respectively. I will come to get you at a quarter to eight to meet Miss Jaqueline. At ten, you will be presented to His Grace and introductions to the rest of the family will follow, as he dictates. He will tell you what duties are expected of you while you stay."

It wasn't hard to miss that Mrs. Peterson was not pleased that Isabella had already acquainted Lord Bellfourd before the designated time.

"You have from three o'clock onward to yourself, as the nurse will take her duties then. You may explore the grounds outside, as long as you are not infringing on the family. You are expected to accompany Miss Jaqueline to church with the family every Sunday morning, and then you are free to use the afternoon as you wish. Many of the servants use the opportunity to go into town, which is about a mile's walk. All other expectations will be given to you by His Grace in the morning."

"Thank you, Mrs. Peterson," Isabella said, now feeling very exhausted from her journey. "Could you also please tell me how I might mail post?"

She seemed to think this over for a minute, undoubtedly weighing what was proper for such a situation. Of course, mailing post along with the members of the household would not be acceptable. She wasn't quite sure whether leaving it in the servant's hall, as the other staff members did, was quite right for her either. Finally, though, it was what she settled on.

"There is a basket on a small table next to the service entrance. Letters may be left there to be posted."

She bid Isabella a crisp goodnight and left the room. Isabella sat for a few moments on her bed, taking it all in before finally opening her still-gloved hand and replacing the locket around her neck.

Feeling like herself again with her treasured locket adorning her neck, she set about unpacking her belongings. It took some effort to get all her gowns into the small cabinet and she realized again how ridiculous she must have seemed to the marquess, forcing him to lug so many belongings.

For lack of a better place, she lined up her treasured novels along the wall between the cabinet and the metal headboard of the bed.

With most of her last possessions in their places, Isabella managed to get herself undressed, only the third time she had done so on her own, and slipped beneath the soft cover of her bed. She was grateful for a room with a fireplace.

She stared dreamily into its dwindling embers as she wondered if that was why she had been placed in a room so far away from the other staff. Had it been for the extra comfort of the fire? Or was it the access to her pupil's side without interfering with others in the house? Or simply to give her a physical reminder that she was no longer one of the lords and ladies who lived in such a lavished manor nor one of the staff that served them?

Her last thoughts as she fell asleep was if this had been how her father felt when out to sea. Adrift, with land in front and land behind and nothing but a lone ship to carry her. Would she spend the rest of her days lost out at sea as a solitary island or could she find a way to make it to a shore, no matter the one she chose?

The next morning, Isabella woke early to the darkened grey sky greeting her through the small porthole window. She was surprised how well she had slept, no doubt due to exhaustion from the long journey. She was afraid that she might have overslept, as she was not used to waking early. She sat upright with a bolt and quickly tip toed over to the small clock that alone adorned the fireplace mantle.

She poked at the fire, finding a few coals warm beneath the ash, and did her best to use the fuel provided to get it going again. Once there was a small flicker of flame, Isabella turned, hearing a slight knock at her door.

She opened it to find a maid standing with a pitcher of steaming water and basin. She stood aside to let the girl in to set it down on the small stand next to her bed.

"Thank you, that looks lovely, miss..." Isabella trailed off waiting for the girl to introduce herself. She was very young, not more than sixteen.

"Just Betsy, Miss Watts," she said with a thick Scottish accent and a curtsy.

"Are you Scottish, then?" Isabella asked.

"Aye, most of the lower staff is, Miss Watts."

"Please call me Isabella," she encouraged. "Shall I bring my basin down when I am done?"

"Oh no, Miss…I mean Isabella. I shall come and fetch it up when I brin' your breakfast tray."

"That is very kind of you; I am sure it is tedious work to go up and down so many stairs."

"Dinna fash. I dinna mind it one bit. It's a much more enjoyable task than the others." Betsy turned to leave after another short curtsy, but paused just a moment. "I dinna mean to be a bother, but I was a'wonderin' if you happen to need help with your things, dressin' and hair, I mean to say. I would be happy to help you."

"That is very considerate of you, Betsy, but I would hate to ask more of you than you already do, or give you additional tasks. It may take some practice, but I believe I will soon learn to do it on my own."

"You see, you would be doin' me a favor if you let me," Betsy continued. "I want to be a lady's maid one day for a fine house. May'haps even this one. I need the practice first, you see. I heard that you were raised as a lady, so I thought you might help me. Tell me if I was doin' somethin' wrong and the like."

"Well, I suppose I could use some help to make something simple with my hair."

"Aye, that would be great practice for me if ye would allow it."

"Mrs. Peterson won't be mad? I had the feeling she didn't want me speaking with others very much."

"It's not like that. She is just verra particular that all are in their place and none try to be more than they are. It makes it pretty impossible for a lass like me to make much more o' herself. But what she dinna ken won't hurt her much."

"Well, if you are sure we won't be caught," Isabella hesitated. "I suppose it would be fine. I would love to do what I can to help you."

Isabella meant it sincerely, too. It was the first friend she had made in the house and any way she could help Betsy she was willing to. It reminded her of something her father used to say, "a small act of kindness can open the door for great friendships."

Isabella used the warm water to wash and freshen herself before dressing. She found a soft green colored cotton morning dress that she paired with a dark, velvet green spencer jacket. Though the dress was very modest in cut, she still fretted over its look as a practical dress.

She was, after all, hoping to put the right foot in front of His Grace after clearly blundering things with the Marquess the night before. She smartly tucked a fichu into the top of her green gown before putting on the spencer jacket.

Though she had the fire going relatively well, she feared she would never get used to the chill that always seemed present in this northern country. Tucking a cream handkerchief into her long sleeve, she finished just in time for Betsy to knock at the door again.

She came in and set the tray down on the small table beside the port window. Before eating, Isabella sat in the only chair facing the window while Betsy pulled her hair back into a tight chignon. She left a few of Isabella's dark ringlets out to frame her face. Isabella did her best to feel around to assure Betsy she had done a fantastic job, as there was no mirror present in the room.

Seeming happy to have gotten some practice in, Betsy thanked her again then took the water basin and left Isabella to eat her breakfast alone.

She had just finished her toast and rejuvenating cup of tea when a knock came to her door again. This time, it was Mrs. Peterson, and she was very accurate with her timing. Without so much as a good morning, she turned on her heels, expecting Isabella to follow after.

Isabella supposed that this was a common habit of Mrs. Peterson. Not only did she feel everyone had their place to be, but also the use of words that didn't need to be spoken were a waste of time. She quickly walked to catch up to Mrs. Peterson for the second time in two days to start her new beginning as governess.

CHAPTER 5

Isabella made her way down the narrow stairway and ended on the second floor of the main house. She followed Mrs. Peterson along the Turkish-rugged hall listening to the soft pads of their feet on the ground and swishing of skits.

She was surprised that, for such a large house, filled with not only the family of the house but at least a hundred servants downstairs and not all the tables were even full, it was so quiet.

Where was everyone else? She had expected to see maids bustling about and hear the clank of breakfast silverware in the distance, but it was complete and utter silence as she walked. Perhaps it was just that the west wing of the manor was far off from the rest of the house, she thought to herself.

The wing was basically a rectangle shape with a walkway that outlined the rectangle. Off the walkway, numerous doors sprouted along the walls.

The middle, however, was open, with four enormous chandeliers hanging down from the ceiling. Isabella took a second to look over the railing on their walk and saw the most magnificent ballroom she had ever set her eyes on. It took up the whole of the bottom floor.

The chandeliers, as well as at least a dozen standing candelabras dotting along the floor, were all covered with sheets, as was a section in the far corner that was no doubt used for a live orchestra. She imagined royalty might very well dance in that hall on occasion.

As she walked, she learned that her quarters were the farthest west and left edge of the manor, her small port window looking out at the left side of the property.

She had gotten so mixed up walking the downstairs corridors that she hadn't realized which way she was facing. She remembered seeing the front of the manor in the dark and mentally pictured the three sections. Her left side held the grand hall and a significant amount of what she assumed were guest rooms above it.

The middle section was, no doubt, the main part of the house with studies, libraries, sitting and drawing rooms. Most likely, in a house this size, it also boasted a smaller hall for more intimate affairs and the various dining rooms.

Then, lastly, she pictured in her mind, the east wing of the manor. She wondered if it shared a similar large hall and rooms that housed the family or if it was completely different from the beauty she was walking along.

Finally, they made their way all the way from the bottom of the attic stairs along the straight walk to the other end of the wing. Here, there was a small half circle alcove that led to two rooms on either side of the end of the rectangle and a grand staircase that lead down to the lower floor of the central portion. It was a sensational foyer, with painted ceilings squares, another large chandelier, and marble floors. Isabella stopped for a moment to look at the grandeur of it all.

She saw the large double doors that lead from the outside into the foyer, as well as an exquisite matching staircase opposite her. She did see a single maid dusting one of the vases that adorned the great room along with several marble statues. It was unimaginable to Isabella that this house was lived in. It looked like a royal estate, more magnificent than any she had ever seen.

"Miss Watts, if you please," Mrs. Peterson said with impatience. She motioned to a third door from the small half circle alcove.

No doubt these rooms, closest to the main house, were meant for children. They were far enough away as not to be a bother to the lords and ladies that graced the house, but close enough to come when needed. Isabella smiled at the thought of how many little eyes had spied over the walkway banister to lavish balls below.

Mrs. Peterson opened the door without knocking, and Isabella followed in after her. She found herself in a large room with a small library of its own on either side of a crackling fireplace. There were comfortable chairs seated near the fire, no doubt for reading.

There was a long wall facing outside to the back of the estate. Lush curtains in velvet green draped between the windows that showed vast, manicured gardens and even a large pond. Next to the windows were a small table and four chairs, probably for lunch. And all the way to the right side of the room was a child-sized table where one timid little girl was sitting quietly with her hands folded on top.

Next to the girl stood a woman just past middle age. She was wearing the cream-colored dress and apron of a nurse, as well as a bonnet with large ruffles framing her kind-looking face. She motioned for her charge to stand at the women's entrance and the little girl did as she was told.

"Mrs. Murray," Mrs. Peterson started, "I am pleased to introduce you to Miss Watts, our new governess. She will be relieving you of your duties during the day."

"Ach, they are not much of duties with this little angel," Mrs. Murray said in a thick Scottish accent.

The little girl smiled up at her nurse with affection. It was clear she didn't understand much of what she said. She was a young girl and seemed small for her age. Very petite and thin. She had golden blonde ringlet hair and still had the round face of a small child. She looked shyly at the newcomer.

"Miss Jaqueline De'belmount," Mrs. Peterson said a little louder than before, "this is your governess, Miss Watts."

Mrs. Peterson, ever the proper lady, made the formal introduction to the child. Isabella laughed a little to herself. The child spoke a different language; she wasn't hard of hearing. Isabella stood before the young girl, then kneeled down to Jaqueline's level.

"Enchante. Je m'appelle Mademoiselle Watts."

Jaqueline's little face lit up. "Parlez-vous français?"

"Oui," Isabella answered with a small smile.

This poor little girl had probably felt so alone and isolated in this house. Indeed, she was well loved by her nurse, but Isabella couldn't imagine leaving one's home and being surrounded by a new culture and language.

Mrs. Peterson cleared her throat, "Though all members of His Grace's family are fluent in French, the duke would prefer if the child learns English."

"Of course," Isabella said, standing back up.

The young girl slipped her hand into Isabella's and Isabella smiled down at her, giving her hand a gentle squeeze.

"If you please, I would like to meet with my pupil and see what she already has learned."

"Of course," Mrs. Peterson said, already leaning toward leaving the room. Surely, she had much more pressing matters at this time. "I will return to escort you to His Grace."

Isabella nodded in understanding and waited for Mrs. Peterson to leave. She turned to Mrs. Murray who hadn't gone yet.

"Mrs. Murray, if you have a moment before you go, would you please share with me how you and Miss Jaqueline have been spending your day."

"I dinna mind at all. Miss Jaqueline is a verra sweet child. Sadly, she doesn't know much to say. She does enjoy playing with her dolls. We go on walks after luncheon to enjoy some fresh air. I expect His Grace will desire her time in nature to continue."

"That would be fine. It would give us some time to explore natural science. I understand that Mrs. Peterson wants Jaqueline to focus on learning English, but I hope you will allow me to discuss what she knows thus far from her previous education. To do so, we would need to speak in French."

"Och, don't you worry about that. Mrs. Peterson is a stickler for the rules. What she dinna ken won't hurt her. I will sit right here," she said as she took a spot in a chair by the fire. "I've been working on some winter mittens for the wee lass. I'll be able to hear when Mrs. Peterson comes up the hall and give ye warnin'."

"Thank you, Mrs. Murray," Isabella looked down into the little hand still clasped in hers, "Shall we find some dolls to play with then?" she asked in French.

Jaqueline's small eyes lit up. Tugging on Isabella's hand,

she took her past the table and through a door that lead into a nursery. She collected some dolls and brought them before the fire at her nurse's feet, something she had apparently done on a regular basis.

Isabella followed along and took her place next to the child on the floor. While they played, they discussed where Jaqueline grew up and what she liked to do.

She was just five years old when her mother told her that she would be leaving France and spending time with her grandparents. She spoke lovingly of her mother, but from what she said, her mother seemed to be of a certain profession.

"Grandparents?" Isabella asked.

"Oh aye, Jaqueline is the daughter of the late Marquess of Bellfourd." Mrs. Murray said not looking up from her work. "Lord James, God rest him, was an honorable man. I ken him since he was a young boy of twelve. He could be a bit free-spirited, but not any more so than others of his upbringing. Two years ago he came home from a hunting expedition that had taken a turn in the weather. He never recovered from it," she finished softly.

"Papa?" Jaqueline asked softly of Mrs. Murray, only

understanding a few words of what her nurse said. She nodded to the girl.

"Your Papa was a verra good man, lass; no kinder heart could be found. You see," she said turning back to Isabella, "about a year after his passing His Grace received a letter from a Madame De'belmount of Paris. She claimed that Lord James had fathered a child by her and had been giving her a living. She asked that the child continue to be provided for, as she struggled to do so on her own. His Grace agreed under the condition that she be brought here and raised as a proper young lady."

"What a kindness considering her...her..." Isabella didn't want to say with the child present, whether she understood the words or not.

"I suspect that after the heartache of loss; you see, His Grace was verra close to his eldest son, he was hoping for a chance to have a bit of 'im back."

"And certainly he feels blessed to have her here," Isabella said, looking down at Jaqueline who was softly singing a French lullaby to her doll.

"Many of us do," Mrs. Murray said without explanation.

It left Isabella wondering who wouldn't be happy to have such a polite little girl in the household. She supposed that her parentage might cause some discomfort. She would never be considered a lady of the peerage, but growing in the duke's house and having an exceptional education, she would be a fine lady someday.

Isabella spent the remainder of the morning playing with the child asking her questions here and there to see what amount of instruction she had thus far. She didn't expect much at the tender age of six but was surprised that the girl's mother had spent every night reading to her from quite beautiful books.

She felt a pang of sorrow for this little girl who too had lost her mother, even if just by the separation of land. She couldn't imagine having such happy memories with her own mother and then being forced to leave her.

"Have you written to your mother since coming here?" Isabella asked her in perfect French.

"Yes, Aunt Abigail is kind to me. She writes letters for me, and reads back what my mother sends me."

Isabella was happy to hear that she was able to keep correspondence with her mother, at least.

"Soon, I can show you how to write your own letters and words and then you may write to your mother all on your own."

Of course, Isabella knew writing fluent letters, even in French, was a way off for a girl of six, but it was at least the start of a goal they could make for her education.

"Miss Watts, I believe I hear footsteps. I suspect it is Mrs. Peterson coming for ye. It is mid-morning, and I am sure His Grace is ready for you now."

Isabella stood and made sure her skirt was in proper order. Jaqueline came to hug her waist before she left. Already, in just a few short hours, this child was endeared to her.

Isabella was out the door just as Mrs. Peterson reached the top of the stairs, much to her surprise. Without many words, however, she merely turned around, expecting Isabella to follow. Isabella shook her head with a soft laugh. She wasn't sure if she would ever understand the complexity of Mrs. Peterson.

Want to know how the story ends? Tap on the link below to read the rest of the story

http://amzn.to/2FKQ3n1

Thank you very much

BE A PART OF THE ABBY AYLES FAMILY...

I write for you, the readers, and I love hearing from you! Thank you for your on going support as we journey through the most romantic era together.

If you're not a member of my family yet, it's never too late. Stay up to date on upcoming releases and check out the website for all information on romance.

I hope my stories touch you as deeply as you have impacted me. Enjoy the happily ever after!

Let's connect and download this Free Exclusive Bonus Story!

(Available only to my subscribers)

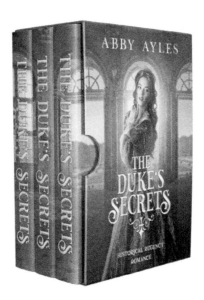

Click on the image or on the button below to get the BONUS

BookHip.com/NVGCDD

ALSO BY ABBY AYLES

- The Lady The Duke The Gentleman
- A Broken Heart's Redemption
- Falling for the Governess

ABOUT THE AUTHOR

Abby Ayles was born in the northern city of Manchester, England, but currently lives in Charleston, South Carolina, with her husband and their three cats. She holds a Master's degree in History and Arts and worked as a history teacher in middle school.

Her greatest interest lies in the era of Regency and Victorian England and Abby shares her love and knowledge of these periods with many readers in her newsletter.

In addition to this she has also written her first romantic novel, **The Duke's Secrets**, which is set in the era and is available for free on her website. As one reader commented – *'Abby's writing makes you travel back in time...'*

When she has time to herself, Abby enjoys going to the theatre, reading and watching documentaries about Regency and Victorian England.

For more information you can contact Abby Ayles Here:
https://manychat.com/l3/abbyaylesauthor
abby@abbyayles.com

Printed in Great Britain
by Amazon

24181907R00293